A gk

✐ **W9-BXB-464**

"Are you really planning to shoot me?"

Roz came right out and asked. "I think I have a right to know. I am not going to lift a finger to help you until you answer me."

Eli propped himself on one elbow and scowled at her. "Remind me to be more particular the next time I take a hostage. I swear that mouth of yours is bigger than you are."

"Answer the question," she snapped.

"Don't push your luck, lady," he said ominously.

She matched him stare for stare and said, "Well? I'm waiting for your answer."

"You just don't know when to back off, do you?" He scowled.

"No, I don't."

Eli expelled an exasperated sigh. "No, damn it, even if I am provoked into shooting you, if only to shut you up, I need your help. And you need mine...whether you believe it or not!"

* * *

The Last Honest Outlaw
Harlequin Historical #732—December 2004

CAROL FINCH

The Last Honest Outlaw

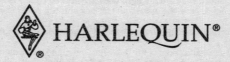

HARLEQUIN®

TORONTO • NEW YORK • LONDON
AMSTERDAM • PARIS • SYDNEY • HAMBURG
STOCKHOLM • ATHENS • TOKYO • MILAN • MADRID
PRAGUE • WARSAW • BUDAPEST • AUCKLAND

ISBN 0-373-29332-1

THE LAST HONEST OUTLAW

Copyright © 2004 by Connie Feddersen

www.eHarlequin.com

Printed in U.S.A.

Please address questions and book requests to:
Harlequin Reader Service
U.S.: 3010 Walden Ave., P.O. Box 1325, Buffalo, NY 14269
Canadian: P.O. Box 609, Fort Erie, Ont. L2A 5X3

This book is dedicated to my husband, Ed, and our children, Kurt, Shawna, Jeff, Christie, Jon and Jill. And to our grandchildren, Kennedy, Brooklynn, Livia and Blake. Hugs and kisses!

A special thank-you to my editor, Ann Leslie Tuttle. It is a pleasure to be working with you!

Chapter One

Denver, Colorado
1878

Rozalie Matthews proudly extended the newspaper article that she had thoroughly researched and carefully proofread to her father, owner and editor of the *Daily Chronicle*. "Read this over and see what you think," she requested.

Charles glanced up from setting type and frowned curiously. "What is it?"

"After I finished writing the obituaries and society pages you assigned to me," she explained, wrinkling her nose distastefully, "I felt compelled to investigate the details of Albert Thompson's murder." She pointed to the third paragraph of her article. "I included the description of the accused man that three eyewitnesses described to me."

Without bothering to read the story, her father handed it back to her. "I don't want you involved with this sort of investigation, Roz. We have discussed this several times."

"But I feel this is my calling," Roz insisted, trying to control her frustration. "I believe that I'm at my best, journalistically speaking, when interviewing witnesses and—"

Her father flung up his hand to forestall her. "Your time and efforts would be better spent making arrangements for your wedding to Lieutenant Harper. He came by this morning to ask for your hand and I gave my permission."

Roz's temper hit its flash point in one second flat. "John Harper is barely more than an acquaintance! I don't even like the man all that much. I got the distinct impression that his true interest in me is my ability to open doors for him into society. He badgers me constantly for introductions to the most prominent members of the community and then he proceeds to butter them up."

When her father shrugged off her comments as inconsequential, another wave of frustration flooded through her. "How could you possibly think I want to spend the rest of my life with Harper when I only *tolerate* him as an escort to the parties *you* insist I attend so I can write my columns for the society page? The lieutenant cannot have my hand or anything else!" she declared adamantly.

His blond brows flattened over his pale green eyes. "Now you listen to me, daughter. You are twenty years old and it's high time you settled into a normal life."

"Normal for complacent, unassertive females, you mean," Roz muttered resentfully. "Surely you realize by now that I have greater aspirations than finding a husband. I want to launch my career as a journalist."

"You won't have any hope of a career if you don't wed the lieutenant," her father countered. "Your mother plans to marry you off to that pompous dandy that she handpicked for you. You'll be stuck back East permanently."

Roz reared back when her father's booming voice ricocheted off the office walls. Her gaze swung to her corner desk. "You read Mother's letter?" she said accusingly.

He scowled and busied his hands with arranging the type on the manual printing press.

"You know I have no interest in going back East," Roz reminded him. "I didn't want to be dragged to Philadelphia to live with my maternal grandparents six years ago when you and Mother decided that you got along better with a half a continent between you, either."

No matter how often Roz had begged to return to Denver—the only place that felt like home—her mother had denied her requests. Sophia Matthews had been determined that Roz make all the proper social connections and attend a private finishing school. Roz had been miserable and her life had seemed dull and meaningless. Not to mention how much she had missed her father when her parents separated.

At the moment, however, she was having trouble remembering how fond she was of him. Suddenly, he had become as demanding as her mother.

Roz had finally convinced her mother to allow her an extended stay with her father two years ago and she had no intention of returning to Pennsylvania. She refused to be sucked back into the restrictive confines placed on aristocratic women in Eastern society. Denver provided the freedom and opportunities she craved, and she was not giving that up.

Roz was ready to break free of the unreasonable decrees of her parents, who always seemed to be at cross-purposes where she was concerned. For years Roz had held herself personally responsible for her parents' separation. She had carried a burden of guilt until she had matured enough to realize that she had nothing to do with Charles and Sophia's differences of opinions and conflicts of interests.

She was tired of someone else making all her decisions for her, and her parents' rocky marriage was reason enough to avoid the pitfalls of wedlock. This was *her* life, after all. She was not going to live it according to the dictates of her parents who used her as a pawn to retaliate against each other—and left her floundering in the middle.

"That woman is making sure you return to the East by arranging your wedding," her father said, breaking into her thoughts. "She deprived me of the chance to watch you grow up. I want you here with me permanently. If you marry Lieutenant Harper, that scheming mother of yours can't uproot you and repot you in Philadelphia soil."

Roz positioned herself in front of her father, demanding his undivided attention. "Is that what this attempt to marry me off to John Harper boils down to, Papa?" she asked pointedly. "Do you want the exact opposite for me that Mother wants, just to irritate her?"

Her father clamped his mouth shut, refusing to reply.

"I've been caught in your tug-of-war for years.

Mother constantly tries to influence my opinion of you and you try to influence my opinion of her. I'm tired of being caught in the middle,'' Roz burst out in exasperation.

"And furthermore, I am not marrying anyone, just to please you or Mother,'' she told him in no uncertain terms. "All I want is a career in journalism. If you won't print my story then I will march myself over to one of the rival newspaper offices and apply for a job. I will also tell Judge Milner that you are being difficult and he will be here in a flash to take my side the way he usually does!''

Judge Milner was her father's longtime friend who, having no children of his own, had declared himself Roz's honorary uncle. She had confided her frustrations with her parents to him over the years, and the judge had been her champion on several occasions. No doubt he would come to her defense again.

Charles scowled at Roz's threats and wagged his finger at her. "Don't you dare use the kind of tactics to get even with me that your mother is famous for!''

His voice thundered, but Roz didn't so much as flinch. She was as aggravated as her father was. She met his gaze head-on and said, "I am declaring my independence here and now. I intend to have the final say in decisions that affect my life. I do *not* intend to marry that stuffy lawyer Mother picked out for me and I won't marry the pretentious lieutenant you picked out for me, either. In fact, I'm not sure I want to marry— ever. I just want to be my own person and make my own choices for once in my life!''

Wheeling around, Roz stamped over to her desk to

snatch up the letter from her mother. She ripped it to shreds in symbolic defiance then stared meaningfully at her father. "Wedding engagements are not important to me, but this article is, Papa. Albert Thompson's daughter, as you well know, is my dearest friend in Denver. I want to see Albert's murderer captured and punished. Writing the obituary is not enough. He was a prestigious hotel owner and leading citizen and I intend to keep his name in print and on the mind of your subscribers until the case is solved. Surely someone else in this town sees the need to report the details of Albert's demise!"

"Someone should, but not *you*. Damn it, girl, where are you going? And it better not be to one of my rivals... Rozalie Beth Matthews, get back here this instant!" her father called out as she strode toward the door.

Roz didn't break stride, just hurried onto the boardwalk to grab the reins to her horse. She was so frustrated that she wanted to scream. She slung her leg over the saddle to ride astride and trotted the horse around the corner, then down the alley before her father could determine which direction she was going.

She passed her father's two-story brick home that sat two miles west of town—and she kept right on riding. She needed to regain her composure, and galloping at breakneck speed, with the wind in her face, seemed the only cure for the jumble of emotions that hounded her.

When Roz noticed two riders approaching, she veered off the road and headed toward the river. The last thing she wanted was to encounter the rougher elements of Denver society and fend off attack. She simply wanted to be left alone with her thoughts.

Roz dismounted from her winded steed and ambled along the river's edge. The setting sun reflected off the water, nearly blinding her. She whirled around to pace back in the direction she had come and muttered several oaths to vent her annoyance at being denied the chance to prove herself in her chosen career.

She felt as if her decisions and choices had never been her own and she wanted to make something of herself. She needed to be reassured of who and what she was. There were times when she wished she had been born a man! She had half a mind to pack her belongings and take the stagecoach west—all the way to the Pacific.

Perhaps newspaper editors in San Francisco weren't averse to hiring a female reporter.

Despite her inner turmoil, Roz squared her shoulders and inhaled a fortifying breath. She *was* going to make something of herself, woman or not, she vowed resolutely. She wasn't going to acquiesce to her mother's decree to return East and she wasn't going to agree to her father's demand, either. But she *was* going to remain in Denver because that was exactly where she wanted to be.

She glanced westward to admire the grandeur of the mountains. This mile-high city bustled with prospectors, businessmen, cowboys, ranchers, gamblers and various shysters. 'The community offered the kind of diversion, adventure and challenge that Roz craved—and wanted to be a part of. Here she felt alive.

Although she had been educated in Philadelphia, at

her mother's insistence, Denver was truly where her heart was—here on the last frontier. Most Easterners and foreigners were fascinated with the West. This was the place where life was what you made of it, and Roz had no interest in adhering to the restrictions women encountered in the East when they dared to be different.

Rozalie Matthews was going to be her own woman, with her own identity. She longed to be a journalist who tackled the gritty stories, not reported on the social activities of the nouveau riche who had made their fortunes by investing in the gold and silver industry.

Roz was *not* backing down on this matter when she returned to town to confront her father again.

The thud of hooves pounding on the road jostled Roz back to the present. She grabbed the horse's reins and walked toward the piers beneath the wooden bridge so she wouldn't be seen or disturbed.

After the rider passed by, Roz intended to return home to continue her discussion with her father—with a bit more diplomacy than she had used at the office. Charles Matthews was usually a sensible man—unless her mother got him riled up. Roz would sit him down and make him understand that she had always wanted to follow in his footsteps and pursue a career in journalism. She didn't need to marry Lieutenant Harper to do that.

When the sound of clattering hooves on the bridge startled her horse, Roz reached out to soothe the jittery animal. The last thing she wanted was for her mount to break and run and force her to hike home after dark.

"You, there! Hold up! I want to talk to you!"

Roz frowned curiously when a muffled male voice mingled with the sound of hoofbeats. Apparently another rider had approached—from which direction she couldn't say because she couldn't see who was on the bridge above her. More hoofbeats resounded like thunder on the bridge. She flinched when she heard a gunshot explode overhead.

A second gunshot rang out, followed by an agonized howl. A third gunshot cracked the sudden silence and Roz predicted a duel had broken out above her. She quickly tethered her skittish horse then scurried away from the underside of the bridge to see what had happened to the two combatants.

Roz swallowed a shriek of alarm when she saw a man topple from his horse and plunge into the river. To her stunned disbelief she saw the second man—who was identically dressed, right down to his moccasins and doehide leggings—keel off the bridge and land with a splash.

Roz froze to the spot when it dawned on her that both men fit the description of the outlaw accused of killing Albert Thompson—she should know since she had heard the desperado described three times by eyewitnesses. She watched in amazement as both men, garbed in buckskin breeches and blue linen shirts, floated facedown on the river. Two similar sombreros drifted downstream with the swift-moving current.

Roz scampered along the river's edge, wondering what she should do. The fast current was propelling both men downstream and neither one was close enough for her to latch onto. If she raced off to summon assistance she couldn't predict for certain where the men might end up. And in the gathering darkness she wasn't sure how long she would be able to keep an eye on the men.

Glancing over her shoulder, hoping someone would miraculously arrive on the scene so she wouldn't have to go for help, Roz scanned the hilly terrain. There was not another soul in sight and there was only a thin sliver of moon hanging in the sky. An outlaw's moon, she mused as she scanned her surroundings. There was barely enough light to lead the way back to town.

When Roz pivoted around she was surprised to note that one of the bodies was drifting gradually toward shore. Roz sidestepped down the incline to take a closer look.

Suddenly the man burst from the water like the Loch Ness Monster rising from the deep. Roz was so startled that she stumbled backward and tripped over the trailing hem of her gown. Icy fear paralyzed her when the man lunged toward her and snaked his hand around her ankle to jerk her roughly toward him.

Roz opened her mouth to scream bloody murder, but a wet hand clamped over the lower portion of her face. Six foot two inches and two hundred some-odd pounds of hard muscle surged over her, flattening her like a flounder, forcing her breath from her chest in a whoosh. Roz froze in terror when she felt the prick of the knife that appeared, as if by magic, in his free hand. The sharp blade pressed perilously against her throat. Roz had no doubt whatsoever that she had come face-to-face with Albert Thompson's vicious killer—and quite likely her own.

Dear Lord! What irony that she had waited to announce her independence on the day of her death, she thought. She would never have the opportunity to launch her career as a renowned journalist. She was going to die a horrible death—right here in the grass and weeds that lined the river. Her mutilated body wouldn't be discovered until long after this ruthless murderer escaped.

"Don't make a sound, or else…" the outlaw snarled at her.

The ominous threat echoed in her head like a death toll. Roz was afraid to struggle for release for fear it would be the last thing she ever did.

She swallowed with a strangled gulp when the man's shadowy face, surrounded by long wet hair, full beard and mustache loomed over hers. Blood from the superficial wound on his scalp dribbled onto her neck.

It could be *her* blood that was spilled if she angered this criminal, she reminded herself bleakly.

"Now we're going to get up, slow and easy," he growled at her. "Then we're going to fetch your horse and get the hell out of here—pronto."

When he moved his hand away from her mouth, she choked out, "You'll have a better chance of escaping alone. I'll only slow you down, and kidnapping me will only make matters worse."

He muttered what she was sure was a foul oath in Spanish as he hurriedly levered her into a sitting position beside him. "You're coming with me for your own good," he said on a ragged breath.

Her own good? Roz gaped incredulously at him. Obviously this murdering criminal was as crazy as he was vicious. How could being abducted possibly be a good thing for her?

"You're also going to patch me up when we find a safe place to hide," he added as he snaked his arm around her waist.

Roz blinked, bemused by his comment. This place seemed safe enough to her. The outlaw had obviously shot his look-alike and there was no one else around to pounce on him. The man was mentally unstable and suffering from paranoia, she decided.

When he hoisted her to her feet she noticed the bloody wound on his thigh. She felt him hobbling unevenly on his injured leg while he leaned heavily against her to approach her horse. That explained the three shots she'd heard, Roz mused as she struggled to gather her scattered wits. Obviously, this outlaw was a better shot than his unfortunate look-alike—who was floating lifelessly down the river, destined for a watery grave.

Roz glanced over her shoulder to note the other man had sunk completely out of sight. No doubt, the undercurrent was carrying him far from the scene of the deadly duel.

Roz chastised herself for haring off after her confrontation with her father. Her need to clear out had led her straight into disaster. At the moment, the prospect of marrying the stuffy Winchester Chapman the Third or the dull and uninspiring Lieutenant John Harper sounded a hundred times better than ending up as another victim of this murderer's merciless killing spree.

When the outlaw stopped abruptly to brace himself

against the supporting beam of the bridge, Roz accidentally collided with him. He was as solid as the beam, though obviously a bit unsteady because of his wounds. She didn't waste time feeling sorry for the scoundrel, however. He had killed her best friend's father, murdered his look-alike and he obviously planned to kill *her* when she no longer served his purpose. Roz predicted she would only remain alive long enough to treat his wounds—and then would be disposed of.

The abysmal thought sent another blast of fear coursing through her.

Knowing her hours were numbered, she vowed to devise a method of escape. Until then, she would deceive this desperado into thinking she posed no threat to him.

"Climb aboard. And no funny business, lady," he muttered as he limped toward the horse.

She pulled up the hem of her skirt and stuffed her foot in the stirrup. She squawked in offended dignity when the outlaw planted his hand on her derriere to boost her hurriedly into the saddle.

"That was *not* necessary," she said, scowling as she leaned forward to untie the reins. "I can mount up by myself."

"Not fast enough to suit me, you can't" came the gruff voice beside her. "We've got to get the hell out of here."

Roz stiffened in alarm when the fugitive swung up behind her and his damp, muscular body practically surrounded her. His masculine thighs flanked her hips. His broad chest was plastered against her back and his powerful arms closed around her waist as he took control of the reins.

When his knife blade sliced into her petticoat Roz instinctively opened her mouth to shriek in terror, but his free hand clamped over her mouth before she could utter a sound.

"Keep quiet," he growled against her ear. "Tie that piece of fabric around my thigh to stop the bleeding."

Hands shaking, pulse pounding like a tom-tom, she fashioned a makeshift tourniquet from the strip of lacy cloth and wrapped it tightly around his injured left thigh. Her nerves already standing on end, Roz practically leaped out of her skin when the outlaw let loose with a howl—that was reminiscent of a coyote—so close to her ear. She heard the clatter of hooves on the bridge above her as the outlaw nudged her horse forward, following the meandering path of the river.

Several minutes of silence passed before Roz heard the muffled hoofbeats approaching from the rear. She glanced around the outlaw's broad shoulders to see the dark silhouette of a horse, laden down with supplies, following in their wake. Apparently the coyote howl was the signal for the desperado's well-trained steed to come to heel.

Roz hoped the hombre would slide over to his own horse and grant her breathing space—and the chance to make a fast getaway—but he stayed put and kept his left arm clamped around her waist, refusing to let her leap to freedom.

"What's your name, lady?" he asked a mile later.

There was no way Roz was going to identify herself, just in case the scoundrel decided to hold her for ransom and extort money from her father. "Mary Smith," she lied.

She felt a chuckle rumbling in his massive chest. "Right. Well, I'll say one thing for you, *Mary Smith,* you've got a brain in your head and you know how and when to use it. I wasn't sure your kind did."

"My kind?" Roz muttered, offended. "And what *kind* are you referring to?" No doubt, this hombre considered women as incapable and useless as the rest of *his* kind.

"Females," he replied. "Most white women can't fight their way out of a feed sack and are prone to tears. They usually faint at the first sign of trouble."

Roz jerked up her chin, stiffened her spine and said, "I do not faint. I have never fainted in my life."

"Good for you, Mary Smith. The last thing I need right now is a squeamish female who keels over when forced to dig this bullet out of my leg."

"Far as I'm concerned, it can stay where it is," she burst out spitefully.

Damn, when was she going to learn to keep her mouth shut? It was her worst fault. Well, except for her instinctive need to be alone until she cooled down after dealing with the unreasonable dictates of her parents.

"Figured you'd feel that way, but you're going to take out this bullet nonetheless," he insisted sharply.

That was the last thing he said to her for five miles. Even in the darkness she could see the towering, snow-capped peaks to the west and she presumed her captor was heading for the cover of timber in the foothills. She hoped he passed out first. Then she could reverse direction and haul him back to town. She would make sure that he was stuffed in jail and charged with the murder of Albert Thompson and the unfortunate look-alike that pitched off the bridge.

In light of the incident she had witnessed, Roz presumed this man and his accomplice had conspired to be in two places at once—in an attempt to provide an alibi for Albert's death. But the identically dressed villains had obviously had a falling-out and cruel fate had left Roz in the survivor's company.

The prospect of ending up like this man's dead cohort sent another snake of apprehension slithering down Roz's spine. She might not be the only one around here who ended up sinking into the depths of the river if she didn't devise a method of escape—and fast!

Elijah McCain battled nausea and light-headedness as he reined the horse toward the thicket of trees that lay a mile ahead. His head was pulsing in rhythm with his heartbeat and his left leg was throbbing like a son of a bitch. The sweet scent of the woman who was pressed against him was damn distracting. She was also full of sass and spunk, despite her fear and mistrust of him. Eli figured this feisty female would pound him over the head with the butt of his own rifle if he lost consciousness for even two seconds.

In short, she was as much of an asset as a hazard.

Although Elijah had no clue why that imposter had framed him for murdering a man he had never met, he knew for certain that the imposter wasn't working alone. Eli hadn't expected his look-alike to draw and fire when ordered to halt—but he had. The bullet had plugged Eli's thigh. Before Eli could return fire, a rifle blast had erupted from the underbrush and hit the imposter squarely in the chest.

If Eli hadn't sprawled over the back of his horse—instead of twisting in the saddle to see where the shot had come from—the second rifle blast would *not* have grazed his head. It would have finished him off with a bullet through the *heart*.

Eli didn't know what the hell was going on, but he knew for a fact that the mysterious man in the underbrush was a crackshot. Definitely an enemy to be reckoned with. The incident had alerted Eli to the possibility that someone had *hired* the imposter. The unidentified mastermind might have decided to remove all evidence—*after* Eli had spotted his look-alike riding away from town.

When dizziness threatened to close in around him, Eli leaned forward to take another whiff of Mary Smith's enticing scent. He had never been near a woman who smelled as good as she did and felt so perfect in his arms. But then, his associations with females had been brief, at best.

This woman, however, was sharp-witted and unafraid to speak her mind. It hadn't taken but a few moments to realize the lady hailed from a higher class of society than the women Eli usually encountered.

His conscience had badgered him when he was forced to intimidate the woman to gain her cooperation. But in his weakened condition—not to mention the unknown whereabouts of the bushwhacker—Eli didn't have time to be courteous and polite. He had needed to make a speedy getaway.

Considering that he was wanted for murder—by description if not by name—he didn't expect the woman's willing cooperation. And why she was out here alone in the middle of nowhere to become a victim of circumstance—same as he was—Eli didn't know. On one hand he was damn glad there was someone here to patch him up. On the other hand, the bushwhacker might have seen her—which put her life in jeopardy.

"My name is Elijah McCain." He introduced himself as he veered toward the cover of the trees. "And just so you know, I haven't shot anyone…not lately anyway."

In his line of work, shooting in self-defense was commonplace. But he hadn't planned to shoot the imposter, just ask a few questions before he hauled him to jail.

Too bad Eli hadn't had the chance to find out what the blazes was going on.

"You are obviously delusional if you expect me to believe you didn't shoot your look-alike and send him catapulting off the bridge," she said, then smirked. "I heard three shots. Two of them hit you. Simple math implies *your* shot hit its mark." She grabbed a quick breath then asked, "Who was the other man that was floating down the river? Your accomplice?"

"No. I've never seen him before," Eli replied.

She twisted slightly in the saddle to toss him a disbelieving glance, but Eli's attention dropped to the lush curve of her mouth. He wondered if she tasted as sweet as she smelled, but he expected he would get his lips bit off if he yielded to the forbidden temptation of finding out. Besides, he had more pressing concerns than kissing this spirited female. He needed to bandage his aching head and treat his leg wound before infection set in.

The instant Eli reached the protective cover of the trees in the foothills he reined the horse to a halt. He slid to the ground with a grimace and groan. Putting pressure on his left leg sent sharp pain knifing into his thigh. Panting for breath, he pulled his waterlogged pistol from the holster on his hip and pointed it at Mary Smith—or whoever she really was. He hoped she wasn't familiar enough with firearms to predict the weapon probably wouldn't fire, even if he did pull the trigger.

"Climb down," he ordered in his gruffest voice. "Fetch the saddle bags off my horse and don't try anything heroic or we'll both be sorry."

She flashed him a go-to-hell glare—he could read that look easily enough in the darkness—then untied the two leather pouches. Eli sank gingerly to the ground and sighed in relief. The jarring motion of the horse had compounded the pain in his head and his thigh. Sitting on the ground was better—somewhat.

Although he kept his pistol trained on the woman, he saw her glance this way and that as she approached him. He suspected she had debated about making a run for it and decided it was too risky. He glanced up and frowned when she halted in front of him and tossed the saddle bag on the ground beside him.

"Are you really planning to shoot me?" she came

right out and asked. "I think I have a right to know."
She stared down at him and her chin tilted up a notch.
"I am not going to lift a finger to help you until you
answer me."

Eli propped himself on one elbow and scowled at
her. "Remind me to be more particular the next time
I take a hostage. I swear that mouth of yours is bigger
than you are."

"Answer the question," she snapped at him.

"Don't push your luck, lady," he said ominously.

She didn't quake or quail, just matched him stare for
stare and said, "Well? I'm waiting for your answer."

"You just don't know when to back off, do you?"
He scowled.

She crossed her arms over her chest. "No, I don't."

Eli expelled an exasperated sigh. "No, damn it, even
if I am provoked into shooting you, if only to shut you
up, I need your help. And you need mine, whether you
believe it or not."

"Why did you shoot Albert Thompson?" she fired
at him.

"Who? Is that the man I supposedly killed in Denver?"

She nodded curtly.

"I wouldn't know the man if he walked right up to
me," he insisted. "I've only been in and out of Denver
for two months. Mostly out. Despite what you think,
I'm not the bad guy. My look-alike shot me before I
could demand answers about why he was dressed like
me."

When she eyed him skeptically he added, "The last
two shots you heard came from a rifle, not a pistol, in

case you can't tell the difference. The imposter and I
were ambushed, which is why you and I had to get the
blazes away from there before we both got gunned
down. I did you a favor.''

''Well, it didn't feel like it to me.''

''Just take my word for it,'' he muttered.

''Can't think of one reason why I should.''

In a show of faith, Eli retrieved his dagger from the
sheath on his right leg and handed it to her, butt first.
''Cut a slit in my breeches so we can see if this wound
is as bad as it feels.''

She scrutinized him for a long moment before she
shifted her attention to the dagger clutched in her fist.
Eli suspected she was contemplating whether to defy
his pistol and bury the blade in his chest or rip open
his buckskin breeches. He breathed an inward sigh of
relief when she sank to her knees, grabbed a handful
of the sturdy fabric then cut the seam to expose the
wound.

''Dear God!'' she croaked. ''This is not good.''

''You're telling me, sister.'' Eli wasn't squeamish at
the sight of his own blood and this wasn't the first time
some mean bastard had used him for target practice.
But he knew a serious wound when he saw one.

Bracing himself, he poured the whiskey that he had
fished from the pouch onto the wound. Beads of sweat
pooled on his flesh as the alcohol set flame to his injured leg.

''Damn, that hurts,'' he wheezed. He tipped the bottle to his lips and took three quick gulps. ''I might pass
out while you're digging around there, but don't quit
until you get the bullet out.''

"I think we should wait until daybreak," she said shakily. "I can't see what I'm doing in the dark."

"I could bleed to death by then. You'd be stuck out here all by yourself without protection and I'd have your death on my conscience. No, we're going to do this my way."

"You sound just like a man," she grumbled resentfully.

"I am a man," he shot back. "But I don't plan to be a *dead* one, so get started."

She glanced around then bounded to her feet. "I'm going to start a small fire to provide a little light. I am absolutely *not* going to try primitive surgery in the dark."

Eli scowled while Mary-Quite-Contrary scurried off to gather twigs. Where was Simon Foster when he needed him? Simon would have removed the slug and packed the wound already. But Eli had to rely on this headstrong female—and hope he lived long enough to reach Simon's mountain cabin.

After she retrieved the tinderbox from the saddle bag and ignited the small fire, she poised herself above him. Eli's hand stalled as he reached for a leather strap to bite down on. His thoughts stalled when he got his first glimpse of Mary Smith in the flickering campfire light. Damn, she was breathtaking with those luminous green eyes that were rimmed with spiky lashes. Pale blond hair formed a halo around her bewitching face, giving her a cherubic appearance.

Eli was sure he was staring rudely, but he had never seen such rare, sophisticated beauty or such delicately refined features. Never in his nomadic life had he been this close to physical feminine perfection. The woman looked like an angel hovering beside him.

All that ruined the vision was the knowledge that this particular female was full of sass and indomitable spirit.

Giving himself a mental shake, Eli gestured his useless pistol toward the wound and demanded gruffly. "Get to work, Green Eyes. I don't have all night."

Chapter Two

Roz shook herself loose from the hypnotic trance that assailed her when she got her first good look at Elijah McCain—accused murderer and known kidnapper. His bronzed complexion indicated that Spanish or Indian blood—or maybe both—flowed through his veins.

She didn't recall any of the three eyewitnesses mentioning that fact.

A black beard and mustache concealed the line of his jaw and the shape of his mouth, giving him a rugged, uncivilized appearance. Long, coal-black hair skimmed his wide shoulders. An odd-looking bead-and-silver necklace encircled his neck.

She recalled that the eyewitnesses hadn't mentioned that, either.

He appeared wild and untamed—the kind of man that would give her mother a fit of the vapors if she knew Roz had the slightest association with him. Eli appeared to be the farthest thing from a gentleman as a man could get.

Therefore, there was not one reason why Roz should feel the slightest concern, interest or attraction to this man. Yet, when she stared down into those vivid blue eyes that were framed with long thick lashes and saw the look of hope and expectation—and masculine appreciation—it affected her strongly.

On one hand, she sensed Eli was dangerous. She felt the instinctive need to escape, as fast as she could. On the other hand, she wondered if her assumptions about his guilt were ill founded. His claims of innocence and the inaccuracy of the eyewitnesses' descriptions niggled her. And yet, she was reluctant to believe his fantastic story of bushwhacking and conspiracy.

Quite honestly, Roz wasn't sure what to make of this man. But, guilty or innocent, compassion refused to allow her to abandon him while he was seriously injured.

She wondered if he would have returned the favor if the situation were reversed.

"My real name is Rozalie, but people call me Roz," she said, though she wasn't sure why she confided the information to him.

"That fits you better." He inclined his shaggy head toward the task at hand. "There's an old Indian custom stating that if you save a life it belongs to you. If the time comes that you need a favor then all you have to do is ask. I will do my damnedest to set things right for you."

"Ah, so you do have an Indian heritage," she mused aloud. "Nice to know there is a code of ethics among Indians and outlaws." Roz came to her knees then gently eased his leg sideways to expose the wound to the flickering campfire light. "Brace yourself, McCain.

I'm sorry to say that I don't have the slightest idea what I'm supposed to do.''

She saw him flinch at the first touch of the blade on his tender flesh. Her stomach somersaulted as she tended the unpleasant task of prodding and poking to locate the bullet.

Eli bit down hard on the leather strap and perspiration popped out on his forehead, but the only sound he made was a guttural groan. Roz was sure *she* would have screamed in agony and lost consciousness immediately. But Eli's stamina and ability to endure pain testified to the fact that this wasn't the first time someone had dug a bullet out of him.

It made her wonder what line of work he was in, if not a gunslinger that made a habit of parting his victims from their money—and their lives.

After what seemed an eternity Roz finally located the slug that was embedded against bone. She glanced up to see perspiration dribbling down Eli's face, which was contorted in excruciating pain.

He looked straight at her and wheezed, ''I want to apologize in advance for whatever I say or do to offend you when you dig out that slug. Now get on with it, damn it.''

Roz drew in a steadying breath and angled the blade into his flesh. When he hissed in pain and cursed the air, Roz retracted the knife.

She recoiled reflexively when his hand folded over hers and he stared grimly at her. To her amazement he guided her hand—that was clamped on the butt of the knife—to the wound to pry loose the slug. His panting moan testified to the level of pain he was enduring and she felt his hand quiver upon hers.

"Jesus, God A-mighty, that hurts!" Eli groaned as he sagged to the ground. "Need more whiskey."

"For you or for antiseptic?" she asked shakily.

"Both," he said on a seesaw breath.

She grabbed the bottle and pressed it to his lips. After he took several large gulps she poured whiskey on his thigh. He bolted into a sitting position and let loose a string of obscenities Roz had never heard linked together quite so creatively. Sympathy washed over her as he collapsed back to the ground, his big body shuddering with the aftereffects of the torture.

"Get the damn thing out," he demanded raggedly.

Gritting her teeth, Roz scraped the slug from the wound. When Eli reached for a small tin that he kept in his saddle bag she frowned curiously. "What's that?"

"Indian remedy," he panted as he dabbed salve into the wound. "There's a needle and thread in the pouch to stitch me back together."

Roz rooted into the bag to retrieve the needle and thread. Although her stomach was pitching and rolling, she set to work. Dizziness threatened to distract her, but she had sworn to Eli that she wouldn't faint and she would be damned if she made a liar of herself.

"Thanks," Eli wheezed when she finished her chore. "Now fetch my pallet so you can bed down and get some shut-eye."

"No, you need the comfort of the pallet more than I do," she insisted. "I—"

"Damn it, woman. Just do what I tell you," he snapped grouchily.

Roz had heard those words too many times the past few years. "I am quite finished with people telling me what and what not to do," she rapped out, then smiled guiltily when Eli gaped at her, obviously curious about what prompted her outburst. "*I* will sleep on the ground and *you* will sleep on your own bedroll because you are injured."

When he opened his mouth—to object, no doubt— she wagged her finger in his peaked face. "Don't argue with me, McCain. This is for your own good and you know it."

Eli squinted up at her, a hint of a smile playing on his ashen lips. "Are you always this demanding and snippy or are you just ticked off because I dragged you along with me?"

She shot to her feet to fetch the pallet. "I'm sorry for lashing out at you. I'm sensitive about being ordered about and it affects my temper."

"Gee, I never would have noticed if you hadn't brought it to my attention," he teased.

"Well, it's not as if you don't have a few faults of your own," Roz countered as she shook out the bedroll beside Eli. "You're bossy and abrupt. You go around shooting people for no good reason and you take defenseless women hostage."

"Defenseless? *You?*" He hooted. "I told you, loud and clear, that *you* were in danger of being gunned down by that sniper. Plus, I did *not* shoot Albert Thompson, and I intend to prove it when I get back on my feet."

Roz positioned herself behind his head to ease his shoulders and torso onto the padded bedroll. When she circled around to grab his good leg, he grimaced and swore as she shifted him sideways. That done, she dribbled whiskey over the wound on his scalp and listened to Eli hiss several more inventive oaths—before switching to Spanish to voice what she assumed were juicy expletives that she was glad she couldn't translate.

The ones she *could* understand were certainly ripe enough.

Roz grabbed the discarded knife and cut away another portion of her petticoat to form a bandage to cover the head wound.

After a moment he said, "Thank you for what you did. I owe you, and I always repay my debts."

When Roz fluffed the Indian blanket and settled it over him, Eli stared at her for a long moment. "Whether you believe it or not, you *are* in danger. I don't advise trying to escape during the night. You're safer here with me."

"My father is going to wonder what became of me," she insisted. "I need to get word to him."

"Well, it can't be tonight." Eli winced as he tried to settle more comfortably on the pallet. "Tomorrow perhaps. Just…don't…leave…tonight," he added emphatically.

Roz watched Eli sink bonelessly onto the pallet. She didn't know if he had fallen asleep or passed out from the pain. Indecision furrowed her brow—she wondered if she should seize the moment and run. Or stay put.

She glanced uneasily around her. Perhaps fleeing in

the darkness wouldn't be a good idea, as Eli cautioned. But this was definitely her golden opportunity to escape.

Roz took two steps toward her horse. But she halted when Eli's warnings buzzed through her mind. What if he *was* telling the truth and some unseen assailant was lying in wait, intent on silencing her because she had witnessed the shooting on the bridge? What if Eli *had* been framed for murder and truly needed her help to survive his injuries so he could return to Denver to clear his name?

And what if he was only trying to frighten her to make certain she remained nearby to nurse him back to health?

Confusion and uncertainty tormented Roz as she wrestled with her decision. The emotional pandemonium of arguing with her father, being kidnapped and then dealing with the stress of performing surgery on Eli's leg suddenly caught up with Roz. She was dead on her feet, she realized as she sank to the ground. The need to rest overwhelmed her.

As her lashes fluttered shut and she breathed an exhausted sigh, she wondered if good judgment had failed her where Eli was concerned. If he had used fear to manipulate her with his claims of innocence, she was going to be hugely disappointed in herself.

That was her last thought before she fell asleep.

Charles Matthews paced back and forth across the parlor of his home then glanced anxiously at the grandfather clock in the corner. It was one in the morning and there was still no word from Roz.

Reversing direction, Charles wore another path on the carpet and scolded himself for brushing off Roz's news article, as if it counted for nothing. He had purposely turned the conversation to Lieutenant Harper's request to marry Roz to avoid a debate over her insistence on tackling stories that were usually written by men. But he hadn't handled the encounter well at all, especially while he was seething from reading Sophia's letter. Now Roz was perturbed with him and he had no idea where she had gone.

Blast it, if only she had agreed to marry Lieutenant Harper, he mused as he paced. He could have successfully countered Sophia's attempt to ship Roz to Pennsylvania to become Chapman's bride and sever Charles's personal contact with his one and only daughter.

Charles halted in front of the dining room bureau, pulled open the top drawer and retrieved the photograph of his estranged wife that lay facedown. A twinge of frustration pricked him—as it always did when he stared into that lovely face that still tormented his dreams.

"Confound it, woman, this is as much your fault as it is mine. It's no wonder Roz craves independence. We have restrained and frustrated her. She has become what we have made of her. Curse us both for that!"

Charles expelled a loud sigh and shook his gray-blond head. "*Six years, Sophia.* I should be over you by now. You weren't satisfied living in the West and I craved being on hand while history was being made."

Tossing aside the photograph, Charles plunked down into the nearest chair. His tormented feelings for Sophia were the least of his troubles right now. No one he had contacted, not even Gina Thompson and his close friend, William Milner, had seen Roz all day.

True, she spirited off in a bit of temper occasionally, but she always returned when she cooled down and they worked out their differences. He wished she would show up so he could tell her that he *was* going to print her story—because it was actually quite good. It was his way of apologizing for sounding demanding and tyrannical.

Charles shot another glance at the clock. One-thirty. He suspected Roz had checked into a hotel. What else could she have done and where else could she possibly be? First thing in the morning he would track her down, announce that her article was due out in the evening paper and give her what she wanted—the chance to write stories that she was passionate about.

He supposed he should be pleased that Roz shared his passion for the newspaper business. But he still had to counter Sophia's arranged marriage that was designed to drag Roz where she didn't want to go. Sophia was not going to take Roz away from him again, he vowed.

Charles veered into his room to stare at the bed he had once shared with Sophia. "Damn the woman," he muttered to the room at large. "Couldn't live with her. And can't live *without* her. Now there's irony for you."

Charles prayed that the best thing he and Sophia had created together would soon come home where she belonged.

Eli awoke at dawn, unable to quell his shaking. Cold chills chased up and down his spine and his leg pulsed painfully when he tried to move. When he pried open his eyes, he saw Roz hovering over him like a glorious guardian angel. He really had expected her to leave while he was incapable of stopping her. But here she was, safe and sound, frowning worriedly at him.

"I think we should return to Denver and have a physician check your wounds," she advised.

"No," Eli croaked, amazed that his voice sounded like a bullfrog's. "It's a day's ride to Simon's cabin. He'll nurse me back to health. Then we can head to town together. But you can't go anywhere alone until I'm certain you aren't in danger because of your association with me. Even when I'm well enough to figure out what's going on, we still have to watch our backs."

"Who's Simon?" she questioned curiously.

"My mentor. A substitute father of sorts."

He expected Miss Inquisitive to interrogate him further, but she surprised him by rising to her feet and walking over to fetch the coffee that was warming over the small campfire.

"I found trail rations among your supplies," she said as she poured him a cup of coffee. "You need to keep up your strength." She set the pot back on the fire then tossed him a surreptitious glance. "Do you really think you can stay in the saddle for a full day's ride in rugged terrain? You're not in good shape, McCain."

Eli fought down a wave of dizziness as he levered up to sip the coffee. Then he choked down the pemmican she offered him. When he eased into an upright position, the world tilted sideways and turned gray around the perimeters of his vision.

"Gawd, surely dead feels better than this," he mumbled.

"I'm sure it does," she agreed. "Which is why we need to get you to a doctor." She stared pointedly at his left leg. "If gangrene sets in, you won't be worth shooting."

"Can we argue about this later? I'm not up for it right now," he said raggedly.

Eli rolled onto his good leg then tried unsuccessfully to push himself to his feet. Pain speared his thigh like a lightning bolt and he swore he was about to lose his breakfast.

"Oh, for heaven's sake," Roz muttered as she clamped an arm around his waist and hoisted him to his feet. "I told you this is not a good idea. If you pass out, I will have no clue where we're going. Plus, I'm not sure *you* can get there without your condition going from bad to worse."

"Thanks so much for cheering me up," Eli grumbled crankily. "Nice of you to remind me that I have one leg in the grave already." He gestured toward a fallen branch. "Hand me that tree limb for support."

Roz cocked a brow at his demanding tone then strode off to fetch the limb that would serve as a makeshift cane.

Eli leaned heavily on the crutch and made slow, excruciating progress toward his horse. "Snuff out the fire before you mount up."

"Yes, master," she said smartly. "Anything else?"

Eli sighed audibly, all too aware that his manners and etiquette were so far below Roz's expectations that it was laughable. He was accustomed to spouting orders that needed to be obeyed immediately, because he dealt with life-and-death situations repeatedly. He wasn't a *please* and *thank-you* kind of man, which usually offended females—especially one as feisty as Roz.

"*Please* snuff out the fire," he said as he struggled to put weight on his left leg so he could mount up. Eli clamped hold of the pommel before his injured leg folded up beneath him.

"Outlaws must have some sort of death wish," Roz said as she hurried over to lend support. "And if you had the sense God gave a flea, you would spend the day recuperating on your pallet."

"And wait for that bushwhacker to pick us off? No thanks. I'll be just fine." That was an outright lie. He felt like hell and he barely had the energy to remain upright.

Roz cast him a withering glance as he leaned heavily against his horse. "You aren't anywhere close to fine," she contradicted. "You are noticeably unsteady on your feet and you look like death warmed over."

"I'll manage," he said determinedly.

Roz peered into his face that was surrounded by tangled raven hair and asked herself why in the world she felt sorry for a man she wasn't entirely sure she believed or trusted. He kept insisting that he had kidnapped her for her own good and she was hesitant to strike off on her own for fear his theory of a bushwhacker who might have marked her for death was true.

If she raced back to Denver, ignoring his warning,

she might be walking into a deadly trap. Yet, if she accompanied Eli west there was no telling what perils she might encounter.

Despite the indecision and uncertainty swirling around her, Roz gathered the supplies, tied them in place behind the saddles then assisted Eli onto his horse. "If I don't get word to my father, I expect he will send out the cavalry—literally. And my soon-to-be fiancé will be leading the charge. Lieutenant Harper—"

"Harper?" Eli jerked up his head then gave a distasteful snort. "You plan to marry that idiot? Talk about a man who doesn't have the sense God gave a flea."

Roz blinked in surprise. "You know John Harper?"

Eli nodded his ruffled head. "I've guided, scouted and hired on as a guard for army patrols hauling supplies to other posts while I've been in this area of the territory. Harper has little tolerance for half-breeds like me. I'm a second-class citizen to him and he has no use for my opinions and advice.

"Harper nearly got his men and me killed last month because he wouldn't listen to reason," Eli elaborated. "He went charging into a nest of outlaws instead of retreating. If you ask me, the man's military training is seriously lacking. He doesn't know a damn thing about guerilla warfare or how to counter it. Only when we had our backs to the wall did he let me handle the situation."

Roz didn't rush to John's defense because she'd had a lukewarm reaction to his courtship. Learning of John's prejudice didn't endear him to her, either. Although she felt guilty about aiding and abetting the man accused of killing Gina's father, Roz was unwillingly intrigued with Eli.

Although Roz had yearned for adventure and excitement and longed for the chance to test her strengths, this wasn't exactly what she had in mind. Yet, if she had been dragged into the conspiracy surrounding Eli, the best course of action was to hide out for a few days and keep a low profile when she returned to town.

Roz cast her ruggedly handsome companion a discreet glance and reminded herself that no matter what fate awaited her, this uncertain alliance with Eli McCain was a novel experience. And not because she might be traveling with a cunning fugitive from justice. Dealing with Eli was vastly different from the men she usually encountered in her social circle.

She had been whisked from the drawing rooms of the privileged and forced to face life-and-death situations in the wilderness. Her life was no longer predictable and mundane. She wasn't stuck writing columns about the latest social events, doing obituaries or printing advertising flyers for local businesses. She was *living* a sensational story of potential danger. She was facing critical decisions and testing her mettle.

"There," Eli murmured, jostling Roz from her meandering thoughts.

She glanced down the tree-choked hillside to see a small stagecoach relay station beside the winding road.

"If you want to send a message to your father, now is the time." With effort, Eli braced himself upright in the saddle. "I'll wait for you here." His vivid blue gaze zeroed in on her. "Don't make a rash decision that might cost your life," he warned grimly.

Roz guided her horse through the trees, faced once again with the choice of leaving Eli on his own and saving herself from untold danger. She drew her mount to a halt beside the corral then glanced in the direction she had come to see Eli's shadowy silhouette poised on the hill above her. Part of her wanted to flee to the safety of home. Yet, another part of her was convinced that Eli McCain had been misjudged and would inevitably suffer unless she discovered the circumstances surrounding Albert Thompson's death.

Assailed by conflicting emotion, Roz dismounted then approached the log cabin that served as an isolated stage stop.

Eli heaved a sigh of relief when Roz emerged from the crudely built cabin and mounted her horse. He knew he had asked a lot of her. Most decent folks wouldn't have given him the benefit of the doubt, especially after he had dragged Roz away from the scene of the ambush in an attempt to protect her.

In most instances, when dealing with white society, Eli's mixed heritage was a strike again him. Which was why he avoided civilization as much as possible. Being accused of murder and targeted for death—for reasons he didn't understand—left him feeling more isolated and alienated than usual. Being weak and injured also left Eli feeling that his contradicting birthright was even more of a burden and a curse.

Right now, he desperately needed a friend and companion. Roz's decision to rejoin him was obviously a difficult one for her, but it did wonders for his sagging spirits.

"You came back," he murmured as she halted her horse beside him.

Roz stared directly at him, her expression somber. "I've waited years to make my own choices," she confided, then glanced pensively at the stage station. "I wonder if my first crucial decision is the right one."

"It is," Eli assured her as he reined toward higher elevations. "Thank you for believing in me when most whites wouldn't have."

"I'm not judging you by *what* you are, McCain," she replied, then tossed him a wry smile. "But if you betray my trust in you, rest assured that I am never going to let you hear the end of it."

Eli chuckled. "I don't doubt that for a minute."

Two hours later, Roz noticed Eli weaving unsteadily atop his horse. His face had turned another alarming shade of pale. It was beyond her how he could remain in the saddle in his injured condition. Apparently he was concerned about the same thing himself because he grabbed the coiled rope tied to his saddle and fashioned a harness to hold himself in place.

"See that middle peak straight ahead of us?" Eli rasped. "If I pass out, make sure we stay on course."

Roz's mouth dropped open as she scanned the craggy precipices that loomed ahead of them. She had always wanted to explore the mountains where trappers and prospectors sought their fortunes. But she wasn't sure she wanted to go exploring with an injured and unconscious guide. If she got them lost, they were both doomed to disaster.

"I'm not sure..." Her voice trailed off when she glanced sideways to see Eli slump forward on his horse.

Dear Lord, she had the uneasy feeling that she was about to be tested to her limits. It was one thing to *imagine* that she was bursting with boundless potential and her parents had held her back, but it was another matter entirely to face a challenge—and meet with defeat.

Roz twisted in the saddle to stare back in the direction they had come. A moment of panic assailed her and she asked herself what the blazes she thought she was doing. She didn't have a change of clothes and they had only a few provisions and meager food. She might be eager to get to the bottom of this unsolved murder case...but at what cost?

If Eli was telling the truth about being set up as a murderer, then he needed to recuperate before returning to Denver. He *needed* her help.

Inhaling a fortifying breath, Roz set her sights on the towering peak where snow glowed incandescent white in the sunlight—even in midsummer. They might succumb to the cold temperatures at higher elevations—if they weren't attacked by animals first.

Roz glanced around apprehensively as she led the way through a thick grove of trees. While it was true that she had ventured between Denver and Philadelphia by stage and train a few times, she had never faced the hardships of the wilderness.

She sent a prayer heavenward that she might rise to the challenges that awaited her.

Chapter Three

Charles Matthews's first order of business the morning after Roz's disappearance was to send off a telegram to Lieutenant Harper at the garrison. An hour later a military patrol arrived at the newspaper office. The blond-haired lieutenant was the picture of authority as he posed rapid-fire questions. Unfortunately, Harper seemed more focused on reminding Charles of his military rank than showing concern about Roz's unexplained disappearance.

Charles wondered if he had been too hasty in giving Harper his blessing when the man asked for Roz's hand in marriage.

"Do you think Rozalie might have been abducted?" John asked. "Considering the rough elements of Denver society, she could have been set upon by some drunken scoundrel."

Charles grimaced at the appalling thought. "I don't know what happened to her. I checked with my good friend Judge Milner, but Roz didn't show up at his home. I have asked around town, but only the barber remembers seeing her heading west on horseback." He threw up his hands in exasperation. "How is it possible that in a town of more than five thousand citizens someone can't tell me where she is?"

"When was the last time you saw her?" John inquired.

"Just before dark." Charles glanced away and shifted restlessly from one foot to the other. "We had a disagreement and Roz stamped off half-mad. Ordinarily she cools down quickly. When she didn't come home last night I presumed she had stayed with her friend at Thompson's Hotel. But she didn't check into *any* hotel in town."

"Did you contact the city marshal?" Harper questioned.

Charles nodded. "I also printed handbills offering a reward for information, but no one has come forward.... Oh, my God!" he crowed when an unnerving thought bombarded him suddenly. "There was another murder yesterday evening, just before dark. It was committed by the same man who killed Albert Thompson." Charles swallowed hard. "What if that bastard happened onto Roz while she was alone and unprotected?"

John drew himself up like a soldier on parade, the heel of his gloved hand resting on the butt of his saber. "I will do my best to find Roz. My patrol will keep searching until she's home where she belongs."

Charles appreciated that. However, he was concerned that the lieutenant's *best* wouldn't be good enough, not if a wily criminal had abducted Roz. This job required a seasoned hunter or guide who knew the area west of town like the back of his hand.

After John performed an about-face and strode off, his troop at his heels, Charles closed up the office and went in search of a skilled guide. He found two willing takers then handed over the handbills with Roz's description on it.

He did not, however, send off a telegram to inform his wife that Roz was missing. That was exactly the kind of ammunition Sophia needed to make double-damn certain that Roz returned East to marry that foppish lawyer.

Back in the office, Charles plunked down at his desk and stared sullenly at the wall, seeing nothing but the superimposed image of Roz's face floating above him. If something dreadful happened to that girl he would never forgive himself—and his wife wouldn't let him forget it, either.

Charles loved his daughter dearly and he wanted her with him in Denver—and not just because Sophia wanted to ship Roz back East. Charles probably hadn't told Roz often enough how important she was to him. If she returned safe and sound, he would become more receptive to her needs and more sensitive to her desire to become a journalist.

And he was never going to let her out of his sight again!

Eli came awake with a soundless groan. It took a moment for his muddled brain to register the fact that unfamiliar voices rang out around him. The one voice he did recognize was Roz's. She sounded angry, indignant and a mite panicky. Eli pried open one eye to find the midmorning sunlight filtering through the trees. He discreetly appraised the situation without alerting the intruders that he had regained consciousness. He spotted two woolly-faced prospectors, dressed in tattered clothes. They were leading a mule that was laden down with provisions and equipment used to filter gold dust from streambeds.

"Kindly get out of our way." Eli heard Roz say in a demanding tone.

"That your husband sprawled out there?" one of the prospectors asked. "He looks half-dead...or full drunk."

"He is perfectly fine, just catching a well-needed nap," Roz snapped—and Eli wished she would watch that sassy tone of voice. She wasn't dealing with that egotistical moron who went by the name of Lieutenant John Harper.

"My husband is very protective of me," she went on boldly. "If he wakes up to find that you have waylaid us for no good reason, then he is liable to shoot now and ask questions later. And believe me, gentlemen, you won't be the first men he has blown right out of the saddle."

Eli heard the ruffians snicker.

"Don't look like much of a threat to me, lass," the red-haired miner commented. "For the right price we'll let you pass. You're on our claim, after all."

Eli didn't like the sound of that. Nor did he like the leers directed at Roz. Well, hell, he thought as he discreetly watched the burly men close ranks on Roz. Sounded like he was going to have to come to life and expend what little energy he could muster to stave off an attack.

While the two men focused their lusty attention on Roz, Eli inched his hand toward the leather sling that held his rifle. When the red-haired miner made a grab for Roz, Eli reared up and jabbed the rifle barrel against the man's ribs. The miner yelped in surprise and froze in midlunge.

"Hands off," Eli snarled threateningly. He grabbed his useless pistol and aimed it at the other man's chest. Two pairs of wide eyes swung to Eli. "You heard my wife right. I don't share her with anyone."

"Hey, no call to get all riled up, friend," the red-haired miner cajoled. "We don't often git to socialize with females in this neck of the woods. Can't blame a man for wantin' to have hisself a little fun, can ya?"

Eli stared stonily at both men. "Yes, I can. If you don't want to become supper for varmints then back off!"

To his relief, the men eased their horses away. But to his surprise, Roz snatched the pistol from his left hand and aimed it at the red-haired miner. "I think we should just shoot them and take their supplies," she spouted vindictively.

Eli decided Roz was nothing if not feisty, daring and determined to put up a threatening front to discourage future trouble from these prospectors. Although he admired her spunk—in an exasperated sort of way—he preferred to avoid an all-out gun battle. If she got herself shot, they would be in a worse mess than they were now.

"Take it easy, lady," the gray-haired prospector beseeched as he eyed her warily.

"I *never* take it easy when I'm angry and offended!"

she shouted at him. "Now get out of my way before I start shooting. Do you hear me!"

Who couldn't hear her? Even the birds roosting in the trees took flight.

"I'll give you to the count of three to make yourself scarce," Roz said sharply. "One...two..."

She made a big production of cocking the trigger of the useless pistol and Eli held his breath—he was pretty sure the waterlogged weapon would do more damage to *her* than to the scruffy prospectors if she tried to fire it.

"Okay, take it easy, lady. We're leaving," the gray-haired miner chirped. He cast a quick glance at Eli. "You got my sympathy, mister. This wife of yers is about half-loco."

"That's why her father begged me to take her off his hands," Eli insisted, then gestured to the wound on his head. "You can plainly see what happened when I stumbled home drunk and set fuse to her temper."

The comment served its purpose. The miners took off lickety-split. Eli breathed a gusty sigh of relief as he reached out to retrieve the pistol from Roz.

"Where the hell did they come from?" he asked.

Roz shrugged uncertainly. "They appeared from the trees and caught me unaware." She slumped in the saddle then glanced curiously at him. "Just how desperate *are* these prospectors for female attention?"

Eli holstered the pistol and urged his mount forward. "I rode into a mining camp near Devil's Point to see a shovel and pickax lashed together like a cross. It was decorated with a woman's hat and calico gown." He glanced meaningfully at Roz. "Four miners were dancing around the effigy and singing a ditty that you wouldn't want me to repeat. Does that tell you anything?''

''Good gracious,'' she gasped, appalled.

Eli ducked beneath a low-hanging branch. ''I was impressed with your performance, by the way. You aren't an actress by chance, are you?''

''No, I'm...not.''

Eli stared curiously at Roz, wondering what she had started to say. ''You live with your father, right?''

When she nodded, her pale blond hair glistened in the sunlight. Eli wondered what it would feel like to run his fingers through that mass of curly tendrils that reminded him of the color of corn silk.

Now there was a really bad idea, he scolded himself. He had already made the mistake of speculating what it would be like to kiss those dewy lips. The thought had entered his feverish dreams the previous night. Considering her hostile reaction to the advances of the two prospectors, Eli suspected Roz would have grabbed his rifle and finished him off for daring to take liberties with her.

''What?'' Roz demanded when Eli studied her speculatively for a long moment.

''Nothing important.'' Eli focused on the winding trail that led higher into the mountains. ''We'll stop to rest in an hour or two.''

Exhausted, Eli curled forward to rest his cheek against his horse's neck. The encounter with the prospectors had zapped his energy. He hoped an hour's nap would revive him. He definitely needed to muster the strength to clean and reload his pistol so it would function properly. If Roz decided to shoot the blasted thing he didn't want the gunpowder to backfire and mar her bewitching face.

Roz was also in need of a crash course in target practice, he mused. The way she held the pistol indicated she wasn't familiar with weapons. Eli smiled tiredly, impressed that what Roz lacked in practiced survivor skills she more than compensated with her defiance and daring. She had made a believer of the two miners when they tried to tangle with her.

Eli groaned miserably when an unseen hand jostled his shoulder, shaking him awake.

"It's been two hours," Roz told him. "I let you sleep for a while, but this looks to be the perfect place to rest."

Eli braced a hand on the pommel and pushed upright. He noticed they had reached the rippling stream located a half-day's ride from Simon's cabin. Although they were behind schedule, because of his slow pace, Eli decided to take a much-needed break to cleanse his wounds and eat. With effort he dismounted then clung to his horse for support.

"Fetch me another crutch, will you?"

When Roz raised a challenging brow and stared pointedly at him, he quickly tacked on, *"Please."*

She approached him a few moments later with the likeness of a cane, then rolled out his pallet. "Sit," she ordered.

Noting that Roz didn't always practice polite etiquette herself, Eli grinned wryly. He nearly fell off his feet when an impish smile curved her mouth upward and put a twinkle in her mesmerizing green eyes. Damn, but the woman radiated beauty and mischievous spirit and he couldn't help but be affected by her.

"Please sit," she requested. "While you're resting I want to refresh myself in the stream and wash out this gown."

The prospect of seeing what lay beneath the soiled blue gown hit Eli like a shotgun blast. He marveled that he still felt the stirring of desire, in spite of his weakened condition. He decided that Roz was one of those rare females who could even arouse a man who was in more pain than anyone should rightfully have to tolerate.

Just his luck that it was *this* particular woman who had been hovering on the riverbank when he came ashore the previous night. He had desperately needed her assistance, but she was proving to be a distraction of the worst sort.

"You are doing it again," Roz chided, jostling him from his erotic thoughts. "Why are you looking at me like that?"

Eli sighed audibly. "You have only to glance in the mirror to know the answer to that. You're too damn attractive and I would have to be dead a week not to notice."

He expected the candid remark would set her off, but to his amazement she said, "I'll take that as an honest compliment since you've been rendered harmless, McCain. I have no fear for my virtue since I know I can run circles around you." She pivoted toward the stream, then glanced back to peer at him from beneath a fan of long lashes. "I...uh...like the looks of you, too, McCain."

When she smiled radiantly at him, his heart flip-flopped in his chest.

"If I were in the market for a husband, which I absolutely am not," she added emphatically, "I would find you more interesting that the lieutenant my father wants me to marry or the stuffy lawyer my mother selected for me."

"And if I were in the market for a wife, which I absolutely am not," he said with an answering grin, "I would prefer someone with your spirit and gumption than the dull-witted females I have encountered during my travels."

He waved her on her way as he leaned on his improvised cane. "If you can't swim then don't venture too far from shore. If I have to come to your rescue while you're naked I might get distracted."

Roz chortled as she ambled toward the picturesque stream that tumbled lazily over the rock bed. Eli McCain was a fascinating contradiction. Oddly enough, she felt relaxed and at ease around him—even if he *did* turn out to be as bad as she predicted when he had taken her hostage.

She ducked behind a clump of bushes to remove her dress and petticoats then mulled over her ever-changing perception of Eli. True, he was plainspoken and rough around the edges—a far cry from the aristocrats her mother had tried to foist off on her. Also true, she had discovered that Eli had a ruthless, tough-as-nails streak that appeared in times of danger and desperation.

Yet, if he was to be believed, he had considered it

crucial to *her* safety that he whisk her away from the bridge and the unseen sniper. He had also come to her defense when those oafish prospectors tried to manhandle her. That definitely said something about his character and integrity.

Dressed in her chemise and pantaloons, Roz strode toward the stream. She asked herself if she truly believed Elijah McCain was capable of the brutal robbery and murder that had taken Albert Thompson's life. She knew for a fact that the money stolen from Albert's office was not among Eli's possessions—because she had looked.

Honestly, it was hard to imagine that this man— who, despite his pain and misery, had dragged himself upright in the saddle to protect her from harm—would commit premeditated theft and murder. If Eli had no scruples and no concern for her whatsoever, he would have played possum while the prospectors dragged her away.

No, Roz assured herself sensibly. There *had* to be more to Albert's murder than the three eyewitness accounts. She had seen for herself that someone had impersonated Eli's style of dress, right down to the moccasins and sombrero. No one, however, had noted Eli's mixed heritage or described the bead-and-silver necklace he wore. Those descriptions were cause for doubting his guilt.

However, she couldn't actually verify his story about an unidentified sniper because she didn't know the difference between the shots fired by a pistol or rifle and she had been hiding beneath the bridge. She had been too distracted by shouts, the clatter of hooves and the sight of two look-alikes pitching off the bridge to see where the shots came from.

Fleetingly she wondered if Gina Thompson and her mother would be as open-minded to Eli's claim of innocence. Already there were warrants out for McCain's arrest. Wanted posters, with his sketch and description, had been placed around town. There was also a price on his head. Roz knew that for a fact because she had checked before writing her detailed account of the murder. If Eli McCain returned to Denver he might be strung up and hanged before his case went to trial.

It wouldn't be the first time vigilantes in Colorado took the law into their own hands.

Until two days ago, Roz probably would have been part of the lynch mob because of her close ties to the Thompsons. Now Gina and her mother would likely think Roz had taken leave of her senses by questioning Eli's guilt and lack of involvement.

Roz dashed into the icy water when an inhuman snarl erupted behind her. Teeth chattering, she whirled around in midstream to see a dark, shaggy-haired animal that resembled a bear cub. When the growling beast scurried to the water's edge, Roz reflexively screamed Eli's name at the top of her lungs. The vicious-looking creature bared its teeth and spat at her. She treaded water, hoping the blasted varmint would give up and go away.

When she heard a loud thrashing downstream, she glanced sideways to see Eli hobbling on his crutch, his rifle braced against his side. When he spotted the snarly critter he balanced himself on his good leg and took its measure down the sight on the barrel. One well-aimed shot dropped the animal in its tracks—and testified to Eli's deadly accuracy with weapons.

"What is that strange animal?" she asked as she sank down to shield herself from view and shivered from the water's chill. "At first I thought it was a bear cub, but at close range it doesn't really look like one."

Eli leaned heavily on his cane. "That's a wolverine. It's one of the most vicious and powerful animals for its size that I have ever encountered," he told her. "Trappers detest wolverines because they kill for the pleasure of killing. Not unlike some men I've met," he added meaningfully. "Wolverines also have a clever knack of stealing bait from a hunter's trap without getting caught."

He glanced from the lifeless creature to Roz, his gaze roving intimately over her. "Getting cold yet?"

"Freezing," she said through chattering teeth.

"Then I suppose I should make myself scarce so you can come ashore."

"Either that or just shoot me and put me out of my misery." She eyed him steadily. "This is your second chance to get rid of me, you know."

Eli cocked his head and studied her for a moment. "You still don't believe I'm innocent, do you?"

"I—" Roz clamped her blue-tinged lips together then decided to be honest with him. "The jury is still out, McCain. If I put blind faith in everyone I have met I shudder to think where I would be now."

She predicted he would take exception to her candid remark, but he simply nodded. "Fair enough. I wouldn't be alive myself if I had fallen prey to every deception I have encountered. I always figured that blind trust was the last step you took before you ended up *dead* wrong.''

When he disappeared from view Roz paddled ashore to retrieve her wet gown and petticoats. Ah, what she wouldn't give for a set of dry clothes, a cup of hot coffee and a soft bed, she mused whimsically.

Her enthusiasm for adventure was wearing thin. That realization came as a crushing disappointment to Roz. She wanted to be a free spirit who made a place for herself in this man's world. But, at the first sign of inconvenience and trouble, she was yearning for the luxuries and comforts of home.

''Brace up, Rozalie,'' she told herself as she wiggled into her clinging gown. ''What doesn't kill you is supposed to make you stronger. You wanted to count for something and this is your chance to prove that you are made of sturdy stuff.''

Roz rallied her flagging spirits and hiked back to camp.

Eli glanced up from disassembling his pistol when he heard Roz approach. He inwardly groaned when he noticed her wet gown clinging to her voluptuous curves and swells like a coat of paint. It was bad enough that his imagination had been running rampant after he had seen her treading water in midstream. But this was ten times worse!

He definitely wasn't as bad off as he thought if forbidden desire could affect him like this. Not that he was going to do anything about it, of course, he told himself sensibly. That green-eyed siren didn't trust him completely and she was reluctant to believe his story of trumped-up charges. Not to mention the fact that she was so far above his social station that she was completely unattainable to him.

If he knew what was good for him he would look upon her as just another temporary traveling companion. Just because she was more intriguing and attractive than the ones he usually encountered shouldn't matter.

Things would be easier when they reached the cabin, he reassured himself. Simon would be on hand to make sure Eli didn't forget his place at the bottom of the social totem pole. A woman like Roz certainly deserved better than a reckless fling with a tumbleweed half-breed that never stayed in one place long enough for grass to grow beneath his moccasins.

Eli breathed a sigh of relief when Roz wrapped herself in the Indian blanket. The visual torment of seeing the rigid peaks of her nipples straining against the damp fabric inspired way too many ideas on how to while away time during this rest stop.

"You need to learn to shoot," Eli blurted out with the second thought that popped in his head. The first thought was entirely too erotic to voice.

"I thought I gave a passable impression of being able to handle a weapon when those miners showed up," she replied as she shivered beneath the quilt.

Eli leaned out to retrieve his saddle bag then tossed her one of his shirts. "You'll never warm up in those wet clothes. Give them to me and I'll hang them up to dry."

The shirt disappeared beneath the blanket. Eli forced himself to concentrate on cleaning his pistol while Roz squirmed out of her clothes. When he tried to rise up on one knee to grab her wet garments she waved him off.

"You sit and rest. I'll tend to my laundry."

Eli's breath logjammed in his chest, nearly strangling him, when she emerged from the quilt like a butterfly from a cocoon. The oversize shirt cascaded to midthigh, exposing well-shaped legs and skin that looked so soft that it made his mouth water and his body harden—competing painfully with his tender head and aching leg.

He watched her walk away, tormentingly aware there was nothing between her shapely body and that shirt. "Are you purposely trying to drive me crazy?" he asked more sharply than he intended.

When she reached up to drape her clothes over the tree limbs, the shirt rode dangerously high on her thighs. Eli forgot to breathe. "Damn it, Roz!" he croaked when he recovered his powers of speech.

She pivoted toward him and braced her hands on her hips, unintentionally emphasizing the trim indentation of her waist. "Just because you're irritable and cranky doesn't mean I'll let you take it out on me, McCain. And I am not trying to drive you crazy. I just don't expect you to wait on *me* when the very reason for this stop is to allow *you* to rest. And really, you act as if you've never seen a woman half-dressed before."

She eyed him meaningfully. "I might not be entirely convinced of your innocence, but I am not so gullible as to believe *that!*"

Eli peeled off his shirt, leggings and moccasins then rose inelegantly to his feet. Wearing nothing but his breeches, he took grand satisfaction in noting that

Roz's attention had shifted to his bare chest and that she was looking her fill. He also noticed the pink tinge that rose from her neck, to her cheeks and then stained her hairline.

Well, good, it was nice to know that he wasn't the only one around here whose sap was rising. She was staring at him as if she had never seen a shirtless man before. It gave him a fierce sense of pleasure to know that he probably *was* the first and that she was as intensely aware of him as he was of her.

"I'm going to take a bath." Cold water should cure what ailed him, he hoped. "Grab the rifle and shoot anything that moves, except the horses…and me. I have enough bullet holes in me already." When he limped past her, she was still staring at his bare chest in trancelike fascination. "Close your mouth, woman. You look like a fish," he teased as he hobbled toward the stream.

Roz wilted onto the pallet and watched Eli disappear into the underbrush. She could feel her face pulsating with heat and she scolded herself fiercely for becoming rattled by the sight of his broad shoulders, the hard bands of whipcord muscles on his chest and washboard belly. Except for the scars on his shoulder and arm he was absolute male perfection.

Sweet mercy! She had seen statues of Greek gods that didn't compare to him. Eli McCain was a perfect study of masculinity. She had been assailed by the outrageous urge to reach out and explore the corded tendons and textures of his bronzed skin. He intrigued her and she wanted to see even more of him….

What the devil was wrong with her? she wondered,

aghast. She had never found other men wildly interesting or sexually stimulating, so why was *he* the one
who had become the object of her feminine curiosity
and fascination?

Probably because he didn't treat her like some frag-
ile china doll and didn't patronize her as if she were
dim-witted. He didn't fuss, fawn and ply her with ef-
fusive flattery, the way most of her escorts did. She
liked that about him. A lot.

That, and his incredible masculine chest that her fingers itched to explore...

"Stop it," Roz scolded herself.

But it didn't do any good. Her gaze drifted to the
place where Eli disappeared and her imagination ran
wild. She suspected that seeing Eli McCain in all his
masculine glory would be an impressive sight to be-
hold.

Roz admitted that she had been plagued with insa-
tiable curiosity since childhood. The whys, whens,
wheres and hows of journalism seemed second nature
to her. Never having seen what a man looked like in
the altogether, she supposed it was only natural that
she wanted to find out. Why not appease her curiosity
with the most appealing masculine specimen that ever
crossed her path?

Even if wicked temptation and tantalizing speculation were tormenting her to no end, she was not going
to spy on Eli to appease her feminine curiosity.

Annoyed with the wayward direction of her
thoughts, Roz made a beeline for her damp clothing
and hurriedly dressed. Then she rolled up the pallet and
secured it to the saddle. She gathered the bulging sad-

dle bags and tied them in place. She intended to be ready to ride the instant Eli returned to camp because she suddenly couldn't trust herself. Feminine desire was making its presence known—and felt. These unwanted tingles were disturbing and she felt the need for the kind of distraction that riding through the rugged terrain provided.

She glanced skyward to note the afternoon sun was playing hide-and-seek with the clouds that were piling up on the towering mountain peaks. A cool breeze drifted over her and Roz shivered in her damp clothes. If she wasn't mistaken, a storm was heading in their direction.

When Eli limped back to the campsite he frowned curiously at her. "What's the rush to leave, Roz? I was going to give you shooting lessons before we rode off."

"Let's postpone target practice until tonight," she requested. She gestured skyward, careful to stare anywhere except at his bare chest. "A storm is building and you insisted that we had several miles to cover to reach the cabin."

"I need a fresh shirt before we leave," Eli requested.

She fished a shirt from his saddle bags. When she pivoted to hand it to him she noticed the odd brand on his right arm. A circle the size of a silver dollar, inset with a half-moon, had been etched on the skin above his wrist.

"What is that?" she asked, pointing to the tattoo.

Eli stuffed his arms into the shirt. "The mark of Cheyenne," he said as he buttoned the garment. "It's been there for as long as I can remember. It's part of my heritage that was lost when I was a child too young to recall much about my mother who was of Indian and Spanish descent.''

''And what of your father?'' she questioned curiously.

He shrugged. ''I was ten years old the last time I saw my white father. All I remember was that, in the middle of the night, he came stumbling toward me—probably so drunk that he could barely stand up. He tossed me on the back of my horse and slapped it on the rump. I had to hold on for dear life to stay aboard.''

''He just left you to fend for yourself?''

Roz was outraged by the very idea of sending a child out alone in the darkness. She had dealt with squabbling parents who put half a continent between them, but Eli had been cast out alone. Who would do such a cruel thing to a child?

''Did you try to find your way back to your father?'' she asked.

''It was impossible during the snowstorm in the mountains,'' he replied as he hobbled toward his horse. ''Luckily, Simon Foster found me the next morning and took me under his wing. He taught me the fur trapping and trading business. I spent several summers with the Ute tribe because Simon insisted that I should know something about my mother's culture, even if it couldn't be with the Cheyenne that had migrated to the Dakotas to avoid the white invasion. Simon is the only father I remember clearly.''

Sweet merciful heavens! Roz thought. Eli was a man without knowledge or a link to his past. No wonder he roamed the mountain range like a lost soul. He didn't know where he belonged.

"I'm sorry," she murmured sympathetically.

"Don't be." Eli hauled himself onto the horse. "You don't miss what you never had. Besides, Simon did right by me, which is more than some white men might have done if they had stumbled onto a mixed-breed child that was injured and nearly frozen to death."

Roz watched Eli veer west and then she counted all her blessings. She thought it was incredibly sad that Eli had no real contact with his mother's family and no idea why his father had sent him racing off into the unknown without a word of explanation.

Whoever this Simon Foster person was, Roz wanted to hug the stuffing out of him for undertaking the responsibility of raising an abandoned child of questionable heritage.

Chapter Four

"So tell me about yourself," Eli entreated as he took them deeper into the forbidding mountains. "Raised with a silver spoon in your mouth, were you? What was that like?"

Eli was anxious to turn the focus of conversation to Roz. He didn't know why he had shared his uncertain past with her. He had never divulged that much of himself to anyone except Simon. And he sure as hell had felt self-conscious when those luminous green eyes looked upon him with sympathy and concern.

That was the very last thing Eli wanted from this beguiling female. But he quickly reminded himself that what he wanted wasn't what he would allow himself to have. He would protect Roz as best he could while he recuperated. Then he would return to Denver to determine who had paid his look-alike to set him up for murder.

"It *was* an easy way of life," Roz agreed as they rode side by side. "I was educated in the East, lived in a spacious home with my mother and grandparents and never lacked for food or clothing."

She wrinkled her nose. "Unfortunately, I yearned to return to Denver after my parents separated. The social life that my mother relishes seems superficial and inconsequential to me. Wealth, title and breeding are important to my mother and my grandparents."

Eli could just imagine how appalled Roz's family would be if they knew she was tramping around alone with a man who had no blue-blooded pedigree whatsoever.

"Mother refused to tolerate the life Denver had to offer because, at that time, the upstart community afforded none of the luxuries and cultural entertainment she thrived on. She insisted on returning to Pennsylvania where she was raised. My father, however, refused to be sucked back into the kind of life he had purposely left behind. He craved the adventure of watching the foundling town grow up around us."

"Ah, so that's where you get your craving for challenge. It must be nice to know where you inherited your traits," Eli muttered. He had secretly wondered where he had acquired his good and bad traits. Unfortunately, his hazy memories of his father were twenty years old and viewed through the eyes of a child. Eli remembered even less about his mother and her family.

"What does your father do for a living?" Eli questioned as he absently rubbed his throbbing leg.

He frowned, bemused, when Roz shifted uneasily in the saddle. He recalled that she had been hesitant to tell him her last name, too. Now he wondered exactly who she was and how it was going to affect the charge of kidnapping he would inevitably face when they returned to Denver.

Never mind that he had taken Roz along for her own protection, as well as her assistance. No one was likely to believe a half-breed who was already wanted for murder.

"You might as well tell me who you are," he prodded impatiently. "I need to know what I'll be up against when I ride back to town."

"My father is Charles Matthews," she said eventually.

Eli winced. He wasn't familiar with many folks in Denver, but he definitely recognized that name. "The Charles Matthews who owns the *Denver Daily Chronicle?*" When she nodded he groaned aloud. "Hell! There will be handbills posted all over town, not to mention at every mining camp this side of the Great Divide!"

His annoyed gaze landed squarely on Roz. "Damn it, woman, the bounty on my head is probably sky-high already. If someone links us together it will be even worse. You should have told me who you were right off."

"I didn't tell you because I thought you were a murdering thief. I was afraid you might try to hold me for ransom," she flung back at him. "I certainly had no intention of doing you any favors when I presumed that you planned to leave me for dead after I had served your purpose."

Eli glared at her. "Considering my background, do you think *I* would leave anyone for dead?"

"How was I supposed to know that you might be sensitive about such things?" she retaliated defensively. "You only told me a few minutes ago that you had been abandoned as a child."

Eli huffed out his breath. "Fine. You had no call to trust me or to know what I might be capable of doing. But I suspect your father wallpapered every business in Denver with your picture and offered a reward for your return—*before* your message has a chance to reach him. No doubt, he *did* notify your would-be fiancé to send out patrols to track you down." He growled sourly. "Is there more good news you'd like to share with me?"

"No, that about covers it. Except..." Roz averted her gaze then added, "I wrote a story about Albert Thompson's murder and offered readers a detailed description of you that I compiled from three eyewitnesses."

Eli howled in dismay. "God A-mighty, you're a journalist?" He glared accusingly at her. "Don't tell me. Let me guess. Our misadventure is going to make front-page headlines. Damn it, Roz, you deceived me!"

"I did no such thing. Besides, *you* kidnapped me," she countered.

"I did not! I saved your hide. You should be thanking me for it!" He stared at her in annoyance. "Just exactly what did you say in the message you sent your father? Or dare I ask?"

"I assured him that I was safe and unharmed, but I didn't want to divulge my whereabouts for a few days," she informed him. "With luck, Papa will call off any search he might have requested when he receives my message.

"You know, this could work to your advantage,"

she said after a pensive moment. "If I am convinced of your innocence, then I am not only the *journalist* who can tell your side of the story, but also the *witness* who saw you and the imposter pitch off the bridge."

"Well, that is one story you aren't going to write," Eli said with finality. "I don't want or need to have my tale of woe splashed across the front page of the newspaper. I want to find out who framed me. Then I intend to get the hell out of Denver for good."

"If it's any comfort, the story I wrote about your alleged involvement in the robbery and murder didn't make it to print. My father discarded it and we got into a shouting match about *my* desire for a career in journalism and *his* desire to see me married—to counter my mother's decree that I should return to Philadelphia to marry Winchester Chapman the Third."

"But now that you have disappeared your father probably feels guilty and printed your story," Eli muttered in speculation. "I have no idea if my look-alike washed ashore to catch the blame for the murder."

Thunder boomed overhead, punctuating Eli's frustration. He had definitely taken the wrong woman along with him. He was a wanted man with the bounty the size of a king's ransom on his head and she was an aspiring journalist, the daughter of a man whose business it was to spread information far and wide.

Fate, it seemed, could be as cruel as polite society's distaste for half-breeds, he thought sullenly.

"Well, I guess it could be worse," Eli said, trying to regain a positive attitude—difficult though it was, considering his condition and the situation. "Your father could be a judge who is out for revenge..." His voice trailed off when he noticed the odd expression on Roz's enchanting face. "Now what?" he asked, though he wasn't sure he wanted to know.

"Judge William Milner is my father's oldest and dearest friend," she confided. "He is my godfather and honorary uncle."

Eli recoiled when a huge raindrop slapped him in the face and Roz's last comment settled over him like impending doom. Damn, the day had started out badly and it had gone downhill in a hurry. Eli wondered what else could go wrong, but he felt so lousy at the moment that he wasn't sure he wanted to find out.

It might be even more depressing.

Lightning flickered across the evening sky and thunder boomed overhead. Roz instinctively ducked then glanced apprehensively at Eli. His condition had grown steadily worse during the strenuous ride that led them up a rugged mountain trail. Roz noted the taut lines that bracketed Eli's mouth, the waxen color of his face, his hollow-eyed stare and the telltale bloodstains that seeped through the bandage on his thigh to discolor his buckhide breeches.

"I think we should stop for the night," she recommended in between rumbles of thunder. "You need to rest."

"I can make it a little farther," Eli insisted.

Roz rolled her eyes at his relentless determination. "This ride is sapping what's left of your strength. The sky is about to open up—"

No sooner were the words out of her mouth than huge raindrops pattered against the leaves of the towering trees and the temperature dropped a quick ten degrees. Roz took command of the situation when she spotted an overhang of rock that could offer protection from the storm that had been looming on the horizon for the past several hours.

When Eli slumped over his horse, Roz grabbed his reins and veered off the winding path. Leaving Eli asleep—or unconscious, she didn't know which—she dismounted to gather an armload of firewood before the pounding rain soaked everything in sight.

She muttered an oath when she brushed her hand over Eli's forehead and discovered he was burning up with fever. "And you call me stubborn? You'll catch your death of cold and never survive to present your side of the story," she grumbled at him as she unfastened the rope harness that secured him to his horse.

Bracing her feet, Roz tugged on Eli's arm until he rolled from the horse. Teeth gritted, she staggered beneath the excessive weight then jostled him hard enough to rouse him. With a groan Eli wobbled unsteadily then half stumbled as Roz guided him toward the shelter provided by the jutting stone ledge. When Eli accidentally tripped on the hem of her gown they tumbled to the ground in a tangle of arms and legs. Roz found herself sprawled beneath him, her face mashed into his massive chest.

"Sorry," Eli mumbled groggily. He shifted sideways. "Damn leg is as stiff as a fence post. You okay?"

"I'm fine," she assured him.

The fact that he was considerate enough to ask, despite the terrible shape he was in—due in part, no doubt, to her inadequate attempt at primitive surgery—left Roz wondering how this man could possibly be a cold-blooded killer.

A half-breed, who was a newcomer in Denver, made a perfect mark to take the blame for robbery and murder. In addition, Eli's style of dress, borrowed from the Indian, Spanish and white cultures, made him easy to describe and impersonate. In short, he was a perfect mark to divert suspicion from someone who had plotted to commit murder. The question that Roz was at a loss to answer was why had Albert Thompson become the target?

The moment Eli rolled away, Roz bounded up to retrieve the pallet and supplies. While rain formed a curtain over the ledge she set up their meager campsite. Despite the chill of being soaked to the bone, Roz started the fire near the stone wall, hoping the rock would absorb the heat and provide much-needed warmth for Eli. That done, she divested Eli of his damp shirt and tucked him beneath the Indian blanket.

"Some kidnapper I turned out to be," he said hoarsely. "Might as well be the other way around since you're having to do all the work and take care of me."

The half smile that pursed his ashen lips tugged at her heart. The poor man, who had been ostracized by society and unjustly accused of a crime, was feeling guilty because he was in no condition to take care of *her*....

Unjustly accused. Roz stilled, realizing that her indecision had fallen by the wayside. For some reason—and don't ask her why, because she couldn't rationally explain it—she *believed* Eli.

Someone should, she mused as she blotted his damp shirt against his feverish brow. Hard-bitten and dangerous though Eli could be when the situation demanded, he still had a good heart and soul. He simply didn't fit the profile of a merciless outlaw, and she was not going to doubt his innocence again. She was going to make it her personal mission to discover who was responsible for setting him up as the prime suspect and figure out why Albert had been marked for death.

"Water...please," Eli wheezed as his disoriented gaze drifted to her.

Roz retrieved the canteen and held it to his lips. When he drank his fill, Roz took a sip then turned her attention to his leg wound. When she unwrapped the bandage her stomach rolled. Infection had definitely set in with a vengeance, turning his flesh an angry red. The strain of riding up treacherous inclines—that were more suited to mountain goats—caused the wound to bleed profusely.

Hurriedly she rooted into the saddle bag to locate the whiskey bottle then dribbled the amber liquid over his leg. Eli came off the ground with a tortured howl then collapsed on the pallet. He treated Roz to a liberal dose of obscenities. The juiciest curses had her name attached to them.

Roz didn't take offense. She predicted she would have sworn up a storm herself, if she had been in his moccasins.

"Curse me to your heart's content," she said as she grabbed his knife and held it over the flickering flames. "But I have to clean out the infection."

She saw the look of bleak resolution settle on his

pale features as he gave her the go-ahead. Hands much steadier than they had been the previous night, Roz offered him a stick to bite down on. Impulsively, she leaned down to press her lips to his perspiring brow. She didn't recoil when his hand curled around her neck to bring her lips to his.

"Humor me with a little pleasure before the inevitable pain," he whispered raggedly. "Truth is, I've wanted to kiss you since I laid eyes on you."

The moment his sensuous mouth moved beneath hers a delicious warmth spread through her veins. Then his lips opened on hers and he explored the recesses of her mouth, traced the edge of her teeth with his tongue for a long breathless moment. He kissed her as if he were dying and she were providing his last breath.

Fiery sensations blazed through her, compelling her to return the mushrooming need that built with unexpected intensity. Roz had been kissed a time or three but never with such a lack of restraint. And most assuredly, she had never felt as if the world had come crashing down around her when she was in a man's embrace.

Pleasure pinwheeled through her as his darting tongue tempted, teased and explored. The lean fingers clamped on her neck brought her body in close contact with his. She couldn't draw breath without breathing him in, without feeling his muscled contours meshed intimately to her.

Roz swore that she had been struck by lightning. Electrifying sensations sizzled through every nerve and muscle in her body. If she had ever been this aware and attuned to a man she couldn't recall when—or whom—it might have been. There was simply something about Eli McCain that drew her eager response. It didn't take but one heart-stopping kiss to remind her that she was very much a woman and he was all man.

One kiss was turning out to be one too many, Eli thought dazedly. He had kissed his fair share of women, but none of them had tasted like Roz. Although he knew he was burning with fever, he was cognizant enough to tell the difference between that and the white-hot ache that overcame him the instant his lips touched Roz's.

It was as if she'd been born to match this well of passion that bubbled up inside him. That was ridiculous, he tried to tell himself. Roz wasn't his soul mate—if he believed in such a thing. And he shouldn't be affected by such sensations while she was pressed against him.

He had never experienced such an uncontrollable response to any woman, even though he knew she wasn't the kind of woman a man like him should be kissing in the first place.

What the hell are you doing, McCain? The voice of conscience roared in outrage. *Back the hell off. Now!*

It took every ounce of willpower Eli could muster to release his possessive hold on Roz. He swallowed hard, wishing he could drown in the intoxicating taste of her. And damn it, why was she staring at him with that startled sense of wonder? One look at that lush mouth, swollen from the intensity of their kisses, and he wanted to treat himself to another taste.

McCain, you idiot, you should have left well enough

alone. When she inflicts pain, it's going to be exactly what you deserve.

Roz was sorely disappointed when Eli pulled away long before she was ready to give up the feel of those warm lips moving expertly over hers and the tantalizing pleasure of rock-hard muscle pressed against her sensitized flesh. She blinked as if emerging from a trance to note the hint of a scowl on his bearded face. It made her wonder if she had disappointed him. The exact opposite was true for her. Roz's senses were still reeling from the erotic impact he had on her.

"Go ahead and torture me within an inch of my life. Do your worst, Green Eyes," he murmured before he clamped the twig between his teeth.

It took a moment for her senses to clear so she could focus on cleansing the wound. Like a swimmer about to dive underwater, she drew in a deep breath and set to work. But it was next to impossible to concentrate on her task when Eli stiffened and groaned, testifying to the agony she was inflicting on him.

"Brace yourself for the sting," she warned as she grabbed the whiskey bottle again.

His body shook as the liquor seeped between the stitches and he clamped down so hard on the twig that it snapped in two. His breath came out in ragged spurts while Roz fished into the saddle bag for the poultice. After she had packed the wound she tore off another strip from her petticoat to wrap his thigh.

"I owe you a new dress, as well as my life," he panted. "Never been beholden to a woman before. If something happens to me, tell Simon that I want him to give you—"

She pressed her forefinger to his lips to shush him. "Stop yammering and rest, McCain," she ordered.

"Bossy female." He smiled faintly—and then passed out.

Roz reached out to smooth the tousled raven hair across his forehead then kissed his brow. It astonished her that her opinion of Eli had completely reversed itself in the course of the day. Furthermore, she hadn't voiced the slightest objection when he practically kissed her senseless. She had never let another man this close—physically or emotionally. But *he* got to her without even trying. He impressed her most because he was making *no* effort to impress her, yet her fascination with him had increased tenfold.

"Ill-fated attraction, if ever there was one," she murmured as she eased away from Eli.

The prospect of marrying Winchester Chapman the Third and living in the lap of luxury held no appeal for her. Wedding Lieutenant John Harper didn't interest her, either. No, she was rapidly developing a soft spot in her heart for a man who had scratched and clawed for what little respect society granted him. To make matters worse, a conniving killer had decided Eli would make a perfect suspect to take the blame for murder.

Well, if nothing else came of her unusual association with Eli McCain, Roz vowed to help Eli prove his innocence and redeem his reputation.

The thought caused Roz to wince. By rising to Eli's defense she would be betraying her long-standing friendship with the Thompsons. A riptide of emotions hounded her as she shed her wet gown then cuddled up beside Eli to provide them both with enough warmth to endure the chill of the rainy night.

As the mountain trail turned into a swift-moving stream and rain came down in torrents around them, Roz closed her eyes and prayed that her newfound allegiance to Eli wasn't a disastrous mistake.

If Eli McCain had cleverly manipulated her, plied her with deceptive lies and used his wiles to insure her cooperation, she could lose the one true friend she had. Gina Thompson would never understand why Roz might side with a nomadic half-breed who was suspected of ruthlessly ending her father's life.

Charles Matthews stared in disbelief at the message from Roz that had arrived with the driver of the evening stage. "'I'm safe and unharmed, but I can't divulge my whereabouts at the moment,'" he read aloud. "Why the hell not?" he asked himself.

He had no clue what to make of this unexpected missive from his daughter. Frustrated, Charles paced his office, unsure whether to call off the two search parties that were combing the area around Denver. What if Roz had been taken captive and *forced* to send that message? What if the next message he received was a ransom demand?

Charles stopped short and stared out the window, watching the throng of passersby file down the boardwalk. Even if he decided to call off the searches it would be difficult to get word to Lieutenant Harper and the trail guides he had hired.

Whirling around, Charles snatched up the article he had written about Roz's mysterious disappearance and read it again. Concern for his daughter's safety compelled him to print the story, despite the baffling message from Roz. Only when the search parties caught up with Roz could he be absolutely certain that she was safe and had not been bent to the will of a ruthless desperado.

The thought of Roz being used for some hombre's perverted pleasure had Charles swearing a blue streak. If any man touched his daughter, he would pay with his life!

Tormented by worst-case scenarios and driven by purpose, Charles manned the printing press. He was going to see to it that every citizen and traveler in the area knew Roz was missing. He would increase the reward for information about her, too, Charles decided immediately.

Only when he saw his daughter *in person* and heard *her* tell him that she truly *was* safe and sound would he believe it. And not one moment before!

Eli awakened the morning after the rainstorm feeling bone-weary and completely wrung out. His leg was throbbing something fierce and piling onto his horse had been nothing short of excruciating. Every jarring motion of his steed, as it scrabbled up the steep inclines, left Eli wincing in discomfort. Yet, an odd sense of peace stole over him, knowing Roz was right beside him, her concern evident on her enchanting face.

It shouldn't have mattered, he told himself sensibly. He didn't really need a traveling companion because he was accustomed to being alone. But being a wanted man was a new twist, and battling pain wasn't helping,

either. Then there was the fact that he had succumbed
to the insane urge to kiss Roz during a momentary
lapse of good judgment.

Eli tried to blame his impulsiveness on delirium, but
he knew himself well enough to admit that was only
an excuse. Right or wrong—and it was definitely
wrong—he was fiercely attracted to this feisty female.
Now that he had dared to taste her dewy-soft mouth
and feel her lush body molded familiarly to his, he
wanted more.

*You are completely out of your mind, McCain. The
fever has fried your brain,* came that niggling voice of
logic.

It was only that he felt weak and vulnerable and
craved security and contentment, he diagnosed. Just
like those early days when he had been an abandoned
child. He had instinctively reached out for moral support, even when he had been wary and cautious of Simon. Now it was happening again. But if he knew what
was good for him he would keep an emotional and
physical distance from that green-eyed siren or his life
would become more complicated than it was already.

It didn't help that Roz was all sweetness and concern
each time she glanced in his direction. Certainly, she
was still strong-willed and spirited—couldn't cure her
of that—but this morning she had stopped staring at
him in confusion and distrust.

She hadn't come right out and said that she didn't
believe he was responsible for the murder of her
friend's father, but her attitude toward him had
changed. Sick as he was, he still noticed the loss of her

antagonism and the end of those wary, suspicious glances.

Eli's stomach flip-flopped, as it had been doing off and on all morning, and he shifted uncomfortably on the saddle. *A few more hours,* he chanted silently. He could let his guard down completely when he reached Simon's secluded cabin.

"We should stop so you can rest," Roz announced as she thrust out her hand to grab his reins. "Forgive me for saying so, but you look awful."

Eli shook his head, astonished at the amount of energy the gesture required. "No, we have to reach the cabin."

"Or die trying?" she said, and scoffed.

"Thank you for the encouragement," he said crankily. "It makes me feel ten times better."

"You should at least have a bite to eat," she insisted. "You refused breakfast."

Yes, he had. The thought of food made him nauseous. Sipping water occasionally was the best he could manage.

Eli nudged his horse with his good leg and led the way around the tumble of fallen rocks. "We'll keep moving, just in case search parties are following us."

He heard her exaggerated sigh of exasperation and smiled faintly. There was one thing you could say about Roz Matthews. She didn't hesitate to make her opinions known. She thought this jaunt was foolhardy and that he would collapse long before he reached the protection of the mountain cabin.

Yet, she seemed more concerned for *him* than for herself. Now that was a novel experience. Most folks viewed him as a dispensable commodity. His presence was tolerated if he could save someone's hide, but that was as far as most of his associations in civilization went.

Furthermore, he couldn't allow Roz's attentiveness toward him to change his perspective toward her. And he would not kiss her again, no matter how much he wanted to. She was doing him a tremendous service by trying to nurse him back to health, and he was not going to repay her by taking what could never belong to him. If he had a brain in his head he wouldn't forget that, either.

Two hours later Eli uncurled his sluggish body from his slouching position over his horse and pushed himself upright in the saddle. He mumbled a prayer of gratitude to the powers that be—both Indian and white—when he saw the crude log cabin that was surrounded by a canopy of towering pines.

The place had been home to him before a severe case of wanderlust grabbed hold of him and sent him searching for his long-lost father. Eli had taken one job after another as a guide, army scout and stagecoach guard, moving from one locale to the next in search of his past. But never in ten years had anyone been able to point Eli in the direction of the man he had described, who went by the name of Marcus McCain.

"I sincerely hope this is our destination," Roz said as she gestured to the mountain fortress that was perched on an outcropping of stone.

"Home sweet home," Eli confirmed.

"Good, because I don't think you can survive another two hours."

"Again, thank you for the moral support," he said caustically.

"Blast it, McCain. I'm worried about you!" she burst out in true Roz Matthews fashion. "Simon damn well better be a miracle worker if we are going to save that leg. You have pushed yourself to the limits for two days."

Eli hated to admit that he, too, was gravely concerned about whether he still would have a left leg when all was said and done. If the infection festered again he would have little choice but to resort to amputation.

His horse halted in familiar territory, waiting for Eli to dismount. Before he could drag himself from the saddle Roz was beside him, offering support. The last time she had tried that they had ended up in an unceremonious heap on the ground. This time Eli made an effort not to trip them up.

Eli frowned curiously when Simon didn't immediately appear on the stoop to greet them. He glanced toward the lean-to, noting Simon's mule wasn't in its stall. Damn the luck. Where was that old coot when Eli needed him?

Leaning heavily on Roz, Eli staggered toward the cabin. His good leg threatened to buckle as he climbed the steps. When he felt himself teetering he thrust out a hand to grab the supporting beam.

"I cannot wait to get you in bed," Roz muttered.

Eli cocked a brow and managed a grin when Roz's exquisite features turned a becoming shade of pink.

When he met her embarrassed gaze, the vivid memory of their first kiss triggered sensations that Eli was frankly surprised he could feel while fever wracked his body. It didn't seem to matter how awful he felt. The woman had a fierce and lasting effect on him.

"I can't wait for you to get me in bed, either," he said wryly. "It will give me something to look forward to…if I survive."

"I wish I had kept my mouth shut," Roz grumbled as she propelled him across the porch. "That didn't come out the way I intended."

"Keep that smart mouth shut? Now there's an impossibility," he teased.

Her blush faded and she smiled at him as she reached for the door latch. That smile of hers nearly knocked the breath out of him. Weak and miserable though he was, her expression was like sunlight piercing through the gray thunderclouds that his life had become.

Once inside the cabin Eli hobbled unsteadily toward his corner bed. Every smidgen of energy and determination to make it to this isolated refuge deserted him. He literally collapsed onto the bed and groaned in relief.

"Where is the Miracle Man?" Roz questioned as she surveyed the cabin, then focused on the shelf of leather-bound books that were Simon's pride and joy. "Out hunting?"

"Dunno," Eli mumbled into his pillow.

"I'll get a fire going and make some stew," Roz volunteered.

"I can—" Eli tried to lever onto his elbows, but it

felt as if a hundred-pound weight were strapped to his back.

"*No,* you can*not,*" she contradicted. "You are going to rest. I'll wake you when the meal is ready. I don't want to hear another peep out of you until then."

Eli didn't argue with her. Couldn't. He sagged bonelessly onto the straw mattress and fell asleep immediately.

Chapter Five

For two days and nights Roz worked tirelessly to combat the delirious fever that raged through Eli's body. His head wound had healed properly, but she'd had to swab his leg injury repeatedly to control the infection. In between bathing and caring for her patient she had tidied up the cluttered cabin, tended the horses and took short hikes around the panoramic countryside.

Roz found it oddly disconcerting that the cabin where Eli was raised held no sentimental mementos. No doubt this house was merely headquarters for two men who spent more time in the wilderness than in the shelter this modest home provided.

Each time Roz stared into Eli's pain-ridden features another corner of her heart crumbled. Eli was a man without true ties to his past, roaming the country in search of a connection to his heritage—and finding none. That aroused her suspicions and her curiosity. How was it possible that no one in this area knew what had become of his father? Had the man ventured farther west, choosing to discard the responsibility of a young child that would only slow him down?

Eli's quiet moan jostled Roz from her pensive musings. She pivoted away from the cookstove where she had been heating stew for their noon meal. She noticed that Eli looked more alert than he had in days.

"Welcome back," she greeted as she sat down on the edge of his bed. She cupped her palm over his forehead and smiled in relief. "I think your fever has finally broken."

Dazed blue eyes fixated on her then scanned the tidy quarters. "You cleaned up the place. Simon won't be able to find a thing, but it does look better than it has in years." He frowned curiously. "How could you have accomplished so much in such a short amount of time? And where the devil is Simon?"

"I haven't seen him. You've been asleep for more than two days and I have had plenty of time to give this cabin a thorough cleaning."

"Two days?" Eli crowed in amazement. "And Simon still hasn't showed up? Damn, I hope he's all right."

When Eli tried to sit up, Roz shoved the heel of her hand against his shoulder, forcing him back down. "You stay put," she demanded. "I have invested considerable time and effort in tending that infected wound. You aren't getting up until I say you can."

Eli grinned wryly. "Why is it that you have so much trouble remembering that *I'm* the one who is supposedly holding *you* hostage?"

She smiled mischievously, relieved to note that a hint of color had finally returned to his cheeks. For the first time since she had met him, he didn't look like the living dead. "In case you haven't noticed, I'm not very good at being submissive."

"I noticed that right off," Eli replied. His attention shifted to the stove. "Is that food I smell? I'm starved."

That was an exceptionally good sign. Roz hadn't been able to get him to eat more than a bite or two at one setting. He had survived too long on thin broth and sips of water. She bounded to her feet to ladle a cup of stew then spun around to see that Eli had defied her command and had pushed himself upright to recline against the rough-hewn wall.

"You don't take orders well, either," she said as she handed him the stew—and a disapproving stare.

"It comes from living in the mountains where your best friend—and sometimes worst enemy—is Mother Nature. She's the only one I usually answer to," he replied before he tasted the stew. "Damn, this is good. Writing skills, nursing skills and cooking skills, too. I can see why your parents are certain you have excellent marriage prospects." A smile twitched his lips. "Except for those stubborn and bossy streaks, you would make a fine wife. Just what is it about marriage that offends you, by the way?"

Roz settled back beside him on the bed, astounded that she could talk to him with such casual ease. "It's complicated."

"Most things are," he said between bites.

"First of all, I consider myself a new breed of woman," she confided.

"I'm in total agreement with that," Eli commented.

"My entire existence doesn't hinge on finding a man

who can provide security and protection,'' Roz continued then stared pointedly at Eli. ''And the last thing I want is a man who thinks he could control and dominate me. I want to be considered an equal.''

Eli chuckled. ''I hate to burst your bubble, but I'm not sure the world is prepared for your philosophies.''

''Which is why marriage would be a colossal mistake for me,'' she maintained. ''I saw enough of wedlock to last me a lifetime watching my squabbling parents. Growing up in a feuding household makes you question permanent commitment.'' She frowned. ''I think my parents cared deeply for each other, but they held such contradicting goals and aspirations that it was impossible for them to remain under the same roof.''

''So love wasn't the mortar that held them together?'' Eli questioned before he took another bite of hot stew.

''I think they loved each other, but apparently their differences of opinion and separate interests drove a wedge between them.'' Roz smiled ruefully. ''Sometimes it was difficult for me to tell the difference between love and hate in our household. There was considerable shouting and several retaliations to get under each other's skin. There were times when I swore that my existence caused the rift that resulted in their separation.''

Roz stared somberly at Eli. ''My mother would never consider divorce for fear of the scandal it would cause in Philadelphia society. My father has never once mentioned finalizing their separation because I don't think he's ever really gotten over Mother, no matter how crazy she makes him.

"And I can tell you for sure that if I were to have a child, it would never be caught in the middle of an ongoing feud. If complete indifference toward my spouse is the only way to avoid the conflicts in a marriage, then I choose not to wed at all. I have decided that I will make a better spinster than a wife."

"I can see that you have given this considerable thought," Eli remarked as he handed her the empty cup. "More…*please,*" he added when she shot him a stern glance.

"I have given this a *great* deal of thought," Roz emphasized as she retrieved the cup. "Spinsterhood is more widely accepted now that women are becoming better educated and are entering careers once held exclusively by men. In fact, some men claim they want nothing to do with educated women because they don't think they make dutiful, submissive wives."

"Well, it's plain to see that *submissive* will never be a word in your vocabulary," Eli taunted. "As for me, I'm a confirmed bachelor. Not because I don't believe in the existence of love, but because I have never been *in love.* My problem is that I don't have much in common with the weaker sex."

Roz slanted him a disapproving glance, and then realized he was teasing her. "And who has been flat on his back, delirious with fever and completely dependent on me, hmm? Weaker sex, indeed!" she sniffed.

"Figured that would get a rise out of you. Now fetch me some more stew. For a pampered aristocrat, your culinary skills are amazingly good."

She rose from the bed, unable to take offense at his backhanded compliment—especially when he delivered it with that endearing, lopsided smile. "You might be surprised to learn that those of us who eat with silver spoons have abundant talents," she said with the kind of aloof aplomb that would have done her mother proud. "Sometimes you just can't find good help and have only yourself to rely on, you know."

Eli's rumbling chuckle caused a coil of awareness to tighten inside her. What was it about this man that fascinated her so? He was an enigma, a walking contradiction to be sure. His unconventional upbringing and background intrigued her. He was articulate and spoke with just a hint of a Southern accent. He was also knowledgeable and intelligent.

He was *not* what society chose to label him, that was for certain.

Eli McCain was very much his own man, a warrior's warrior. He had scruples that were uncommon among the elite who would stab you in the back for the almighty dollar. Power, position and wealth didn't seem that important to Eli. If it was money he wanted, he could easily have sent a message to her father, demanding a ransom rather than allow her to send the missive herself.

Roz stopped in her tracks, her hand hovering over the ladle in the stew. It suddenly dawned on her that Eli had *trusted* her to send a message to her father without making demands or stipulations. She could have told her father who her traveling companion was and given Eli's description. Eli wouldn't have known until it was too late. Did that sound like the mind-set of a ruthless thief and murderer? Definitely not!

Eli cocked a curious brow when Roz stared at him overly long. "Now what?" he asked.

Roz shook herself loose from her meandering thoughts and filled the tin cup. "Nothing, McCain. Just eat your stew and regain your strength so I don't have to wait on you hand and foot. I can't dally around in the mountains indefinitely. I have obligations in society, you know," she added with a melodramatic air.

Eli snickered as he accepted the soup. "You know, you *would* make an exceptional snob if that was your aspiration, princess."

"Thank you, kind sir." She batted her eyes at him, struck a dignified pose and flicked an imaginary speck of lint from her gown. Then she made a spectacular production of settling her tattered skirts as she seated herself beside him once more. "My mother would be ever so pleased to hear you say that."

Eli leaned over to press a kiss to her cheek and said, "Personally, I like you just the way you are, so don't go putting on airs on my account."

Another jolt of awareness, mingled with uncontrollable desire, rippled through her. Roz had never experienced such a quick and volatile reaction to a man. She simply couldn't come within ten feet of Eli without responding to him.

"I shudder to think what it's going to be like to be eternally indebted to an uppity debutante like you," Eli teased, while sipping the hot broth. "No telling what you will have me doing to repay my debt of gratitude."

The comment caused Roz to purse her lips thoughtfully. "*Eternally* indebted, did you say? I will have to give serious consideration to that. Having a genie grant my fondest wishes provides me with stupendous power.''

"Don't get carried away," Eli cautioned. "I *will* draw the line if your newly acquired power goes straight to your head."

"A fiancé of my choosing is what I need to counter my parents' demands," Roz burst out suddenly. "I should have thought of that sooner. Instead of rebelling against their decrees, I should have *acted,* not *re*acted."

The color Eli had regained waned as his hollowed blue eyes locked with hers. "Don't look at me, princess. I'm the last man you need to pose as your fiancé." He flicked his wrist, shooing her away. "Go clean something and, while you're at it, think of another way for me to repay you. You don't need a half-breed with a price on his head posing as your betrothed."

Roz rose to gather the cooking utensils then set them to soak in the pan of sudsy water on the homemade sawbuck table. While she washed the dishes, she contemplated the prospect of having a temporary fiancé to run interference for her. Having Eli as a buffer between her parents' demands seemed the perfect solution.

He *did* owe her a favor, after all.

Except that he was a murder suspect. But if she made it her mission to investigate the incident thoroughly and managed to clear his name, he *would be* the perfect candidate.

Eli McCain wasn't interested in elevating his social position, as Lieutenant Harper was. Neither was he concerned about following Eastern protocol by merging one elite family with another the way Winchester

Chapman the Third was. Eli had no ulterior motive or hidden agenda. He *was* perfect, whether he thought so or not.

Roz smiled to herself as she tidied up. First she would help Eli solve this mysterious conspiracy and make certain the trumped-up charges were dropped. Then she would hold Eli to his offer to repay her for nursing him back to health—by insisting that he help her discard her two would-be fiancés.

And then they would be even, she decided as she glanced back to see that Eli had fallen asleep again.

She tiptoed over to tuck the quilt around him then skimmed her lips over his forehead. Oddly content, away from the hustle and bustle of town, Roz ambled outside to admire the spectacular landscape that seemed to extend to the far horizon.

By nightfall, Eli was feeling better than he had since the shoot-out on the bridge. Roz had insisted that he eat every few hours to regain his strength, and he felt like a stuffed turkey. But thanks to her persistence and nursing skills, Eli managed to stand on his own two feet for a few minutes without light-headedness and nausea forcing him back to bed.

All that stood between him and another step toward full recovery was cauterizing his leg wound. He had hoped Simon would show up to handle the task, but he knew he couldn't wait much longer. He was going to have to ask for Roz's assistance—again. And there was no telling what preposterous demand she would make for repayment this time.

Fiancé? Eli shook his tousled head at the very idea

of pretending to be betrothed to the daughter of one of Denver's leading citizens. Roz would be laughed out of town, scorned by society. What the hell was she thinking?

Eli glanced out the window, watching Roz stake out the horses on another area of thick grass. Although he questioned her reasoning at times, he had to admit that she was an amazing female. She had met every challenge and obstacle thrown in her path without breaking stride.

Beauty, brains and willful determination, he mused. What man wouldn't want to claim her as his own? Who wouldn't want to spend his days gazing into that exquisite face and spend his nights worshiping that voluptuous feminine body?

Eli cursed when ungovernable desire pulsed through him. "Watch what you're thinking, McCain," he growled at himself.

Just because he had to linger in bed with nothing to do did not mean he would permit erotic thoughts to roost in his head. Rozalie Matthews was so far off-limits, it was laughable. He definitely needed a distraction to reroute his fantasies. Sealing his seeping wound was the ticket. Nothing like more excruciating pain to take the edge off those unattainable daydreams that were getting him all steamed up.

The moment Roz entered the cabin Eli tugged open the ripped seam on his pants leg then unwrapped the bandage. "I need your help," he requested.

"For what?" She eyed him warily. "I just cleaned the wound and put on a fresh bandage before I went outside."

"I want to sear the jagged flesh back together before infection sets in again," he declared. "Put the poker in the fire, Roz."

She stood there, her gaze leaping from his determined expression to the exposed wound.

"I can't wait for Simon," he told her grimly.

He watched with admiration as she gathered her resolve around her. Distasteful though the task was to her, she was going to oblige. Which was just one more reason why this woman, who was completely and utterly wrong for him, fascinated him so much. She had courage and gumption, and his respect for her character and personality kept growing by leaps and bounds.

Damn, his life would be so much easier right now if he disliked everything about her and could barely tolerate her company. Unfortunately, the opposite was true.

When Roz approached him, her delicate jaw set, her shoulders squared, Eli smiled faintly. He wanted to grab hold of her, tumble her across his bed and rake his hands through those curly blond tendrils, for starters. Then he wanted to work his way down every luscious curve and swell of her body and memorize her by taste and touch. But instead, he was going to undergo extreme pain by urging her to brand him like a calf.

That should cure those lusty urges that wracked his body—at least for the night.

When Roz sank down beside him, Eli didn't allow her time for second thoughts. His hand folded over hers. He felt her flinch, but she didn't take her eyes off the exposed wound.

"I really do not want to do this," she let him know in a hurry. "I've hurt you enough already."

His hand steadying hers, he laid the glowing poker to his tender flesh. Eli ground his teeth and tried like the devil to keep from screaming in misery. A wave of nausea rolled over him and stars sparkled before his eyes. His breath gushed past his clenched teeth and his hand fell away from hers to knot his fists in the quilt.

"Again," he said on a hissed breath.

"My God, Eli—"

"Again," he demanded as he stared into that bewitching face, focusing absolute attention on her while pain scorched his leg and dizziness assailed him. He squeezed his eyes shut and sucked in a bracing breath, waiting for the fiery pain that blazed through his leg to subside.

He heard the poker clank onto the planked floor and felt Roz's arms lock around his neck. Impulsively he clutched her to him, nuzzling his chin against her shoulder. He inhaled her sweet essence, letting her appealing scent override the smell of seared flesh. For several moments she clung to him and he clung to her. When she turned her head toward his and kissed him so tenderly Eli inwardly sighed in contentment. And then he kissed her back—soundly.

While he savored the distraction she provided, he remembered that the pain was *supposed* to be the preventative that kept him from doing what he was doing. And what he was doing was clutching her to him as if he never had any intention of letting her go. He wasn't supposed to be saturating his senses with her and pressing her lush body into his masculine contours, either.

But he was—and he was reveling in every forbidden second of it.

When her fingers speared into his long hair and she angled her head to taste him more thoroughly, Eli lost the good sense that Simon had spend years drilling into him. Eli touched her, mapped the terrain of her body and kissed her until his head swam in circles.

When her hand drifted back and forth across his bare chest, pleasure channeled through every part of his being. He pulled her onto his lap, uncaring if she felt the hard throb of his desire against her hip, uncaring if he had disregarded restraint and caution in favor of a few moments of incredible pleasure.

Eli had never wanted anything as much as he wanted the right to teach Roz what uncontrollable passion was all about. He wanted her naked beneath him. He wanted to be inside her more than he wanted his next breath. When she shifted on his lap, his sensitive body tightened with such extreme need that he felt the urge to toss back his head and howl in unholy torment.

No woman had left him feeling so wild and desperate. The self-discipline that had sustained him for years evaporated. Eli twisted sideways, taking Roz to the mattress, allowing him free access to devour her lips and caress the full swell of her breasts. When she arched against his hand he dipped his forefinger beneath the neckline of her gown to encircle her taut nipple.

Her skin was as soft as satin and her heated response was like a gust of wind that fanned a wildfire so intense and compelling that Eli wanted to burn alive in the flames they called from each other.

Baring her creamy breasts to his hungry gaze, he bent his head to flick his tongue against the rosy crest. When her hand drifted to the band of his breeches, he reached down to press her palm to his throbbing length. He was desperate for her touch, and yet, he wanted her to realize that their volatile response to each other put them on very dangerous ground.

"We're playing with fire," he said hoarsely. "Tell me to stop because I'm not sure I have the will to do it—"

His voice dried up when her fingers contracted experimentally around his pulsating length. Damn, she was killing him. He was so close to the edge of restraint that one more caress would send him tumbling into reckless abandon and she would lose her innocence....

The unacceptable thought pierced the fog of need that had blinded him. Eli flung himself away from her and dragged in a shaky breath. He had to get up and get out—now. Another moment and it would be too late.

Despite the pain of placing weight on his leg he pushed off the bed. Half hopping, half hobbling, Eli made an inelegant retreat to the front porch and latched onto the supporting beam to hold himself upright.

"Do I frighten you that much?"

He glanced over his shoulder to see her peering up at him with an expression he couldn't interpret, but he answered her honestly nonetheless. "Yeah, you do, Roz Matthews. You scare the living daylights out of me because I can't trust myself with you. Taking what doesn't belong to me is no way to repay you for believing in me and nursing me back to health. If I touch you again, you have my permission to shoot me, because that's exactly what I deserve.''

On that parting comment, Eli eased down the steps and headed for the nearby stream. He needed to cool off and he needed to drown out the curses his body was shouting at him for backing away from the sweetest temptation he'd ever known.

Halting beside the shallow stream, Eli drew a fortifying breath and closed his eyes, battling the alluring vision of glorious blond hair fanning across his pillow and bare, shapely legs exposed by the hiked hem of a gown. He tried to block out the tantalizing memory of kiss-swollen lips that practically begged to be taken, and a ripe, luscious body that he ached to sink into and take as his intimate possession.

Swearing inventively—and at great lengths—Eli struggled to doff his socks and breeches. Fate, that cruel bastard, had thrust Roz into his life, forcing him to drag her along with him. He had never spent so many consecutive hours with a woman and he had gotten to know Roz too well. Gotten to want her too much.

This, he decided as he sank into the frigid water, was his personal brand of hell.

His conscience was giving him fits while his male body snarled at him from walking away from a woman who felt so right in his arms. But sound logic reminded him repeatedly that she was wrong for him. Extenuating circumstances and close proximity were playing against him. No matter which way he turned, Roz's beguiling face materialized in his mind and unfulfilled desire grabbed him again and again.

Hell! He'd go nuts trying to do the right thing if

Simon didn't show up to act as a buffer. He needed Simon on hand to remind him of his place—outside civilized society. Someone certainly needed to remind Eli that he had not only stepped over the line but that he had dashed across it full steam ahead.

"Just so you know, I'm not the least bit afraid of you, Eli McCain. I'm not afraid of what just happened between us, either."

Eli jerked upright in the stream when Roz's sultry voice drifted toward him. He steeled himself when he heard her approach, but he didn't glance in her direction. He stared into the darkness that had settled over the mountains. Yet he saw nothing but her enticing image, felt nothing but the lingering heat that even a cool mountain stream couldn't douse.

"What nearly happened is *not* going to happen," Eli said resolutely.

"No? And what if teaching me what passion is all about is what I ask in payment for saving your life?" she countered. "Are you going to refuse that request, too? Hard as you might find this to believe, McCain, some men would actually leap at the chance to be my fiancé or my lover."

He half turned to note the impish smile playing on her Cupid's bow lips. "You may be almost royalty, but you are also a mischievous witch with a wicked streak as long as my arm."

"And you are the very devil sometimes," she tossed back saucily. "You abducted me and I expected to be ravished. Instead you tempted me to no end and then walked away. For a man who is reported to be bad to the bone you certainly have a strong streak of honor and nobility." She clucked her tongue playfully at him. "What happened to the code of depraved behavior among ruthless outlaws? Hmm? Can't depend on you wicked types for anything these days, I guess."

Despite her sassy remark, Eli said very seriously, "You know damn well that I'm not the kind of man you need to get involved with, *princess*."

"How do you figure that, McCain?" she countered as she crossed her arms beneath her breasts and stared at him. "You seem to be the misfit *outside* of society and I'm the misfit *in* it. Ever thought of that?"

He watched her saunter into the darkness and felt the gravitational pull that urged him to go after her, to take up where they had left off earlier. The thought sent betraying sensations coursing through him. His need was getting to him again.

She was getting to him.

Eli sat there in the cool water and made a pact with himself. He was going to rapidly recover from his injury so he could accompany Roz back to Denver and deliver her to her father—her innocence intact. No matter how tempting she was to him he was going to resist.

Damn, he hoped that wasn't a shining example of famous last words.

The following evening Roz wandered around outside for several minutes before bracing herself up against a towering aspen. Eli had taken a wide berth around her all day and ignored her every chance he got. Each time she walked into the cabin he was napping—or pretended to be. While she prepared a meal he would lean on his crutch and hobble outside.

Did he really think avoiding her was going to cure the attraction growing between them? It was driving *her* crazy and leaving her speculating on what passion was all about.

Roz licked her lips, swearing she could still taste his kiss from the previous night. Remembered sensations, triggered by his gentle caresses, channeled through her. Sweet mercy, just the thought of Eli's embrace was enough to send her up in flames. Never in her life had she been so tempted to surrender body and soul to a man. Since the day she had physically matured and began to draw male interest she had kept her prospective suitors at arm's length. She had been determined not to fall into the trap that had ensnared her parents.

Right feeling, wrong man, Sophia Matthews had told Roz repeatedly. *Right feeling, impossible woman,* Charles Matthews had insisted time and time again. Roz had her own version to add. *Right feeling, right man. Worst of all possible times.*

She had declared her independence less than a week earlier and had vowed not to marry. Period. But that resolution hadn't stopped her from wanting to explore the incredible pleasure she had only begun to discover in Eli's arms. Of all the men of her acquaintance—out West and back East—*he* was the one who made her wonder how it would feel to cast caution to the wind and experience the full realm of desire.

Roz didn't consider herself impulsive, but rather intuitive. If it *felt* right then more than likely it *was* right—for her. The unprecedented feelings Eli McCain stirred in her definitely felt right. The previous evening he had felt necessary and essential to her happiness, too.

There was simply something about that blue-eyed, raven-haired man that appealed to her, on every level. Chapman and Harper had never inspired her to experiment with passion, but Eli had.

Roz wrinkled her nose in irritation. Too bad Eli was so blasted noble where she was concerned. Had she once believed him capable of vicious murder? A probable molester of women? A greedy thief? He was nothing of the sort and she would bet her life on that.

When the cool evening air settled around her, Roz shivered then turned toward the cabin. For the first time in her life she felt as if she had a meaningful purpose. She could make a difference. Eli had *needed* her to help him recover from his injuries and she was in a position to help him redeem his reputation and clear his name.

What greater reward could she receive than knowing she had saved an innocent man from the hangman's noose? Now if that didn't count for something, Roz didn't know what did.

Roz entered the cabin, noting Eli had doused the lantern and gone to bed. She smiled wryly at the shadowy silhouette on the bed. Eli was afraid of her. Well, he couldn't avoid her if she was right in his face. She desired him and she knew he desired her, too. He preferred to run from that, while she preferred to embrace it, explore it.

"If you are so thoroughly convinced that society would frown on a liaison between us, no one has to know," she said as she came to stand by his bed, fairly certain he was playing possum, as he had done thrice that day. "We are, after all, about as far from civilization as we can possibly get."

"Go to bed," he muttered to her. "I have enough curses looming over my head without doing something I know you will regret later."

"Don't presume to tell me how I might feel later," Roz shot back. "Maybe sharing your bed is exactly what I want, and *I* don't consider that a curse at all."

"No, absolutely not," he said with blunt finality.

"Fine, then at least agree to be my temporary fiancé," she bartered.

"No, absolutely, positively not" was his terse reply.

The dear, sweet, noble man was still trying to protect her. He had been trying to do that since the day they met. "If I asked you to teach me to handle firearms expertly, would you do it?" she asked.

"Without hesitation," he replied.

"If I asked you to teach me to prospect for gold or hunt and trap, would you do it?"

"Certainly."

"But you won't teach me what it's like to be intimate with a man? One learning experience seems pretty much the same as the other. It is an acquisition of knowledge."

Roz didn't know why she was playing devil's advocate—aside from the fact that she delighted in teasing and tormenting Eli. It was a unique experience for her to let go and simply be herself around a man. No pretentiousness. No posturing. No pressure from society to behave like a proper, sophisticated lady.

"Where is that gag when I really need it?" Eli

scowled as he flounced onto his side. "Can't you see that I'm trying to sleep. Go the hell to bed! *Please,* damn it!"

While his voice boomed around the cabin, Roz bit back a chuckle. The snarly bear was all growl and no bite. She knew he would never hurt her, no matter how much she aggravated him. That knowledge made her bold and mischievous.

"All right, I'll leave you alone, but I have slept beside you every night since you abducted me. It didn't seem to bother you *then,* McCain."

"Well, it bothers me *now*. Things have changed. I swear, woman, I'm ready to *pay* your father to take you back."

Roz snickered as she shed her gown then crawled into Simon's bed. Despite Eli's threat, she could detect the underlying smile in his voice. He enjoyed their teasing banter as much as she did. She thought he actually liked her, not because of who she was, but just for herself.

She didn't think John Harper or Winchester Chapman the Third could honestly say the same. To them she was a trophy, window dressing—all those things she had never wanted to be in the eyes of a man.

Of course, there was the possibility that Eli considered her a nuisance and a royal pain. Maybe she was a mite too confident that what he felt for her was more than simple sexual attraction. The uneasy thought worked its way to tongue before she could bite it back.

"Eli, just answer one question."

"Will you clam up if I do?"

Again, there was an undertone of amusement that left her with a warm fuzzy feeling. "Yes, I will."

"Good. What's the question?"

"You *do* like me, at least a little...don't you?"

There was such a long moment of silence that Roz wondered if exhaustion had caught up with him and he had nodded off. Or perhaps he was hesitant to admit that the only thing he liked about her was the fact that she was female and not too terribly repulsive to look at.

"Eli?" she prompted when the seconds turned into a minute.

"I heard the question," he murmured. "I'm just not sure I want to give you the power that comes with the answer. I don't have much control over you as it is. I don't seem to have that much control over myself when you venture too close, either. No need to make things worse."

Roz smiled to herself as she cuddled beneath the quilt. He *did* like her, even though he obviously didn't consider that a good thing. She was beginning to think that his self-esteem had dropped to match society's opinion of him. And if he ever made the comment that he wasn't good enough for her because of his mixed heritage she swore she would smack him upside the head!

She liked him—a lot—and the gold and silver kings of Denver's New Money were *not* going to dictate who she could call a friend...or potential lover....

The tantalizing thought sent a tremor of need rippling through her. Roz stared at the dark silhouette on the bed that was twenty feet away from where she slept, or was trying to. She had become so accustomed to cuddling up beside Eli to conserve warmth and keep tabs on his injured condition that having him on the opposite side of the room felt unnatural.

After an hour of counting sheep and having no luck falling asleep, Roz padded barefoot across the room to ease into Eli's bed. Aware of his reassuring presence beside her, she nodded off immediately.

Chapter Six

Eli awoke in the middle of the night, aware of the warm feminine body snuggled up to his. The woman was trying to drive him insane, he decided. Wasn't it enough that he was drawn to her feisty nature, her quick wit and impish streak? Did he have to desire her until hell wouldn't have it, too?

Even now, he could feel his body harden with forbidden desire and see those wildly erotic images flashing in his mind's eye—as they had too many times already. He had employed the wrong tact with Roz, he mused. He should have made certain that she feared him enough to keep her distance. If he had, she wouldn't be so trusting and confident of him now. But he had tried to protect her at every turn and, by doing so, he had convinced her that she was safe with him, that he had no intention of hurting her.

Knowing he had gained Roz's confidence and trust was humbling and gratifying. Yet it made her exceptionally vulnerable to him. She didn't understand what it was like to be a pariah of society because she was accepted as a member of the upper crust. Her association with him might make her an outcast. She was too young and idealistic to realize the repercussions.

But Eli knew all too well. He had dealt with scorn and rejection most of his life and he cared enough for Roz not to drag her into that demoralizing quagmire.

Yet, that didn't mean he couldn't savor holding her to his heart in the darkness at this remote cabin, and then pretend that he didn't recall cozying up to her the morning after. He was injured and weak, after all. It was the perfect excuse to revel in the only pleasure he could allow himself with this woman who had come to mean more to him than proper society would tolerate.

And so he draped his arm around her waist and tucked her head beneath his chin. He wondered if he would feel her comforting presence in the future, each time he slept alone. When she was beside him, he experienced this indescribable feeling of closeness—of body and spirit—that he never knew existed. If simply sleeping with Roz left him with such a mystifying sense of contentment, he didn't dare consider how it would feel to yield to this compelling need to claim her as his own, if only for just one night.

Eli had the unmistakable feeling that sharing one night of passion with Roz would never be enough to satisfy him. He would want much more. No doubt about that.

Heaven and hell in one, he decided. If he dared to take Roz, polite society would never condone the match. Inevitably she would endure misery and shame. The very last thing he wanted was to see her hurt and embarrassed—especially because of him.

Despite the conflicting emotions roiling inside him,

Eli held Roz against him and told himself that sleeping with her was the only pleasure he could ever share with her. There was that, at least—until they descended from the mountains and he was forced to adhere to the rules of society. A good-for-nothing half-breed would never be considered worthy of a woman who was the daughter of Denver's newspaper mogul.

In the dark hours before dawn Roz gradually came awake to find her cheek resting against Eli's bare chest, her arm slung across his stomach. Her dreams had centered on him, inspired by the arousing caresses and fiery kisses they had once shared. When she had slid into bed beside him, she had been too content to return to her own bed.

Now here she was, lured by some nameless power beyond her control. She relished this close physical contact and she was secure in the knowledge that good judgment had not abandoned her with respect to her feelings for Eli. She wanted him to know that *she chose* to be with him, that she wanted him, despite his concerns about what society decreed was acceptable and proper for a woman of her status.

Her hand drifted over his broad chest, marveling at the lean hard textures, the muscular contours and planes that were such a contrast to her own body. He reminded Roz of a sleek panther—potential strength and formidable power in repose. She had seen his lightning-fast reflexes and she understood that he was a force to be reckoned with. But there was a gentleness about him that utterly fascinated her, too.

She longed to tap into that gentleness, to touch him

freely and to *know* him in ways she had never wanted to know any other man. She wanted to pleasure him, to return the incredible sensations she had experienced, before Eli had pulled away and left her aching for more.

She felt him stir in his sleep as she mapped the width of his shoulders, glided her fingers over the corded tendons of his arm. She pressed her lips to his chest, flicking at his male nipple. Her hand coasted over his hip, ever careful not to disturb the mending wound on his thigh.

When her forearm glided over his abdomen she felt his rigid length respond to her caresses and she smiled at the unfamiliar sense of power she had over his body.

The same power, it seemed, that he held over her.

With feminine curiosity urging her onward, Roz traced the fabric that covered his manhood. His hand suddenly clamped over hers, stilling her caresses. There was no doubt that he was fully awake and fully aroused. Her own body leaped with an answering response. Roz decided, there and then, that she wouldn't allow him to refuse her—not for her own good, at least. She had quite enough of other people deciding what she should and shouldn't do, what she should and shouldn't want.

She could decide for herself, thank you very much.

And what she wanted was this one night with Eli. *Here. Now.* Before the outside world crowded around them and she devoted her time and energy to proving that Eli McCain was not the kind of man who killed for money. She knew him well enough by now to understand that the acquisition of power and wealth didn't motivate him. That was just one of the many things that endeared him to her.

"You don't listen," Eli murmured, his voice raspy from sleep. "I'm not what you need. You're letting curiosity lead you down the wrong path. You might not like what you discover when you get there—"

Her lips slanted over his as her hand moved brazenly beneath his, exploring him familiarly. Eli had learned to say no to all sorts of dangerous temptations throughout the years, but he swore he had just tripped over a stumbling block that utterly defeated him.

Red-hot lust exploded through his veins as her darting tongue mated with his and her fingertips closed tightly around his rigid length. She was turning the sensual techniques that he had used on her on him—and with devastating skill for one so innocent.

The feel of her hand dipping beneath the band of his buckskin breeches, making stimulating contact with his aroused flesh, left him struggling to draw breath. In the time it took to blink, his entire body clenched and he couldn't seem to remember why sharing the most intimate of encounters with Roz was forbidden.

He was every kind of fool for giving her free rein over his body, he knew, but stopping her from touching him was nothing short of impossible. Slowly but surely she was making him a slave to his own traitorous desires and wreaking havoc with his willpower.

When her hand measured him from base to tip and her moist kisses skimmed the pounding pulse on the side of his neck a shudder of indescribable pleasure bombarded his body.

"*My choice*," she emphasized when her lush mouth

returned to his, nipping lightly at his bottom lip. "I choose *you* as payment of your debt to me."

The throaty sound of her voice, the exquisite taste of her, the alluring scent that was uniquely hers and the unruly need of his own body combined their powers of persuasion to devastate him. He could no longer deny the existence of the intense need he felt for her.

"You drive a hard bargain, Green Eyes," he murmured as he eased her down beside him, then braced up on an elbow to study her shadowed face. "But since I owe you my life, what the lady wants, the lady gets."

"Good," she said as she looped her arms around his neck, urging him closer. "I was hoping I wouldn't have to reduce myself to begging."

He stopped just short of taking her mouth and making a feast of it. "Be very sure," he insisted. "In a few more moments I'll be too far gone to stop. There will be no turning back. *Now* is the time to come to your senses and change your mind before it's too late."

Her reply was a scorching kiss and the arching of her upper body to make titillating contact with his bare chest. Eli told himself to be tender and patient, but he still ravished her mouth, feasted on her like a starved man craving nourishment. *She* did this to him, deprived him of common sense when she responded instinctively.

His free hand roamed over her chemise, measuring the trim indentation of her waist, the flare of her hips. He slid his hand upward to encircle her breast and he heard her breath unravel on a moan of pleasure. His name was on her lips as he eased the chemise off her shoulder, and then bared her body in one swift, fluid motion that left the garment drifting carelessly to the floor.

Eli could feel the heat of desire blazing through him as he laved her pebbled nipple with his tongue and lips. He nipped gently at her until she clutched his forearms, her nails digging into his flesh. The pressure she applied to his arms increased as he worked his way down her silky body—one languid kiss and caress at a time. He felt her quiver and sigh as he skimmed kisses over her belly. He felt her melt beneath his caresses as his hand moved lower.

He strung featherlight caresses over her inner thigh and felt her shiver, heard her breath catch. When she instinctively shifted toward him, his fingertips brushed her moist heat. Another bolt of sizzling pleasure exploded through his body. This spirited, independent-minded woman was a dozen kinds of passion waiting to burst free and he ached to be inside her when that happened. He wanted her to be so hungry for him that she welcomed his masculine possession and reveled in the pleasure that awaited them.

Eli stroked her intimately, then dipped his finger inside her and felt the liquid flames of her desire searing him. He teased her and aroused her until his name was a hoarse chant tumbling from her lips. And then he shifted between her legs, his broad shoulders nudging her knees apart until he had intimate access to her body. He touched her in a way that he had never touched another woman. Lifting her hips, he tasted her completely, thoroughly, and felt her shimmering response.

Offering her the most intimate of all kisses was his

silent assurance that she was special to him. For this space out of time, in this isolated place where the world couldn't judge them, they were but a man and woman caught up in a universe of unprecedented sensations and infinitesimal pleasure.

Roz clutched desperately at Eli and he felt the spasms of rapture vibrate through her body and echo through his. She was burning alive with desire that *he* had called from her. Eli wanted to be a part of those wild tremors, to feel her burning around *him.* Bracing on one arm, he pushed down his breeches and kicked his right leg free. The muscles in his left leg protested and pain seared him. But nothing short of dying could have prevented him from gliding inside her at that precise moment, when she wanted him most.

Eli surged forward and felt her blazing hot and tight around him. She tensed momentarily, then melted around him in the most intimate way imaginable and he trembled from the ineffable pleasure of being as close to this remarkable woman as a man could get.

The fleeting thought that he had never felt so connected and attuned to another woman, never felt so mentally, physically or emotionally involved with anyone else flashed across his mind then disintegrated like a shooting star.

He moved with her, teaching her the cadence of passion and marveling at the way she eagerly matched him thrust for urgent thrust. He knew without question that he had claimed her as no man had before—as he had never wanted to claim any woman who had come and gone from his bed.

Her first time might as well have been his first time

because he had never experienced the intensity of feelings and sensations that converged on him while he and Roz moved as one. They spiraled from one plateau of mind-boggling pleasure to another, taking him places he never realized existed until he skyrocketed through ecstasy in her arms.

Her wild cry, the feel of her nails digging into his shoulders sent him cartwheeling over the edge of restraint. He drove into her, hard and deep, his body pulsing with shudder after riveting shudder. Eli angled his head to take her mouth as surely and completely as he had taken her luscious body and made it an integral part of his own.

And then she locked her heels around his hips and drew him in so deeply that he became *her* possession, the extension of her wants, needs and desires.

Regrets, he felt sure, would torment him later—when sanity returned. But definitely not now. This was as close to heaven as Eli swore he could get without actually dying first. And if he did, he wouldn't have voiced a single complaint because sharing Roz's incredible passion was worth the ultimate price.

"Mmm," Roz murmured against his shoulder. "Never let it be said that you don't make a thorough and dedicated effort to repay your debts."

Eli chuckled as he pressed a kiss to the crown of her curly blond head. "I always strive to uphold my end of bargains. So now we're even, right?"

When Roz didn't respond, Eli lifted his head to stare into those mesmerizing emerald eyes that sparkled in the shadows. "Right?" he prompted.

"Well, I did save you *three* separate times, as I recall,'' she replied impishly. "I hardly think one encounter is a fair price for all my time and efforts dedicated in your behalf."

Eli squinted in the darkness to note the mischievous smile on her lips. "You're changing the rules, minx," he reminded her with an answering grin.

"I'll be sure to look over the list of rules you mentioned...much later." Her warm lips moved temptingly over his. "Right now, we need to do it again because I got so distracted that I forgot to pay close attention. Next time perhaps I won't be so caught up in the moment that I lose my ability to think straight."

Eli was amazed that his spent body reacted so intensely when Roz glided provocatively against him. She was definitely a sorceress, he decided. And far be it from him to protest when this enticing little witch demanded another lesson in passion. If they were to have only one night together then he would make the most of it—and savor every magical moment before reality intruded into this phenomenal world that began and ended with the two of them living and breathing as one.

Roz pried open her eyes and stretched leisurely in bed. The first thing she noticed was that Eli wasn't nestled beside her. Her second observation was that sunlight was streaming through the cabin windows, indicating it was late morning.

A contented smile pursed her lips as she reached down to retrieve her discarded chemise. The night she had shared with Eli was definitely a milestone in her life and she couldn't name another man that she would want to initiate her into the wondrous throes of passion.

She was not ashamed or embarrassed to admit that the previous night had given her the most amazing and satisfying moments of her life. She did not, however, presume that Eli McCain shared that sentiment. Honorable and conscientious man that he was, he probably considered their intimate interlude a disastrous mistake.

She wasn't supposed to fall for a man like him—*his* belief, not hers. He insisted that he was the last thing she needed, yet he had become everything she wanted. He had touched her from outer body to inner soul and she had fallen in love with him. She was not going to let him talk her out of it, either, because she *knew* how she felt about him.

Roz dressed quickly then strode onto the porch to inhale a refreshing breath of mountain air. Talk about feeling isolated from the world and surrounded by spectacular scenery, she mused as she panned the rugged landscape. When the frustration of dealing with society began piling up on her, as it did from time to time, this was where she would like to come to regroup.

Her gaze drifted toward the sparkling mountain stream. An overwhelming sensation trickled through her when she noticed Eli was bathing. The man was absolutely magnificent—all rippling muscle and power-packed strength. A bronzed warrior who drew her feminine appreciation and claimed her affection.

Right feeling, right man and all else be damned. Roz marveled at the emotion that bombarded, marveled at the quick about-face in her attitude as she watched Eli wade toward a clump of bushes where he had draped his clean clothes.

A welcoming smile quirked her lips as Eli grabbed his makeshift cane and walked toward her. His leg was healing, she noted. His limp wasn't as pronounced as it had been before. He was definitely on the road to recovery.

"Morning," she greeted as he approached.

"So it is."

Her heart sank when he didn't return her smile, just stared at the air over her head. Apparently Eli's conscience had been beating him black and blue since the moment he awoke.

Sure enough, she wasn't the one with morning-after regrets. *He* was.

"I'm feeling better," he declared as he veered around her to climb the steps. "We're heading back to Denver as soon as I fix us a bite to eat and grab my gear."

"One more day of rest—" she tried to suggest.

"No." His deep baritone voice reminded her of a judge's thumping gavel. "Your father has been anxious over your whereabouts long enough and I want to find out who set me up for murder and why."

Roz couldn't argue with that, but she was disappointed that she couldn't spend one more day in this mountain fairyland where the outside world couldn't intrude.

"I've given some thought to how to handle our return to town," she said as she followed him inside.

"I'm sure you have." He tossed her a smirk as he

parked himself in the chair beside the sawbuck table. "That's what worries me."

"My, aren't you irritable and snarly this morning. Are you sure you weren't raised by grizzlies?" she asked as she strode over to toss two logs into the cook stove.

There was a long noticeable pause before he said, "About last night…"

Roz stiffened. She knew where he was going with this conversation and she damn well intended to head him off at the pass. "I have no regrets about last night. None whatsoever. Obviously you do, though why any man would object to a no-strings-attached tryst I cannot imagine."

"Roz—"

She rushed on, refusing to let him get a word in edgewise until she had said her piece. "I expected you to feel guilty because of your fierce noble streak, but as you recall, *I* am the one who initiated our—" She wasn't sure what to call the magical night that would forever be branded on her heart.

"Our *mistake,*" he quickly supplied. "I doubt your two would-be fiancés will be pleased."

"Well, hang my would-be fiancés!" she erupted as she whirled to face him. "I don't want either of them. Never did. All I wanted was a night with you. More than that actually. But you are in an all-fired rush to dump me on my father's doorstep and pretend we never met."

Hands on hips, she glared at him. "If I am too pre-sumptuous in thinking that you enjoyed last night as much as I did, then this is the time to come right out and say so, McCain. Were you simply doing me a favor because that is what I asked of you for payment?''

Eli glared back at her. "You might not have been experienced, but you know better than that," he scowled. "The point is that last night should not have happened. We come from two different worlds.''

"Oh, really?" She crossed her arms over her chest and arched a mocking brow. "So which star in the galaxy do you hail from?''

"I usually appreciate your quick wit and sass, but right now I would appreciate a little less of your lip," he muttered at her. "You know exactly what I'm talking about. When we return to Denver there can be no association between us, especially not the kind that occurred last night.''

"There *will* be an association between us," she contradicted, "because I plan to help you clear your name.''

"No," Eli said in a tone that expected no argument. She glared fiercely at him.

"If you want a different answer then ask a different man. This one doesn't want to put you at risk again.''

"Object all you want, but I am going to help you," she insisted. "You can talk until you're blue in the face, if you want, but I intend—''

When the door swung open abruptly, Eli reflexively reached for his pistol and Roz snatched a log and held it up threateningly. The bulky frame of a man filled the portal. A thick gray beard and mustache camouflaged his ruddy face. Heavy brows arched over midnight-black eyes. A coonskin cap sat on the crown of his bushy head. He looked every inch a crusty mountain man and Roz had no doubt that she was about to make Simon Foster's acquaintance.

"Don't let me interrupt your spirited argument," he said in a sophisticated voice that held a distinct Southern drawl.

Considering his hardscrabble appearance, it was the last thing Roz had expected. But it explained where Eli had picked up his accent. It also explained the small library of books that lined the corner shelf.

This was the man who had been Eli's mentor and tutor and provided him with the kind of education that most backwoodsmen never acquired. This man, Roz realized, was part of the reason why Eli was such a unique contradiction—a contradiction that made him so intriguing to her.

Simon's sharp-eyed gaze riveted on her. "You must be Rozalie Matthews, daughter of the newspaper mogul, who mysteriously disappeared last week."

Roz blinked in surprise as she watched Simon toss a bundle of fur skins on the bench beside the door. "And you must be Simon. How is it that you know who I am?"

The rugged-looking frontiersman ambled over to nod a greeting to Eli then he plunked down at the table. "I came across an army patrol two days ago. They were searching for a missing woman. The fumbling lieutenant, who led the pack that had gotten lost, gave me a precise description," he explained as he propped up his elbows. "Last night I encountered two trail guides who were searching for the same female."

His obsidian gaze landed squarely on Eli. "They thought the woman might have been abducted by a desperado who fits your description. I hear tell that you are wanted for two murders.''

"Two?" Roz and Eli echoed in unison.

Simon nodded his frizzy head. ''A hotel owner and the proprietor of the general store that outfits prospectors with equipment and provisions. Mind telling me what the blazes is going on?''

While Roz set a pot of coffee on the stove to heat, Eli gave Simon the boiled-down version of the trumped-up charges, telling him of the showdown on the bridge and the tedious journey on an injured leg.

Concern etched Simon's weather-beaten features. ''Let me see that wound,'' he demanded. ''You healing okay, son?''

''Would you excuse us a moment?'' Eli requested of Roz.

She nodded her curly blond head then strode toward the door. ''I'll stake out the horses to graze,'' she volunteered.

''Fine-looking woman,'' Simon remarked as he watched Roz exit. ''From the gist of the argument I overheard on my way up the front steps I would also have to say that you were clashing with a female who knows how to stand up for herself and isn't afraid to square off against you.''

''You got that right,'' Eli grumbled, and wondered exactly how much Simon had overheard.

Simon chortled. ''It's not the size of the woman in a fight, you know. It's the size of the fight in the woman. This one seems to have more spirit than she knows what to do with.''

''Amen to that,'' Eli agreed. ''The confounded

woman seems to have made it her personal challenge to get involved in my problems. I feel responsible for her already because the sniper who shot at me might come after her if he thinks she saw more than she should have that night on the bridge.''

"A conundrum to be sure," Simon said as Eli pushed down his breeches to expose the wound. His dark eyes narrowed. "Looks like she did a damn fine job of stitching you back together and preventing infection. You might not have that leg to stand on, if not for her." He heaved himself to his feet. "I'll fetch the poultice and give the wound another thick coat for protection, since you seem hell-bent on making another trip down the mountain so soon."

He fished the salve from his bags then strode back to Eli. "Must be difficult to give up something that spirited and beautiful. Don't know why you would want to.''

Eli jerked up his head and frowned as Simon applied the healing balm. "You know perfectly well why I can't keep her. Where would I stash her? In the cabin with you?"

Simon grinned devilishly. "You would hear no complaint from me. I may be as old as these hills, but I can still appreciate rare feminine beauty." His dark eyes sparkled. "And she is definitely that."

"She hails from Eastern money and Western prestige," Eli replied. "What could I possibly give a woman who has damn near everything a woman could want?"

Simon chuckled as he bandaged the wound. "Maybe all she wants is you, and last night wasn't enough."

Eli couldn't remember the last time he had blushed, but color pulsed in his face as Simon glanced wryly at him. Damnation, the old coot had heard far more than he should have while he was eavesdropping on the stoop.

"You've gotten idealistic in your old age if you think she and I could find middle ground," Eli said caustically. "For starters, I have a price on my head, and you know perfectly well what society thinks of half-breeds. I'm not about to drag her down to my status."

"Why not? Care too much about her, do you?" Simon asked bluntly.

Eli averted his gaze. "Whether I do or don't is beside the point. You have to help me make her realize that she needs to avoid contact with me when we return to Denver."

Simon glanced speculatively toward the door. "Short of tying her up in her own home, I don't see how you're going to refuse her help. She sounded exceptionally persistent to me."

Eli blew out his breath then fastened his breeches. "Maybe you should hold her hostage here while I ride into town to figure out what the devil is going on."

It was at that moment that Roz surged through the door, sporting a determined look that Eli had seen often enough to recognize for what it was.

And it always seemed to spell trouble for him.

Chapter Seven

"I've come up with a plan," Roz announced as she breezed into the cabin to park herself in the chair beside Simon.

"Let's hear it, girl," Simon invited generously.

"Let's not," Eli grumbled. "Whatever it is, the answer is *no* and I'm not changing my mind."

Roz flashed him a glare that silently demanded that he shut his trap. Then she focused her dazzling charm and attention on Simon. "It seems to me that Eli will have difficulty entering town, dressed in his customary garb, especially since wanted posters are nailed up all over Denver. I suggest an abrupt change in appearance and an introduction into society that will permit him to move freely without arousing any suspicion."

"No," Eli objected, but to no avail.

Simon frowned pensively as he surveyed Eli's ragtag appearance. "Go on," he encouraged Roz.

To Eli's way of thinking it was *never* a good idea to encourage Roz. That was like giving a spirited mustang its head and allowing it to run away with you.

"First off," Roz said, "I can trim Eli's hair to match

the latest style back East. The beard and mustache will have to go, of course.''

Simon eyed Eli critically. ''That will definitely alter his looks and ensure that he doesn't resemble any sketches on wanted posters.''

''Dressing him in the cutting edge of fashion will make a marked difference, too,'' Roz added enthusiastically.

''I will not be trussed up in dandified clothes,'' Eli protested.

He wasn't sure why he objected so strongly. Maybe it was just the principle of the matter. He had accepted who he was and how he looked. Hell's bells, he wouldn't recognize *himself* if Roz dressed him up like some prancing dandy. Secondly, his mismatched garments—the combination of Spanish, Indian and white cultures—served to remind him of his diverse background and that Roz hailed from high society. One of them damn sure needed to remember that, he mused irritably.

Ignoring his adamant objection to impersonating a citified gentleman, Roz continued. ''An ornate walking stick will make a dignified prop and also serve as support for Eli's mending leg.''

''Excellent suggestion.'' Simon said, nodding his wooly gray head.

''I would appreciate it if you two would stop talking about me as if I weren't here.'' He glared fiercely at the traitorous twosome. ''And I sure as hell don't like it when my objections keep falling on deaf ears!''

Waste of breath, Eli thought in exasperation. He

could almost hear the cogs of Roz's sharp mind cranking while she appraised him thoroughly.

"Eli's coloring brings to mind a visiting foreign dignitary I met at one of my mother's parties in Philadelphia. The man was of Spanish and Portuguese descent, as I recall."

Eli knew he was in serious trouble when a sly smile spread across Roz's face and that intriguing twinkle lit up her emerald eyes.

"I'm sure we can pass Eli off as a foreigner," she said, clearly pleased with her inspiration. "I can introduce him as a former acquaintance who is interested in inspecting the local mines as a potential financial investment. My father wrote an article for the paper last month about Englishmen sinking money into Texas cattle companies and the ore-processing industry that has sprung up in the state. Eli's arrival in Denver will sound perfectly legitimate."

"You're a creative young lass." Simon smiled approvingly. "I do believe you are on to something here. This just might work to his advantage."

Eli glowered flaming daggers at Simon. The turncoat was taking sides against him for the first time in his life. *"No,"* he said vehemently. "Guerilla tactics are my forte. I plan to stick to what I do best."

Again, Roz ignored his objections and hurried on. "I know that Eli speaks Spanish fluently. He can toss around a few phrases in public—"

"Here's one for both of you," Eli cut in, and then rattled off a very salty comment in Spanish that suggested where they could go and what they could do with themselves when they got there.

"Be nice," Simon scolded, though his lips were twitching with amusement. "There is a lady present."

Roz smiled triumphantly. "This cover will be perfect. You have an excellent command of the language. Where did you learn that?"

"I taught him," Simon put in. "We've dealt and traded with several Indian tribes and Mexican merchants. I grew up with—"

Roz frowned curiously when Simon stopped short and refused to finish the comment. This obviously well-educated and well-versed man was an enigma to her. Curiosity prompted her to quiz Simon about his background, but now was not the time. Her first order of business was to persuade Eli—mule-headed man that he had turned out to be—to take advantage of the social doors she could open for him in their quest to find the man who killed Albert Thompson and Frank Mason—two of Denver's leading citizens.

"I think this is the perfect charade," Simon seconded.

Roz wanted to hug the stuffing out of him for siding with her. "The fact that two pillars of Denver society were targets for robbery and murder suggests much more than a killer randomly striking a wealthy entrepreneur," she told Eli—who was glaring at Simon as if he were the world's worst traitor. "Whoever this mastermind is, he is clever and cunning enough to place the blame on you. Perhaps because you are a new face in town, one with no local connections."

"You should listen to this girl," Simon advised. "She has a good head on her shoulders."

"Thank you, Simon," Roz said with undisguised triumph.

"Plus, she has connections at the newspaper office, which will prove a valuable resource of information," Simon added. "You can determine who might have the most to gain by eliminating rival competitors. I would approach this investigation from that angle first."

"You are brilliant, Simon," Roz complimented as she yielded to the urge to hug the burly old man. "That *has* to be it. That *has* to be the connection! Point the blame at a newcomer in town. Ruin his name and reputation while you sit idly by, watching the conspiracy unfold and then swoop in to take control of the businesses that might come up for sale."

"Unless the bereaved families decide to carry on the tradition rather than sell out," Eli murmured pensively. "In which case your friend, Gina, might find herself in danger."

The thought sent an apprehensive chill down Roz's spine. It made her all the more determined to find Albert's killer and make sure that he paid for the lives he had destroyed.

"I don't see that you have much choice here, son." Simon stared pointedly at Eli. "I also think the man who set you up to take the blame for two murders most likely walks among the socially privileged. I doubt the sniper who shot you and your look-alike is just some drifter who got liquored up at a saloon and decided to rob two prominent businessmen for the money in their offices. He might be a rich man's henchman, but this sounds too calculated and premeditated to me."

Bad as he hated to admit it, Eli knew Simon was

right. But he still preferred to do his investigating in the cover of darkness. Armed with a list of potential suspects, he could keep surveillance on the comings and goings of men who might benefit from the deaths of Denver entrepreneurs.

Eli didn't care if he had to slither around like a snake, so long as Roz wasn't involved. He wanted her off the streets and out of harm's way until this case was resolved.

"I will agree to posing as a foreign investor, as long as Roz stays here," Eli negotiated.

"You need me as your sponsor," she insisted. "I can verify the background information we concoct. My father will be an excellent source of support and information. The only way to guarantee his assistance is if I return to explain what is going on."

Obsidian eyes zeroed in on Eli. The expression on Simon's face was one that Eli hadn't seen too often. Emotion simmered in those fathomless pools. Emotion that spoke of untold pain and misery.

"Take it from a man who knows, son. If you want to get your life back so that you don't have to pull up stakes and start over on the wildest outposts of civilization, then take what you are offered and be thankful for it. Otherwise, you might as well pack up, turn your back on your recent past and take on a new identity forever."

Silence descended on the cabin. Eli glanced from Simon's grim expression to Roz's speculative stare. She was wondering, as Eli was, why Simon spoke with such fierce conviction. Even Eli didn't know exactly where Simon had been born and raised. It was a subject Simon had avoided since Eli had met him.

According to Simon, the past was a closed chapter that he did not discuss. He wondered if the name Simon Foster was an alias for this man who had become a hermit, in an effort to leave behind a host of unpleasant memories.

Simon surged to his feet. "Now that the matter is settled and out of the way, you need to rest before you trek down the mountain. Tonight Roz can polish up your social manners and offer pointers that will make the transition easier."

He glanced at Roz and grinned. "The possibility that Eli might have become enamored with you when you met two years ago might explain why he decided to check out possible investments in Colorado."

The twinkle of mischief in Simon's eyes caused Eli to tense. If this old goat was trying his hand at matchmaking...

"I *could* use a new suitor to counter my father's attempt to marry me off and my mother's attempt to arrange a wedding in Pennsylvania," Roz told Simon. "Unfortunately, Eli has an aversion to having me underfoot. A shame that, considering that I have saved his life time after time."

Eli wagged his finger at her. "Stop throwing that in my face. We negotiated the repayment of my debt last night—"

Eli snapped his mouth shut so fast that he nearly clipped off his tongue. When a blush exploded on Roz's face, Simon's astute gaze settled on her. A moment later, Eli found himself pinned by Simon's sharp-eyed stare.

Hell and damnation, Eli silently fumed. Simon knew too much already. He did not need to speculate on how he and Roz had settled that debt!

"Parents trying to marry you off, are they?" Simon asked Roz. "I imagine a headstrong woman like you wouldn't take kindly to their high-handed decrees." A faraway look filled his eyes as he stared out the window as if it were a portal into his mysterious past. "I knew a woman once who put up a fiery objection to similar pressure."

"What happened to her?" Roz wanted to know.

The rueful smile on Simon's lips compelled Eli to pose questions that he had never dared to ask. He had the inescapable feeling that Simon knew, firsthand, what kind of catastrophe a star-crossed attraction could create. Which made it all the more puzzling why Simon would encourage Eli's future association with Roz.

"C'mon, lass," Simon said as he clasped his hand around her forearm and urged her to her feet. "Let's give Eli more time to rest and recuperate."

"Teach her to shoot," Eli requested as Simon escorted Roz outside. "She might need to know how to handle firearms if our sniper assumes that she knows more than she should."

"Consider it done," Simon replied. "We'll ride up to Angel's Peak and take target practice."

Eli hobbled to bed, frustrated that his morning activities had depleted most of his energy. He *did* need more recuperation time. But he didn't envy Simon's excursion with Roz because he knew the old man was in for a round of prying questions. Roz was going to grill Simon for all she was worth, he predicted.

Served Simon right for siding with Roz, he thought spitefully.

Eli stretched out on the bed and heaved a weary sigh. He asked himself why he had pitched such a fit about stuffing himself in dandified clothes. It was the perfect cover that would permit him to move freely in Denver. Although he had no particular aspiration to see—firsthand—how the other half lived, it would provide him with the perfect chance to spend more time with Roz.

Unfortunately, it would make her all the more difficult to give up when the time came. The thought caused an unfamiliar ache to unfurl inside his soul. He had the uneasy feeling that nothing was going to fill the void when he walked out of Roz's life for good.

Then his life would be complete, he mused sardonically. He would have visited all seven circles of hell—the worst of which was taking possession of a woman who could never really be his because she was an accepted member of society. Some men were born with birthrights that linked them to the past and to family. Eli was a man without ties and he had spent years trying to find his connection. He was also a suspected murderer with a price on his head, a social outcast who had developed a forbidden fascination for a woman whose life was in danger because of her association with him.

Walking away without looking back would be hard enough, he predicted. But if Roz died trying to save his reputation Eli wasn't sure he could endure it. He needed to know that she was out there in the world—somewhere beyond his reach.

"Seven kinds of hell...and then some," Eli murmured before he pulled the pillow over his head.

His emotions warred with common sense and Eli wondered if running for his life to take refuge in some isolated canyon, deep in the heart of the Rockies, was the best course of action. It had obviously worked for Simon—until someone struck gold and a horde of prospectors crowded in on him to seek their fortunes.

Roz breathed in awe as Simon halted on the spectacular bluff that overlooked a deep, V-shaped valley that was surrounded by sheer rock walls and craggy, snowcapped peaks. A waterfall cascaded from one outcropping of stone to another, sending up a showering mist that danced with dozens of rainbows. She felt as if she were standing atop the world, an arm's length away from the vault of cobalt-blue sky.

"Heaven's half acre," Simon declared as he dismounted.

"The perfect place to commune with the spirit world," Roz commented. "Who was she, Simon, and how did you know her?"

Simon chuckled as he retrieved his pistol from the holster riding low on his hips. "No wonder you give Eli such fits. That mind of yours latches on like a snapping turtle and doesn't let go."

"Even your adopted son doesn't know where you hail from, does he?" She cocked a curious brow and stared intently at Simon. "How long have you been on the run from yourself...or from the long arm of the law? And exactly which is it?''

"Damn, lass, you're worse than a rapid-firing Gatling gun." Simon handed her the pistol, butt first. "Lesson number one—always consider the firing range of your handgun," he said, making it perfectly clear that he had no intention of answering her questions.

"Can't hit what you aim at if you've miscalculated the distance." He clutched her shoulders, turned her around then gestured toward a low-hanging tree branch. "Elbow bent, waist high, feet braced. Keep your eyes wide open. That applies to more than just target practice."

Roz waited while Simon positioned her body and arm in proper firing position. She wasn't sure why, but she had liked the looks of this rugged mountain man the moment he'd strode into the cabin. Perhaps it was because he had made such an admirable commitment to raise a terrified child who had been left for dead. Or maybe it was because he seemed to be such an intriguing riddle that she felt compelled to solve—she couldn't say for sure.

Simon had the manners and speech of a Southern aristocrat, and yet he was a font of experience and knowledge pertaining to survival in the wilderness. Whoever or whatever he was, Roz sensed that Simon's past still troubled him, drove him from civilization and left him wandering the mountains like a lost soul— much like Eli. Except that *Eli's* past was an elusive mystery to him.

"Aim and fire," Simon ordered, jostling her from her pensive reverie.

Roz concentrated on the target then squeezed the trigger. The bullet thudded into the tree trunk, missing its mark.

''Low and to the right.'' Simon repositioned her arm closer to her hip. ''Nothing wrong with shooting low, in case your enemy tries to duck or dive sideways. At least you might slow him down enough to escape him.''

''What will it matter if he's a better shot than I am?'' Roz asked. ''The sniper who bushwhacked Eli and his look-alike was a crackshot. And ultimately, that's who I will have to defend myself against.''

''Stop jabbering and fire the pistol,'' Simon commanded sternly. ''*Concentrate,* lass.''

Roz did as she was told then smiled in satisfaction when she actually hit what she was aiming at. ''How did you get to be such a good marksman, Simon?''

''Practice, which is what you are supposed to be focusing on,'' he didn't fail to remind her. ''Your crusade to clear Eli's name won't be nearly as gratifying if you aren't around to see those trumped-up charges dismissed. That boy will suffer all the torments of the damned if you are the sacrifice made to restore his reputation… Again.''

Roz stared resolutely at her target and listened to every word of instruction Simon offered. The man was a master at diverting attention away from himself, as well as giving pointers during target practice. She had the unmistakable feeling that prying information from Simon would be more difficult than robbing an oyster of its prized pearl. What Simon didn't want to discus did not get discussed. End of story.

Or so he thought. Roz was nothing if not unswervingly persistent.

"One day you are going to tell me, of your own free will, why you came to these mountains," Roz prophesied as she took aim at the target. "Because you are important to Eli, you are also you important to me. If I can be of help to you, you have only to ask, Simon. I think making peace with one's past is necessary if you want to get on with your life. It would certainly be easier if my father could follow that advice."

She cut Simon a quick glance. "And by the way, I greatly admire you for taking Eli under your wing and raising him as your own. It speaks very highly of your character. So...how is it that an educated Southern gentleman such as yourself has become a hermit?"

"Tenacious little witch, aren't you?" Simon teased.

"My father says a good journalist is relentless in digging for facts." Roz fired the pistol, pleased that she hit her mark. Her gaze glued to the target, she prepared to squeeze the trigger again.

"Seeing as how you are in love with Eli and you are determined to be his champion, I just might satisfy your burning curiosity one of these days and tell you what you want to know."

The perceptive comment caught her off guard and caused her to flinch. The shot went astray.

"Lesson number two," Simon said. "Don't allow yourself to be distracted."

Wide-eyed, she glanced up into Simon's sly smile. "Who said I was in love with that stubborn, bullheaded man?"

"*You* did. Not in so many words, of course," Simon

said as he pivoted on his heels to amble toward his horse. "You have come to believe in him and you have taken his side, even when the rest of society has already found him guilty and is eager to hang him high."

He leaned leisurely against his mule and smiled faintly. "But it won't be easy. Eli is dead set against further involvement with you. He thinks the best favor he can do for you is to get out of your life after he has proven his innocence. Unless you can teach him to see himself through *your* eyes, he is going to walk away and tell himself that he is doing what is best for you."

Roz took the advice to heart as she watched Simon climb aboard his mule. "Just one more thing, Simon."

A wide grin crinkled his face. "With an insanely curious woman like you, I suspect there will always be *just one more thing,*" he teased. "Which is exactly what Eli needs to keep his life interesting. Now, climb on your horse. The lesson is over and I'm starving for a home-cooked meal."

"I only wanted to know if you have any objections to my interest in Eli, even if we come from different walks of life," she said as she mounted her steed.

"If it's my blessing you want, then you have it. But I'm not difficult to deal with." He stared down the mountain toward the cabin in the distance. "Eli is another matter entirely. He will try to drive you away for your own good—you can count on it. But I can attest to the fact that you aren't easily dissuaded." Simon stared directly at Roz. "Just don't be surprised if Eli tries to turn your own temper against you. That's what I would do if I wanted to send you running."

Roz followed the weaving path and mulled over Simon's insightful comments. Simon knew Eli better than anyone alive and there was so much she wanted to know about Eli's past.

"What was Eli like as a child?" Roz was compelled to ask. "How did he cope with the loss of his mother and the abandonment of his natural father?"

Simon smiled ruefully. "Eli was a confused and angry child. When I found him, injured and alone, he tried to fight me, tried to scramble away. Since he understood very little English it was difficult to make him realize that I was trying to help him."

Roz could barely imagine how terrifying and bewildering it must have been for a lost child whose world had been shattered—not once but twice.

"It took time to gain Eli's trust," Simon continued as he ducked beneath a low-hanging limb. "I'm not sure he ever got over the fact that his father had thrust him out into the wilderness. It made the situation worse because Eli had difficulty communicating with his father who had come to the Cheyenne camp to take him away after his mother died. According to Eli, he and his father had been together for only six months before he was cast off in the night.

"It was a year before Eli allowed any physical contact or the slightest show of affection. Gradually he came to trust me enough to let me be a mentor and friend," Eli elaborated.

Roz's heart twisted with sympathy for the emotionally isolated and embittered child that fate had made of him. It was a wonder that he had been able to trust in anyone again. She suspected that without Simon's unfaltering dedication and patience Eli would have tried to venture off on his own—and would have perished in the unforgiving frontier.

"I taught Eli to handle weapons, to hunt and trap and to take each day as it came," Simon said as he picked his way down the rugged path. "I taught him to read and write English and speak Spanish so he wouldn't have a problem communicating ever again. I also insisted that he spend time with the Ute tribe. I had gained their acceptance and friendship. Eli needed to get back in touch with his beginnings, even if the Utes weren't his native clan."

"Did you remain in camp with him?" Roz asked curiously.

Simon nodded. "I didn't want to leave him with the impression that I was pawning him off, as his father had."

Roz was relieved to hear that Simon had remained nearby and had reassured Eli that he wasn't going to be discarded again.

"Over the years Eli has taken a variety of jobs as a railroad detective tracking train robbers, a trail guide for miners, wagon-train boss, stagecoach guard—you name it and he held the job." Simon frowned pensively. "I think his widespread travels were his attempt to search for his father so he could find out why he'd been sent away."

"But there was never any trace of him?" Roz asked.

Simon shook his head. "No one Eli encountered during his travels had seen Marcus McCain or heard from him in years. But Eli developed a reputation with the men he encountered. His self-reliance, competence as a mountain man and scout have become legendary,'' Simon stated.

''The hardscrabble types were wary of his fighting skills and his unerring abilities with weapons. They never crossed him, not when they were sober enough to know better, at least. I'm proud of the man he has become. He has conquered almost every difficulty and challenge that he has faced these past two decades.''

Except for the stumbling block that had labeled him a wanted fugitive, Roz mused. And whether Eli thought he needed her help or not, Roz *was* going to be his champion. Perhaps Eli would never love her back—or give himself the chance to care deeply for her—but she was going to find a way to refute the false charges against him and exonerate his name.

Simon swung down from his mule then lifted Roz from the saddle. ''I'll put a meal together while you drag Eli, kicking and screaming, no doubt, through lessons in proper etiquette and protocol.''

Roz tilted her chin to a determined angle and said resolutely, ''You have a deal.''

''Heaven help the man.'' Simon chuckled as he trailed his index finger over the curve of her jaw. ''When you get through with him I suspect he will have more polished manners and sophisticated airs than he can say grace over.''

''Yes, he will,'' Roz affirmed. ''He is going to make a very convincing foreign investor, whether he approves of this scheme or not.''

Eli definitely did not enjoy the pretentious charade Roz had designed for him. Bowing over her hand, kissing her wrist and plying her with rehearsed flattery made him feel like a fraud. By the time she got through with him that evening she had drilled so many rules of etiquette into his skull that he was sporting a king-size headache. She even had him mimicking the accent of the foreign diplomat she had met back East.

When she went to work trimming his hair Eli felt as if he had been scalped. Muttering and grumbling, he shaved off his beard and mustache then turned to Roz for her inspection and approval.

Her eyes widened in surprise and her mouth dropped open. "Good gracious, you are going to cause quite a stir among the ladies," she said as she appraised the drastic change in his appearance.

"The only *stir* I want to cause is bringing that bushwhacker to justice," Eli said, then scowled self-consciously when he took another look at himself in the mirror.

"Don't step out of character," Roz chided. "You are Antonio Miguel Quintana. No scowling allowed. It is beneath your dignity."

Eli looked to Simon for support and found none forthcoming. All evening Simon—the traitor—had agreed with everything Roz had said and encouraged Eli to perfect his manner of speech and behavior.

"The transformation is quite impressive," Simon declared. "You definitely look civilized. I think we should call it a night so we can alternate hot and cold compresses on your mending leg. You have a long ride ahead of you tomorrow, son." He shifted his attention to Roz. "Take my bed and I will make a pallet on the floor."

"That isn't necessary. I can—" She tried to protest.

Simon flung up his hand to silence her. "I insist, my dear. A gentleman always considers a woman's comfort first."

She inclined her head and said, "As you wish, sir."

Eli did a double take. He had never been able to get Roz to acquiesce that easily. He wondered if he would ever learn Simon's amazing knack—and doubted it.

The older man smiled wryly as he scooped up his bedroll and positioned it on the floor. "It's a gift," he said with a snicker.

Eli shook his head—and immediately missed the feel of his long hair fanning the back of his neck. He was counting the days until he could resume his own identity. He was not looking forward to strutting up and down the streets and pretending to be someone he had no inclination to be.

The means justifies the end, Simon had reminded him twice that evening. *Do what you must to ferret out that sniper.* Eli clung to that thought while Simon wrapped a cold pack around the leg wound, and then returned an hour later to replace it with a hot towel he had warmed by the fire.

Even if Simon had sided with Roz, he was here at the cabin to ensure Eli didn't succumb to the compelling need that had overpowered him the previous night. The thought sent remembered pleasure thrumming through Eli's body while he stared up into the darkness. Exasperated, he rolled onto his side—and sorely missed the feel of Roz's voluptuous body cuddled familiarly against him.

While he was adapting to the portrayal of a sophisticated dandy he might as well get used to not having Roz in his bed ever again, he told himself. Their night of passion had been a mistake of gigantic proportions that could *never* be repeated.

Eli sighed heavily, wondering how he was going to teach himself to stop wanting a woman who affected him on so many levels that she colored his every thought.

Chapter Eight

The next morning Roz stared in amazement when Simon exited the cabin with his saddle bags slung over one bulky shoulder and his bedroll draped over the other. "You've decided to come with us?" she asked.

"Partway." Simon strode over to pack his belongings on his mule. "Never hurts to have another pair of eyes and an extra armed guard, especially since patrols are combing the area in search of you. I plan to scout ahead and avoid encounters with unwanted visitors."

Roz was relieved to have Simon along to keep a watchful eye. She made use of the time to drum a few more instructions into Eli's head and perfect his fake accent. But every time she glanced at his clean-shaven face and stylish hair she became hopelessly distracted. Eli McCain truly was a handsome, exotic-looking hunk of masculinity.

He had dimples she hadn't noticed and a cleft in his chin that she hadn't known was there while he was sporting that thick beard and mustache. With his strikingly muscular physique and eye-catching features she predicted that he was going to make a memorable impression on the upper crust of Denver society.

By midday, when they stopped for lunch, Eli's accent sounded fluid and genuine. Even the air of authority and self-importance she had insisted upon had become a part of his mannerisms.

Adaptable, she mused as she appraised him critically. Even when he tried to slip out of character momentarily Roz had only to raise her brow and he stepped back into his role—even though he flashed a disgruntled stare that assured her that he still disliked the scheme.

Simon sent her an approving nod after Eli rattled off his supposed reasons for traveling to the area then mentioned the locations of Spanish land grants that his family held in various parts of the country. Simon was confident that Eli could pass himself off in society, especially if Roz was by his side to prompt him.

Hours later, after Simon had detoured them around the army patrol that was sweeping the countryside, Roz recognized the terrain where she and Eli had spent their first night—and she had performed primitive surgery. She marveled at how drastically her opinion of Eli had changed since that evening. He certainly had *not* turned out to be the ruthless villain she had first thought.

"This is as far as I go," Simon announced as he brought his mule to a halt. "If you can manage another few hours in the saddle you can be tucked safely in Roz's house for the night." He glanced pointedly at Eli. "If Roz's father offers to become your ally, don't let foolish pride undermine you, son. Take every offer of help you can get."

Simon shifted in the saddle then reached out to trace his forefinger over Roz's cheek and smiled affectionately. "Take care of yourself, lass. I've gotten mighty attached to you."

Roz grasped his hand and gave it a fond squeeze. "I will look forward to our future conversation, Simon," she said, flashing him a grin.

He snorted, then chuckled. "*I* won't."

"What was that all about?" Eli asked after Simon vanished into the night.

She shrugged as she nudged her horse forward. "Nothing you need to fret over. You have plenty to think about already, Señor Antonio Miguel Quintana."

He muttered a comment in Spanish that she didn't ask him to repeat, for fear he was wishing her to a place where the hottest of climates prevailed.

An hour and a half later, when they crossed the bridge where Eli had been ambushed, a shiver of unease crept down Roz's spine. She wondered if she would ever pass this direction again without remembering how close Eli had come to death that fateful night. His life had changed dramatically in the course of a week. So had hers. She sincerely hoped her father would be so relieved to see her that he would agree to participate in this charade. If not, she would have to resort to every leverage and power of persuasion at her disposal to convince him that Eli had been wrongfully accused of a crime.

Roz drew in a restorative breath and stared at the distant lights of town. Well, there was only one way to find out if her father would become an ally, she mused. She would wake him up in the middle of the night and ask him.

* * *

Charles Matthews came awake with a start when someone clutched his arm. He opened bleary eyes to see a hovering silhouette that reminded him of his missing daughter. For a moment he swore he was dreaming, but when she bent to press a kiss to his forehead he realized that she wasn't a figment of his imagination. He clamped his arms around her and held her close to his heart, reassuring himself that she *had* returned in one piece.

"Roz, thank God! Where the devil have you been…?" His voice trailed off when he noticed the tall, imposing figure lingering beside the door. "Who the devil is that?"

"He's the man who saved my life," she murmured as she eased down on the edge of the bed. "We saved each other's lives, actually. I didn't suffer a scratch, but he was shot twice. Papa, I would like you to meet Eli McCain."

"McCain!" Charles shot upright in bed. "He can't be McCain. The man is dead. His body washed ashore several days ago and one of the soldiers in town identified him as the scout that had worked with him. He was also the man who shot Albert Thompson and Frank Mason down in cold blood! The pouch of gold that was stamped with Mason's store logo was found on him. I should know because I wrote the article for the newspaper."

"That is not exactly the way it happened," Roz replied, greatly relieved that the imposter had taken the rightful blame for the ruthless murders. She held out her hand, requesting that Eli come forward to make her father's acquaintance. "Papa, this is the real Elijah McCain."

She watched her father hesitantly extend his hand as he squinted to make out Eli's features in the darkness. "You don't look like the sketch that was posted around town," Charles said. "I don't think I know what's going on."

"You will by the time we explain it to you," Eli assured him. "I would like your help in proving my innocence, sir. But with or without your assistance, I intend to find out who used me as a scapegoat and hired an imposter to commit the murders."

"Give me time to dress and I'll meet you downstairs," Charles said as he tossed aside the quilt.

Roz came to her feet to lead the way to her father's study. "I'm relieved to hear the imposter was credited with the crimes. That will simplify the situation."

"It doesn't do me much good if I want to restore my name," Eli muttered then glanced sideways. "Nice place, by the way. I always wondered what the lap of luxury looked like."

"Get used to the place," Roz said as she veered toward the study. "You will be staying here with us until this case is solved."

He clutched her arm to halt her, his piercing blue eyes boring down on her. "I want your solemn promise you won't go haring off without me to sniff out leads. I mean it, Roz. I don't want you hurt or endangered. I'll find a way to get your father to side with me on this matter, the same way you got Simon to side with you. Are we clear on that?"

Roz pushed up on tiptoe to press a kiss to his sensuous lips. "Whatever you say, *Antonio*," she murmured coyly.

Eli lifted her off her feet and held her up so he could stare her straight in the eye. "Do not be so agreeable and accommodating, *señorita*. It makes me suspicious."

The feel of his powerful body molded familiarly to hers sent a shiver of pleasure coursing through her. Roz looped her arms around his neck and kissed him with all the pent-up emotion swirling around her.

This was the man her heart had chosen and she vowed to convince him that he had become vital to her happiness. Simon had warned her that she would have a battle on her hands if she wanted to convince him that he was the only man her heart desired. She only had the time it took to conduct this investigation to prove it to him.

"Ahem…"

Eli set Roz to her feet and backed away when Charles appeared on the landing to interrupt them. Roz met her father's disconcerted stare then tossed him a smile, hoping he would return it. He frowned at her instead.

"The first thing I want to know is what the *hell* is going on?" he bellowed as his accusing gaze landed squarely on Eli.

"Your daughter is a handful. She keeps trying to seduce me," Eli said outrageously. "And not for the first time, either. You really should get her under control."

Charles sucked in his breath so quickly that he nearly choked. He opened and shut his mouth like a drawer but no words came out.

Face flaming, Roz gouged Eli in the ribs. "Behave."

He gave her one of those just-try-to-shut-me-up smiles. "Why? *You* don't. Turnabout is fair play."

Roz was quickly coming to realize that there was another side to Eli McCain that had been overshadowed while he was injured and weak. Now that he had recovered most of his strength he was proving to be an exceedingly dominant force. She liked that about him, she realized suddenly. Men like Lieutenant Harper and Winchester Chapman the Third catered to her whims and provided no challenge whatsoever.

Eli McCain was a different breed of man entirely.

Charles stamped down the steps without taking his gaze off Roz. "You and I are going to have a private talk after we get this mess sorted out," he vowed stonily.

"Good for you, Charles." Eli grinned devilishly. "The lady needs a firm rein that appears to have been lacking. I have been told that highly educated women can be difficult." He stared pointedly at Roz. "Obviously that is true."

Charles cocked his head to appraise Eli for a long pensive moment. Clearly, Eli's accent and the sophisticated manner he projected puzzled him. Now, if Roz could only get Eli to curb his tongue and stop tormenting her, they could get down to the very serious business of conducting this investigation.

"Pay no attention to him, Papa," Roz insisted as she

sailed into the study to light the lantern. "He is only trying to antagonize me because his father and I agreed that this scheme to introduce him into society as a foreign investor touring the area is the most efficient approach. Needless to say, Eli isn't particularly pleased with the role designed for him."

She gestured toward the chair behind the desk. "Please sit down, Papa. You need to hear all the details if you are going to play along with this charade to help us catch a cunning killer."

Charles took his seat then glanced curiously at Eli. "She wasn't this bossy when she left home. Don't see why I have to take the credit for giving her a free hand. Looks like *you* fell down on the job, McCain."

"I was delirious with fever, weak and injured," Eli defended himself. "Fortunately, I'm feeling better now."

Roz was startled by the camaraderie that had sprung up between Eli and her father. Too bad that it came at *her* expense. However, she was enormously relieved that Charles hadn't mentioned the disagreement that had sent her dashing away to collect her wits that fateful night. She wasn't sure, but she suspected her unexplained disappearance had forced him to reevaluate their underlying feelings for one another.

For certain, she still admired and respected him as much as she always had. Even if Charles had tried to sell her down the river to the pretentious lieutenant who saw her as a means of launching him into high society.

Roz sat back in her chair and listened while Eli described the events that had left them hiding out in the wilderness for a week. She silently applauded Eli for making use of the instructions she had provided. He was articulate, concise and impressive. She decided, right there and then, that if it was his want, Eli McCain could move among the socially privileged without drawing suspicion.

She also noted that he had become a commanding force with each passing day of his recovery—which left her to wonder if she would have been as defiant toward him if he had been functioning at full capacity. She decided it was a good thing that she had gotten to know and understand him before they engaged in a clash of wills over how to handle this investigation.

"We have come to the conclusion that these murders were premeditated and arranged by someone who is in position to gain from the passing of the two business-men," Eli told Charles. "Do you know if anyone has come forward with an offer to buy out the hotel and general store this past week?"

Charles shook his head. "No, but that doesn't mean that the families haven't been approached in private. If I had conspired to make you the scapegoat and dispose of my rivals, I wouldn't be too hasty to act or let word get around town. However, I can name a handful of aggressive entrepreneurs and a few unscrupulous up-starts who have been jockeying to monopolize busi-nesses that have been turning impressive profits con-nected to the mining industry."

He leaned forward, his gaze intent on Eli. "What concerns me most is how much danger my daughter might encounter if she is deemed a possible threat to this killer. She is all I have, McCain, and speculating on what sort of trouble and hardships she has faced during her week's absence has driven home that point—in spades.''

Touched by his comment, Roz leaned out to squeeze her father's hand. ''Thank you for your concern, Papa, but I can assure you that I have been in very capable hands.''

Charles stared pointedly at Eli. ''Obviously. But then again, your new acquaintance might be more capable than a protective father prefers.''

Roz noted that Eli didn't so much as wince at the implication—which only went to prove that he wasn't the kind of man who backed down from anyone. That was another trait that she admired about Eli. He didn't go looking for trouble, but he didn't avoid it, either.

''Eli was the perfect guide and protector,'' Roz insisted. ''Even though he was seriously injured, his foremost concern was for my safety.''

Charles turned his attention on Eli to size him up and appraise him thoroughly. Eli didn't even flinch, just flashed a smile that gave nothing away.

Roz waved her hand, requesting her father's full attention. ''Let's not get off track and lose sight of our objective here. Eli will need a wardrobe befitting the fictitious role he will be playing, as well as your approval and sponsorship. I don't think it's wise for him to be seen in public until he is dressed for his role.''

Charles flicked his wrist, dismissing her concern as inconsequential. ''I will take care of the wardrobe first thing in the morning.''

"I have come prepared to pay for the expenses of room, board and clothing," Eli informed him.

Charles waved him off. "I prefer to consider that part of the payment for delivering my daughter home and for acting as her bodyguard." He stared stonily at Roz. "As for you, young lady, you will not be tramping around town alone until this sniper has been brought to justice. This is not negotiable."

When both men stared her down, Roz had no choice but to agree to have one or the other of them dogging her heels.

"Good. The next order of business is to decide what to do about the fiancé that you have made abundantly clear does not suit," Charles declared.

"I know Lieutenant Harper and I've worked with him. He definitely doesn't suit," Eli said, and snorted. "There is also the concern that he, or one of the soldiers from the fort, might recognize me, despite the drastic change in my appearance."

"Short of ducking into alleys, I don't know how we are going to bypass that pitfall," Charles murmured pensively. "One false move and this scheme could blow up in our faces, but we will puzzle all of that out tomorrow. Right now, I would like to have a private word with my daughter. Make yourself at home in one of the spare rooms in the east wing, McCain."

When Eli got up and left, his limp more noticeable after the long ride over rough terrain, Roz girded herself up to answer the multitude of questions that teemed in her father's eyes. "I *know* what I'm doing, Papa," she assured him right off.

"That's what I said before I married your mother,

and you know damn well where that got me,'' Charles countered. ''That display of affection I witnessed at the bottom of the stairs looked a mite too genuine.'' He narrowed his gaze on her. ''So don't try to convince me that whatever is going on between you and McCain is part of the act. You look at him the way you have never looked at other men. You have also taken an interest in his situation.'' He pinned her with another unblinking stare. ''And just why is that?''

Roz fidgeted in her chair, bolstered her courage and spoke from the heart. ''Because I think I might be in love with him, Papa.''

''You *think?*''

''I know,'' she clarified.

Charles steepled his fingers and stared at her for a long moment. ''And what of McCain? Is he planning to offer for you when we get to the bottom of this conspiracy against him?''

Roz squirmed beneath Charles's probing gaze. She was a mite uncomfortable having this conversation with her father. ''I don't know. I doubt it. And to be honest, I think our…friendship…might be more acceptable to both of us if there was no binding commitment.''

Charles gaped at her. ''You love him, but you don't want to marry him?'' he bleated.

''Eli believes that his mixed heritage is an insurmountable problem,'' she explained. ''He has faced prejudices because of it all of his life. But the *man* he is and what he stands for is what impresses me about him. I don't need a piece of paper to justify my feelings for him. It certainly didn't make a difference for you and Mother," she added pointedly.

Charles scowled. Bringing up Sophia always affected his disposition. Roz wished she had kept her mouth shut.

"Having seen the two of you together, I do not like what I'm thinking," Charles said sourly. "Knowing you have been alone together, living in each other's pockets, isn't helping what I'm thinking, either. Just how—?"

"Could we not discuss this right now?" Roz interrupted, battling down the blush that tried to rise to her cheeks. "It has been an exceptionally long day of riding across rugged terrain and an exhausting week. I—"

"Rozalie," Charles cut in warningly.

Roz blew out her breath. "I cannot help what I feel for him and I can't control what you are thinking, either. I can't make Eli love me back. Neither can I foresee the future any better than you could when you married Mother." She tilted her chin up a notch. "But I am not marrying anyone just because it is expected of me. I meant what I said about being independent and making my own choices."

"And your own *mistakes?*"

"Those, too," Roz insisted.

Charles slumped back in his chair and heaved a frustrated sigh. "I promised myself that if you came home safely I would be a better father to you, but I do have my limits. I will also be more attuned to your desire to try your hand at journalism. And just so you know, I did print your story. It was exceptionally good."

He paused momentarily and met her gaze head-on.

''But when it comes to matters of the heart, I would spare you the pain I have endured these past few years. Which is why I thought a marriage to Lieutenant Harper would provide a reason to keep you here.'' He stared solemnly at her. ''Sometimes marrying someone you don't love is far easier. It prevents you from suffering heartache and disappointment.''

Roz leaned forward, intent on making her feelings perfectly clear. ''I would prefer to become a spinster than to *settle* for a marriage of convenience or wed someone who doesn't share my feelings for him. Personally, I think it would be very *in*convenient and dissatisfying. As for Mother, she can make all the arrangements she wants, but I'm staying here. With you. I want my life to be my own. I want the chance to make my own choices and face the consequences of my actions. I don't want to be sheltered and suffocated.''

Charles smiled dryly. ''I do believe McCain is right. You have become a handful.''

Roz returned his infectious grin. ''Perhaps I have. This past week taught me that I can take care of myself, even while I am out of my element. Perhaps I didn't excel, but I did learn to survive. All I ask is that you realize that I have grown up and try to love me for who I am.''

Charles was out of his chair in a single bound. He drew Roz to her feet and embraced her zealously. ''You mean the world to me, sweetheart. If seeing McCain's identity restored and his name cleared of wrongdoing makes you happy then you have my full cooperation.''

''Thank you, Papa,'' Roz murmured as she snuggled

against him. "Eli has had a difficult life already. I cannot stand aside and see him falsely accused of murder. If nothing else comes of our association, I want to see him walk away a free man."

Charles curled his arm around her waist and leaned over to snuff the lantern. "First thing in the morning we will dress Señor Antonio Miguel Quintana fit to kill—" Charles winced. "Bad choice of words. Nonetheless, I will see that he is introduced into society as your former acquaintance."

He smiled down at her as he escorted her up the stairs. "Of course, if he breaks my little girl's heart I'm going to think considerably less of him. Might even shoot him a few times for good measure. It's what any self-respecting father would do."

Roz chortled as she veered toward her room. "He has already been shot twice recently. Do try to be more inventive with your punishment."

Once inside her room, Roz slumped against the door. The apprehension of confronting her father had been much worse than the actual encounter. Charles's support and cooperation were essential. There were enough potential pitfalls awaiting them without her being at odds with her father. But knowing that he planned to stand by her—although he wasn't in total agreement with her—was a vivid reminder of why she adored and respected him so much.

Roz started when she heard the soft rap on the door. She was surprised to see Eli standing in the hall. It took remarkable willpower not to fling herself into his arms and kiss him for all she was worth. Much as she disliked the idea, she was going to have to maintain a certain decorum while they moved beneath the speculative eyes of her father and society. A shame that. Roz had enjoyed the freedom of simply being herself while they were secluded in the mountains.

"Just wanted to make sure you were all right," Eli murmured. "Your father didn't—?"

The door down the hall swung open and Roz craned her neck around the corner to see her father—hands on hips, feet askance—stationed beside his room.

"Did you get lost, McCain?" Charles asked challengingly. "I told you to take a room in the *east* wing."

Eli didn't back down, not even a smidgen. "I was checking to make sure you didn't upset Roz. If something about this arrangement disturbs you then you need to speak directly to me."

Charles narrowed his gaze. "The only one around here in danger of being upset is *me*. My daughter's room is off-limits to you. This is *not* the middle of nowhere and certain rules will be observed!"

Eli's lips twitched when Charles's voice hit a loud pitch. "Protective, I see. Good." He dropped into an elegant bow that impressed the hell out of Roz. "Until tomorrow then, Señor Matthews. *Buenas noches.*"

Smiling, Roz closed the door. It was nice to have her two favorite men under the same roof, being endearingly protective of her. Independent though she wanted to be, it was oddly touching and reassuring to be the object of their concern.

All thought escaped her when she stretched out on her feather bed—and realized she *was* bone-weary and exhausted. Ah, there was definitely something to be said for luxury, especially after several days of camping out on the ground and riding all day—and most of the night.

She wondered if Eli would voluntarily admit that the finer things in life held considerable appeal. She suspected that he would have no complaint about spending the night in the comfort of a warm room and a soft bed.

Roz rolled onto her side to brush her hand over the empty space beside her. She was definitely going to miss having Eli nestled familiarly against her.

Sure enough, tired though she was, it took a while to fall asleep.

Eli paced restlessly around the palatial room where he had spent the night. He was anxious to proceed with the investigation, even if he had to garb himself in the fancy trappings of a gentleman and pretend he was a highfalutin foreigner. That was far better than being caged in a room that represented an alien lifestyle. He did *not* want to grow accustomed to luxury, did *not* need another reminder that Roz belonged here and he belonged in the wilds where he had grown up. But still…

He blew out an exasperated breath and practiced walking without favoring his tender leg. The very idea of asking Roz to give up the life she had known was beyond preposterous. Furthermore, he was not going to get accustomed to lounging on lush furniture and eating fine cuisine. He had no intention of settling down in town permanently.

"You're here for one reason," Eli told himself

sternly. "To get your life back. That's the beginning and end of it."

He wheeled at the sound of a brisk knock on the door. As he anticipated, Charles stood in the hall, laden down with packages and boxes. Grabbing a handful, Eli stepped aside to allow Charles entrance.

"You should be well attired," Charles declared as he dumped the armload of packages on the bed then tossed the walking stick atop the pile. "Frock coats, morning coats, eveningwear and trousers for all occasions. Neckties, top hats and frilly shirts. You name it and I bought it."

"Obviously," Eli murmured as he surveyed the array of stylish clothing.

"A party is scheduled at Judge Milner's home tomorrow night so you won't have to wait long for a proper introduction," Charles informed him. "Word will spread like wildfire that we have an enormously wealthy foreigner in our midst."

He rounded on Eli and his eyebrows swooped down in a sharp V. "Now then, just exactly what *are* your intentions toward my daughter?"

Eli wasn't surprised by the abrupt change of subject. He anticipated that Charles intended to lay down a few more rules, as they pertained to Eli's association with Roz.

Eli knew immediately where Roz had inherited her persistence as he watched Charles position himself in front of him. Despite the difference in their height, Charles somehow managed to make use of every inch of his stature and swell up like a cobra. Eli might have found the attempt at intimidation amusing if Charles hadn't looked so serious.

"Roz's welfare is my foremost concern," Eli insisted.

"Just so you know, if you hurt my little girl, you will answer to me," Charles gritted out. "I am not going to back off until I am satisfied that you don't pose a threat to Roz's happiness."

"What is it you expect me to say?" Eli questioned. He had no experience in dealing with overprotective fathers. Clearly, he was treading deep water.

Charles stabbed him in the chest with his forefinger. "For starters, you can reassure me that you respect Roz and that you don't see her as merely a beautiful trinket to trifle with while you go about your business in town. I made the mistake of overlooking the fact that Lieutenant Harper sees Roz as his free pass into society." His blond brows flattened over his narrowed eyes. "Your motive is essentially the same. You are using her for your benefit in this investigation."

"Not *my* idea," Eli was quick to inform him. "*My* plan was to keep Roz off the streets and under guard until I questioned a few people around town to find out who has the most to gain from the two deaths. This was *her* brainstorm."

He gestured toward the pile of dignified garments and frowned distastefully. "If I had my way, you would return these ostentatious clothes and I would wear my usual attire. But that headstrong daughter of yours decided this was the quickest, most effective route."

"You really should be a politician, McCain,"

Charles said, then smirked. "You are quite good at avoiding a direct question. Now I will ask you again and I want an answer."

"I know exactly where I belong," Eli declared. "And I intend to leave Roz exactly where *she* belongs when I find the man responsible for this conspiracy."

"What if that isn't what she wants?" Charles countered.

Eli plucked up the elegant jacket then stared surreptitiously at Charles. "We don't always get what we want, do we?" He shrugged. "Perhaps it's just as well. What we want and need don't always coincide."

Charles muttered under his breath. "Believe me, I know that all too well.... Next question, McCain. *If* there were to be a permanent association between you and Roz, would you be willing to sign a premarriage contract?"

Eli chuckled. "That won't happen, but if you want me to agree that what's *hers* is *hers* and what's *mine* is *hers,* then I would have no problem with that."

"No stipulations whatsoever?" Charles prodded relentlessly.

"None," Eli assured him. "Any more questions?"

Charles studied him critically and then said, "No, that covers my concerns...for now."

When Charles exited, Eli stared after him. He wasn't sure how to take "the chat" they had just had. However, he seriously doubted that Charles Matthews approved of his connection—temporary or otherwise—to Roz.

Well, the man wouldn't have to fret on that count, Eli promised himself. He had made a pact with himself to maintain a respectable distance from Roz—close enough to keep a watchful eye without tempting himself.

Heaven forbid that he became more attached and involved with her than he was already.

On that uneasy thought, Eli overlooked his distaste and donned the expensive garments Charles had selected. When he looked at his reflection in the mirror he winced, wondering what had become of the man he used to be.

It wasn't Eli McCain who stared back at him, wearing all this expensive finery. It was the fictitious Antonio Miguel Quintana. And why Roz had dreamed up that pretentious-sounding name Eli didn't know. It was definitely a mouthful.

Eli frowned pensively. He had to admit that he was curious to know which man Roz preferred—him or the elegantly dressed aristocrat. Deep down, Eli thought he knew the answer. *This* man belonged in Roz's world.

The real Eli McCain did *not*.

Chapter Nine

Roz knew the instant Eli descended the stairs, drenched in refinement and sophistication, that he wasn't the least bit comfortable in his formal attire. He kept tugging at the necktie and shifting self-consciously from one well-shod foot to the other. But Lord, he looked stunning in the dark clothes that emphasized his masculine physique. The white shirt complemented his bronzed complexion and gave him an exotic appearance. Although Eli had looked exceptionally striking the previous night when they ventured into town, it was nothing compared to his appearance this evening.

Charles appeared at the top of the steps—also decked out in elegant eveningwear. He blinked like a startled owl when his gaze landed on Eli. Roz smiled, aware that her father was as impressed by the their guest's appearance as she was.

Recovering quickly, Charles started down the steps. "Brace yourself, *Antonio,* you are about to brush shoulders with the New Money in Denver. Pretentiousness always reigns supreme at these affairs and *stuffy* does not begin to describe the atmosphere."

"Looking forward to it," Eli said, though his tone of voice indicated he was nothing of the kind.

Politely, he offered Roz his arm, but Charles wedged his way between them and ushered Roz to the door. "Follow my lead and I will make your introductions at the party. Possible suspects included."

The carriage ride to Judge Milner's stately home was made in silence. Eli stared in one direction and Charles stared in the other. Roz fiddled with the folds of her gold satin gown, hoping the evening went off without a hitch.

She had rehearsed her explanation for her disappearance and expected to have to repeat the fabricated tale all around the ballroom. She had already been asked to explain her whereabouts to various acquaintances she had encountered the previous day while she and Eli strolled the boardwalks, before attending a theater performance. She had introduced Eli and assured her friends and neighbors that no harm had befallen her while she was away.

There had been a few tense moments when soldiers passed by on horseback, but none of the men had made the connection between the elegantly dressed gentleman and the rugged-looking army scout.

After her father handed her down from the carriage, Roz squared her shoulders and strode up the steps. Judge Milner met her at the door and hugged her close.

"Where the devil did you get off to, young lady?" the judge questioned. "There were all sorts of wild rumors floating around town. Your father had handbills lining the boardwalks and search parties scouring the hillsides trying to find you."

Roz pasted on a smile and gestured to Eli who towered behind her father. "A former acquaintance that I met at one of Mother's parties back East arrived in town unexpectedly. He requested that I join him while he inspected several of the mines he is considering for possible financial investment," she replied smoothly.

"I left Papa a note on his desk in the study, but the breeze from an open window must have displaced it. We didn't find it until I returned home." Roz waved her arms expansively. "This fiasco has been nothing but an unfortunate misunderstanding."

She half turned to motion Eli forward. "Antonio Miguel Quintana is visiting from Spain. Antonio, this is my father's oldest and dearest friend, Judge William Milner."

On cue, Eli nodded his dark head and greeted William politely. "I regret that I caused a stir, Your Honor," he said, his accent perfect, his manner impeccable.

Then he turned those mesmerizing blue eyes on Roz and every thought flew out of her head. Desire rippled through her as he took her hand to brush his sensuous lips over her wrist.

"I must admit that this lovely young lady was part of my motivation for checking potential investments in the area. She has become even more enchanting and unforgettable than she was when she caught my eye two years ago in Philadelphia."

Charles unclasped Eli's hand from Roz's and quick-marched him through the foyer. "William, do me a favor and keep an eye on Roz while I introduce our houseguest around the ballroom,'' he threw over his shoulder.

The judge chuckled in amusement. ''It appears that Charles isn't particularly pleased with the prospect of your enamored suitor asking for your hand and toting you off to Spain.''

William's observation was lost on Roz. She became distracted when her father halted to introduce Eli to the flock of women who immediately migrated toward him. Sweet mercy, was this *jealousy* that hit her like a blow to the midsection?

So this is what that feels like, Roz mused as she watched Eli's shiny dark head dip to kiss one fragrant wrist after another. There was such a flurry of batting eyelashes and wistful feminine sighs that Roz swore she felt a draft flooding toward her.

Her thoughts logjammed when she noticed Gina Thompson among the bevy of beauties vying for Eli's attention. It was no longer a sense of betrayal that hounded her, as it had earlier in the week when she wavered between Eli's guilt and innocence. It was fierce determination to find Albert's killer and bring him to justice so Gina and her mother could be armed with the truth.

''If you will excuse me, Judge, I would like to speak with Gina Thompson. These past two weeks have been very difficult for her and I haven't been here recently to lend her moral support.''

''Well, at least that vicious scoundrel who shot Albert and Frank met his own bad end,'' William said. ''Gina and her mother can pick up the pieces of their lives and try to put the tragedy behind them.''

"Has Mrs. Thompson decided what to do about managing the hotel?" Roz asked curiously.

William nodded his salt-and-pepper-colored head. "Two local businessmen approached her yesterday about buying the hotel and restaurant." He frowned in annoyance. "One was even so bold as to suggest a marriage of convenience. *His,* mostly. Delbert Brunswick offered to manage the place for her since he owns his own restaurant. The rascal has dollar signs glowing in his eyes and he has made a nuisance of himself already."

Roz recalled that Brunswick was one of the possible suspects her father had mentioned. She glanced through the foyer to note that Charles was leading Eli directly toward the short, stocky entrepreneur who planted himself beside Mrs. Thompson, as if he were staking his claim on her.

When William turned away to greet another guest, Roz threaded through the throng of elegantly attired ladies and gentlemen to locate Gina Thompson. The moment the fetching brunette spotted Roz, she flashed a dimpled smile.

"Here you are at last!" Gina greeted as she gave Roz's hand a fond squeeze. "I was worried sick about you. Speculations that the horrible man who…" Her voice broke and it took a moment for her to recover. "We were left to think the absolute worst. And come to find out, you were hiking around mining camps with that devilishly handsome Spaniard."

Gina's interested gaze locked on Eli, who had been handed a glass of champagne and was engaged in conversation with Delbert Brunswick. "The man is so incredibly handsome that he takes my breath away. Is he as charming as he looks?''

''He has his moments,'' Roz replied, then purposely turned the conversation toward her first suspect. ''Judge Milner was just telling me that Delbert has been pursuing your mother.''

Gina wrinkled her nose in distaste. ''The man popped in three times today. He came, bearing gifts of flowers and confections for Mother, and tried to win her over with flattery. But Ennis Paxton, who owns a rival hotel, has been just as persistent in trying to court Mother.''

A tremulous smile crossed Gina's lips. ''Between the offers to purchase the hotel and trying to put our lives back together, we aren't sure what to do. If I had your self-confidence I would insist on managing the restaurant and ask Mother to handle the hotel. But she has mentioned returning to Boston to live with my grandparents and leaving Denver behind for good.''

''You are certainly capable of running the restaurant. The hotel, too,'' Roz encouraged. ''You know I will help you any way I can. I can also name a handful of women in various communities in the area who have undertaken similar challenges and have succeeded. That is one of the benefits of living in the West. Women have broken through the restrictive barriers that are prevalent in the East—''

Her comment was overridden when the orchestra burst into a lively tune and four prospective dance partners descended on Gina and Roz. The instant she felt her partner's arm glide around her waist Roz found herself wishing that it was Eli who was sweeping her around the ballroom. She didn't know if he could dance and there hadn't been time for that kind of instruction, while preparing Eli for his entrance into society.

Not that her father would allow Eli that close, she mused. Charles had made it crystal clear that he intended to be the chaperon who ensured there were no more of those steamy kisses at the bottom of the stairs—or anywhere else.

If her father knew that she and Eli had been intimate, she wondered if he would drag them to the judge's doorstep and demand that he wed them immediately. If that happened, Roz suspected that she would find herself in a long-distance marriage because, unlike the nouveau riche in Denver, Eli didn't give a tinker's damn about high society and preferred to avoid it as much as possible.

An unfamiliar sensation settled in the pit of Eli's belly as he watched Roz's dance partner twirl her around the ballroom. He had never felt possessive or jealous in his life, but he was bombarded by those emotions now. No matter how many times he told himself that Roz was off-limits, an insistent voice kept repeating that she was *his,* that *he* was the man she had chosen to introduce her to passion. They had been as close as two people could get and that scorching memory was never far from his mind.

Watching a gaggle of men ogle the woman he had claimed as his own was doing nothing for his disposition.

Scowling, wishing he had mastered the skills of dancing, Eli took another sip of champagne. When Roz whirled past him, he noticed her partner's attention had dropped to the full swells of her breasts that were enticingly displayed by the diving neckline of her gold satin gown. He wanted to storm over and break that foppish dandy in half for making a visual feast of Roz's feminine assets.

"He's harmless," Charles said, breaking into Eli's mutinous thoughts. "Roz can think circles around him and she can handle him easily enough." His meaningful gaze zeroed on Eli. "It's the men who challenge her and match her step for step that I worry about."

He grabbed Eli's elbow to tow him forward. "Now, come along, Antonio. There is someone else I want you to meet. Ennis Paxton, who owns the elegant hotel that is second only to Thompson's hotel, is exceptionally proud of his rise to fortune. Expect to be bored with the long-winded details of his success."

Five minutes later Eli realized that Charles had given an accurate assessment of the boastful hotel owner. Paxton droned on and on about his rise from rags to riches, described—in maddening detail—the thirty-room mansion he had built. He prattled about the exclusive soirée that he was hosting in two weeks. The plump-faced entrepreneur, with his beringed fingers wrapped around a champagne flute, waved his stubby arms in exaggerated gestures and called all sorts of attention to himself while he spoke—and Eli swore the man could talk the ears off a corpse. For certain, he was boring Eli to death.

Eli listened for another five minutes to Paxton boast of expanding his business ventures, before Charles crammed a fresh glass of champagne in the beady-eyed braggart's hand to distract him.

"Please excuse us, Ennis," Charles said. "I want Antonio to get acquainted with a few more residents of Denver this evening."

"Of course." Ennis smiled and struck a self-important pose. "If you need the finest accommodations to be found in Denver, stop by my hotel, Antonio. I have a spacious suite that I'm sure you will find to your liking."

"Are self-made entrepreneurs and social parties always this boring?" Eli muttered as he absently tugged at the fashionable necktie that felt like a hangman's noose closing around his throat.

"Usually, but you're doing fine," Charles encouraged. "You have passed several tests already. If Paxton or Brunswick are involved in this conspiracy they didn't seem to recognize you on sight."

Once again, Eli's attention drifted to Roz, who was dancing in the arms of yet another man. She twirled beneath the crystal chandelier's golden light that beamed around her, giving her an otherworldly appearance. A knot of desire unfurled inside Eli and he found himself battling the frustrating emotion that she constantly aroused in him. Eli sincerely hoped Charles couldn't tell what he was thinking at the moment, because there was nothing pure or innocent about his thoughts.

"This must be the young man my wife mentioned seeing at the theater last night," Gunther Rhimes said as Eli halted beside Charles for another round of introductions.

"I expect so," Charles replied. "Antonio, this is Gunther Rhimes. He is involved in railroad expansion and has done exceptionally well for himself."

Gunther frowned pensively as he shook hands with Eli. "There is something familiar about you," he said. "Have we met before?"

Eli tried out his most charming smile, aware that he and Gunther had crossed paths two years earlier, but he wasn't about to give himself away. "Were you in Philadelphia two years ago when I was abroad? Perhaps we met there, *señor*."

"No." Gunther shrugged his thin-bladed shoulders. "Maybe you just remind me of someone."

Charles struck up a conversation about railroad progress through the mountains to divert the man's attention. Thank goodness. A few minutes later, Charles excused himself and led Eli away.

"What was that all about?" Charles asked confidentially.

"I worked as a railroad detective," Eli murmured. "Rhimes was on hand when I brought in two thieves that had robbed his line."

"Do you think he suspects—?"

"Hello, Charles."

Eli glanced over Charles's head to see another fashionably dressed man sauntering toward them. He reeked of wealth and sophistication and Eli disliked the self-important dandy immediately.

"Ah, Fredrick," Charles said as he extended his hand. "How goes the banking business?"

Fredrick rambled on about investing in real estate and the construction of the new addition he was building onto his home. A few minutes later, Charles managed to pry them away to circle around the dancers in the ballroom.

"Damn," Eli muttered. "I'm not sure how much more of this fun I can stand for one night."

Charles chuckled. "That's why I send Roz to these stuffy functions. The filthy rich delight in seeing their name in print. Personally, I prefer intimate dinner parties to these crushes, but the judge is a good friend and I attend his yearly parties."

Charles shepherded Eli toward a tall muscular gent who had his back to him and was engaged in conversation with an attractive older woman. "Our next possible suspect is Jubal Rhodes, the reigning king of gold and silver mining. He's been buying up property in Denver for years. He offered to buy my newspaper three years ago so he could not only *own* the town but *speak* for it, as well."

Eli's attention drifted back to the only person in the ballroom who held his interest. He frowned, disconcerted, when he saw another eager suitor tugging Roz close and whirling her around the room. Eli made a mental note to avoid glancing in her direction again because it only served to annoy him. Jealousy, he was quickly discovering, did nothing for a man's temperament.

Setting aside his empty glass Eli followed Charles around the perimeters of the room—and stopped dead in his tracks. Lieutenant John Harper had obviously received word that Roz had returned to town unscathed and he had arrived to stake his claim before the rest of these panting dandies tried to horn in. Harper was the last man Eli wanted to encounter this evening.

"Charles, I want to step outside for a breath of air before I meet Jubal Rhodes."

When Charles frowned, bemused, Eli gestured discreetly toward the soldier who was cutting a swath through the crowd to replace Roz's dance partner.

"Wise idea," Charles murmured. "Best not to test Harper's powers of observation at close range. We may have to cut our evening short if he is going to be underfoot."

Careful not to catch Harper's eye, Eli veered onto the sprawling terrace where couples were enjoying the view of Judge Milner's well-manicured garden. When a waiter wandered by, Eli accepted another glass of champagne and downed it in two swallows. He was glad to have an excuse to exit the crowded ballroom. He was also dismayed to discover that he had already acquired a taste for the sparkling brew that appeared in his hand each time he polished off a drink.

Propping himself leisurely against the whitewashed column on the terrace, Eli watched several guests filter back and forth through the door. When a tall, expensively attired gray-haired man, who looked to be in his midfifties, swaggered onto the terrace, a hazy memory drifted across Eli's mind. He couldn't recall where he might have seen the pompous gent before, but something about him struck a familiar chord. Something...

Eli shook his head to clear his befuddled thoughts. He had definitely indulged in too much champagne, he mused as he appraised the gentleman. The shape of his eyes, nose and mouth kept shifting as he passed through shafts of light and shadows.

How could he possibly know the man? He was obviously the crème de la crème of Denver society. Eli knew he had seen Gunther Rhimes, the railroad magnate, before but he couldn't place this gent. Eli frowned at the empty glass in his hand, wondering if his overindulgence in champagne was playing tricks on his mind.

"Ah, there you are, Antonio," Charles called out as he ambled across the terrace. "When I saw Jubal stroll outside, I thought it would be the perfect chance to introduce the two of you." He motioned to the gray-haired gentleman who had pivoted around when he heard his name mentioned. "We have a refined member of Spanish nobility in our midst, Jubal. Come meet Antonio Miguel Quintana."

As Jubal approached, an unexplainable sense of recognition buzzed through Eli's mind. Try as he might, he couldn't place the entrepreneur who stood a few inches shorter and struck a pose that implied royalty had arrived.

"A pleasure to meet you, Señor Quintana," Jubal greeted then offered his hand. "Word has it that you absconded with Charles's lovely daughter and whisked her off to the mountains. Which mining camps did you visit with Roz as your companion?"

Jubal's voice didn't ring a distant bell, even though he seemed vaguely familiar. Eli shoved aside his befuddled thoughts and concentrated on portraying his role.

"Rozalie and I took the grand tours around Buck

Eye Ridge, White Feather Gulch and South Cross,'' Eli replied smoothly. ''I found the acquisition and processing of ore quite fascinating. But not as intriguing as my bewitching companion.''

Eli flashed a wry smile at Charles—who looked as if he had bitten into a lemon. ''I considered asking Rozalie to accompany me to my properties in Texas, New Mexico and California. The Spanish land grants have been in my family for more than two centuries and have provided impressive profits. I decided to inspect them while I am abroad.''

''I'm afraid I can't give my permission for Roz's extended travels,'' Charles replied. ''I want my daughter here with me.''

Eli inclined his head every so slightly and cast Jubal a discreet glance. ''The protective father. Very admirable.'' He turned his full attention on Jubal—and felt another twinge of recognition too obscure to place. ''Charles tells me that you own and operate several mines in the region. Are you interested in acquiring investors and expanding production?''

''No.'' Jubal shook his gray head, and another fleeting memory flashed through Eli's mind before he could get a firm grasp on it. ''You will have to inquire elsewhere, *señor*. My company is privately owned and I can afford expansion when I deem it necessary.''

''Antonio!''

Eli glanced past Jubal's wide shoulders to see Roz floating toward him in that alluring gown that had captured too many men's attention this evening. The look in those green eyes hinted at desperation and he reflexively veered around Charles and Jubal to reach her.

"What's wrong?" he murmured—and caught a whiff of her perfume. Lust plowed into him like a locomotive. Damnation, he had broken his hard-and-fast rule about keeping an arm's-length distance between them.

"Lieutenant Harper is what's wrong," she whispered back. "He's behaving as if I'm his personal property and that I'm supposed to ask his permission to do something as involuntary as breathing. He's irate because I spent time with you this week. He also insists on dressing you down for whisking me from town and causing such a disturbance."

Her enchanting face scrunched up with distaste. "The imbecile also proposed to me on the dance floor. I made the mistake of telling him that someone else had captured my fascination and naturally he assumed it was you. I'm sorry. We have to get out of here before the two of you end up face-to-face!"

"Is there a problem?" Charles questioned as he approached.

"Yes, Roz isn't feeling well," Eli improvised. "Perhaps a stroll through the garden will help. Charles, if you would bring the carriage around back, I think we should escort Roz home after she has the chance to walk about without the stifling crowd breathing down her neck."

Charles wavered momentarily. No doubt, he wanted to object to Eli strolling off alone with Roz, but he was aware that a confrontation with Lieutenant Harper might cause complications.

"We'll have you home in a few minutes, sweetheart,'' Charles said, then leaned close to Eli. ''Is Harper the real problem?''

Eli nodded. ''The possessive would-be fiancé. Roz thinks Harper wants to call me out and shoot me a few times.''

Charles tossed him a fulminating glance. ''He'll have to get in line,'' he muttered before he turned on his heel and strode off to fetch the carriage.

Curling a supporting arm around Roz's waist, Eli braced on his walking stick and urged her toward the marble steps. The moment they were out of earshot Roz burst into unladylike curses that he was sure she had borrowed from him.

''I ruined the evening for you. You were doing splendidly,'' she grumbled as she set a swift pace along the flagstone walkway. ''Did Papa introduce you to everyone he thought was a likely suspect?''

''Yes, all five of them. At least I know who to focus on when I doff this getup and take to the streets at night to determine if any of the men have henchmen that do their dirty work for them.''

''And I'm going with you,'' she volunteered.

''No, you are not,'' Eli said firmly.

She stopped short and lurched around to face him. When she opened her mouth to argue, Eli kissed her to shut her up. But he couldn't stop at just one kiss—which indicated that shutting her up was only an excuse.

Before he realized it, Roz was in his arms, crushed familiarly against him. He devoured her for a long moment, while memories of their intimate tryst stirred inside him, leaving him hard and aching for more. Only when he had to come up for air did he find the will-power to set her on her feet.

"Quite the convincing argument," she teased imp-ishly as she fluffed her gown. "I'm glad you see it my way. We will prowl the streets together...or you won't go at all."

"Damn it, woman," Eli scowled. "You are staying home. I don't want to put you in more danger. Why can't you get that through that thick skull of yours?"

"Because I—" She huffed out her breath and glanced toward the sound of the approaching carriage. "Here comes Papa. No doubt, Harper won't be far be-hind when he learns that we have left. I'm going to have to explain to him that, although Papa gave his permission to wed, the choice is ultimately mine."

When Charles appeared, Eli handed Roz into the buggy then sank down beside her. Charles popped the reins over the horses and they took off like a shot.

"I've thought it over and decided to turn this inves-tigation over to the Rocky Mountain Detective Agency," Charles announced as they sped through town. "Things are getting too complicated with Harper lurking about. If he recognizes Eli, this scheme will explode in our faces and there will be all sorts of forth-coming questions about the imposter that washed ashore beside the river."

"No, I plan to be the one posing questions. This is my personal vendetta," Eli said firmly. "Someone on the streets has to know who my look-alike was and who he worked for. I have five possible suspects and the names of their businesses as leads. All I need is an entirely different set of clothes to venture into the saloons and gaming halls to gather information that might lead me to the killer.''

"I still think it's too risky," Roz interjected. "But I definitely think we should wait to contact the authorities. The more people who know we are looking for an elusive murderer the greater the chance that he will get wind of it."

Roz was relieved that her father had backed off and agreed to wait before contacting the detective agency. However, she could tell by the grim set of Eli's lips that he had every intention of sneaking around at night and getting chummy with the local riffraff whose tongues might be loosened with whiskey.

The moment Roz alighted from the coach, she glanced back in the direction they had come. A lone rider appeared in the distance. Lieutenant Harper, no doubt. She sighed audibly.

"Just so you know," Eli grumbled beside her. "I dislike the idea of you confronting Harper."

"Make you feel as if you're hiding behind a woman's skirts?" Charles taunted. "Tough lump to swallow, but there you have it. We do not need Harper crowing that the murderer is still alive and kicking. Not to fret, McCain." He patted Eli's shoulder. "Roz can handle him. I already assured you that she can run mental laps around most of her suitors."

"Thank you, Papa," Roz said, smiling appreciatively.

"You're welcome, sweetheart. But should you have a problem, I will be poised at the top of the steps." He stared pointedly at Eli. "*You* will be tucked out of sight."

"But I won't like it," Eli muttered sourly.

When the two men strode off, Roz grinned in amusement. She knew that hiding out offended Eli's male pride. But sensible was sensible, after all. Harper was *her* problem to resolve. Heaven knew Eli had quite enough on his plate without the risk of being recognized by Harper.

A few minutes later, Harper rapped on the door. Feigning a headache, Roz held a cool cloth to her forehead and let him in. Harper drew himself up to full stature on the porch. Hand resting on the butt of his saber, he strode into the foyer and glanced every which way at once.

"If I didn't know better, I'd swear that Spanish Don Juan beat a hasty retreat before I could call him out," Harper huffed. "Which only goes to prove that he is a coward and hardly deserving of your affection."

Roz planted herself squarely in front of John, who looked as if he intended to scale the staircase in search of Eli. "I will try to put this as delicately as I know how," she said. "While I have enjoyed your companionship at social gatherings—" that was an outright lie to spare his feelings "—I have only looked upon you as a dear friend. Truth be told, I was quite taken by Antonio when I first met him." That was not a lie. That was the honest truth. "Despite what you choose to think, he has done nothing to deserve your animosity. I suggest you turn your attention elsewhere, John. There will not be a match between us."

For a moment he looked as if he would like to slap her. His eyes flashed, his jaw clenched and his fists knotted. "Did you grant *him* intimate privileges during your excursion in the mountains that I wasn't allowed because I don't have his wealth and distinction?'' he asked snidely.

"Not everyone clamors to obtain a foothold in society,'' she snapped back before she could restrain herself. "Surely you aren't so naive to think that I'm not aware of your primary interest in me.''

"I'm sure I don't know what you're talking about,'' John growled. "I have feelings for you.''

"You have the *feeling* that I can open doors for you,'' she countered. "In fact, I overheard you drop my name to Judge Milner to gain entrance to a party where you were *not* invited.'' She gestured toward the door. "You may leave now, Lieutenant. You will no longer be welcome in this house.''

When he stormed out, slamming the door so hard that dust dribbled from the woodwork, Roz sighed heavily. "Well, that was unpleasant.''

Charles stepped from the shadows at the head of the staircase. "My fault,'' he murmured. "Next time I try to arrange a marriage for you, I will be more selective.''

Roz glanced up sharply at him and frowned. When she noticed his teasing smile, she relaxed considerably. "You do that, Papa. At least try to find someone who doesn't have his sights set on the Matthews inheritance.''

Lifting the hem of her gown, Roz ascended the steps to buss a kiss over her father's cheek. "I appreciate the fact that you had enough confidence in me to let me handle that matter myself. While men don't take kindly to hiding behind women's skirts, women don't always prefer to have their fathers doing battle for them.''

"True. *Some* women don't,'' Charles clarified as he accompanied Roz to her room then took a look around to make certain Eli wasn't lurking in the shadows. Charles even went so far as to check under the bed. "Lock the door behind me and keep it locked,'' he insisted on his way out.

Roz rolled her eyes at her overprotective father's behavior then shed her gown. She debated about sneaking down the hall to see Eli, if only to convey her conversation with Harper. Blast it, she missed the closeness they had shared the past week, missed the privacy that allowed her to be herself completely.

Her father was hovering around her constantly, granting her no time alone with Eli. It was frustrating her to the extreme. When this case was resolved Eli would be gone for good and Roz was going to miss him terribly. Confound it, she missed him already, thanks to her father's continual intervention.

"Your father was right. Harper didn't stand a chance against you.''

Roz started at the sound of the hushed voice that drifted across her room. She wheeled around to see Eli—minus his expensive jacket and necktie—ease a hip over the windowsill. Longing swamped and buffeted her as she watched him approach with the silence of a shadow.

Knowing Eli was accustomed to scrabbling up rugged mountains and eluding enemies, she doubted that scaling brick walls posed much challenge to him. She didn't bother to ask how he had gotten into her room or where he had been lurking to eavesdrop on her conversation with Harper. She simply flung herself into his arms and let the scent, taste and feel of him saturate her senses.

"Stay the night," she whispered against his lips. "I want you here."

"Which one of us are you referring to? Me or Antonio?" he questioned quietly.

Something in his voice alerted her that the answer was vitally important to him. She leaned away to peer up into his shadowed face. "You think that I, like all the women at the party, are smitten with that Spanish dandy? Think again, McCain. The fact is I don't care all that much for either set of garb." She smiled saucily. "I like you best when you're wearing nothing at all."

His guttural groan and the swoop of his lips assured her that he wanted her as wildly as she wanted him. His hands moved restlessly over her body, leaving a scorching path of desire in their wake. Roz leaned into him, aching to share the same breath, the same thundering heartbeat and the same skin. She kissed him hungrily and felt the hard evidence of his arousal pressing against her abdomen.

No one else stirred her emotions and tempted her to throw caution to the wind the way Eli did. She wanted to eke every moment of pleasure that she could beg, borrow or steal because she knew as surely as the sun rose each morning that the time would come when Eli returned to his world—and left her alone in hers.

Although Roz was very much afraid that it was only lust that motivated him, that she had yet to touch his heart, she *needed* him tonight. Dancing and conversing with other men had assured her that this was the man who intrigued her, completed her.

"No. We can't do this, damn it," Eli growled softly.

Roz wanted to thump him upside the head when he pulled away and stepped back into his own space.

"Your father has given me a room and meals and agreed to help. I can't betray him by taking what is obviously his most precious treasure." Eli raked his fingers through his hair, muttered under his breath and pivoted toward the window.

Tormented to the extreme, Roz snatched up her pillow and threw it at him—and wished the pillow were an anvil. Her body was pulsing with need. Her heart was breaking because he didn't love her as deeply and devotedly as she had come to love him—and he was walking away.

An amused grin quirked Eli's lips as he plucked up the pillow that had hit him in the back of the head and plunked to the floor. "Temper, temper, wildcat." He clucked his tongue and his white teeth flashed in the darkness.

"Thank you so much for assuring me that appeasing my father is more important to you than I am," she grumbled.

"I'm trying to—"

Roz refused to listen. She went on hurriedly. "Why is it permissible for us to spend the night together in your world, but not in mine?"

He sighed heavily. "Roz—"

"Just leave," she interrupted, shooing him on his

way. "And take that infuriatingly **noble** conscience of yours with you."

He bowed elegantly—damn him. "As you wish, *querida*."

Difficult though it was, she calmly caught the pillow he tossed back to her. She watched him disappear through the window—and felt unfulfilled longing well up inside until she swore she would burst with it.

"Maybe you're right, Papa," she said to the darkness at large. "Loving someone to the very bottom of your soul might not be worth the torment. Damn it, why can't that impossible man find me half as irresistible as he is to me?"

On that exasperating thought, Roz flounced on her bed, covered her face with her pillow and quietly cried herself to sleep.

Chapter Ten

Glancing this way and that, Roz tiptoed down the steps to the dark foyer, trying not to alert Eli or her father that she was disobeying their mandate about leaving home alone, especially at night. But she had picked up a promising lead that afternoon. The man who agreed to answer her questions insisted he would only speak with her if she came alone and met him at a private location where they wouldn't be seen or heard.

Quiet as a mouse, Roz turned the door latch and slipped outside to breathe a sigh of relief. Lifting the trailing hem of her dark skirts, she scurried toward the stables to fetch the horse that she had asked the groom to saddle for her.

Roz kept the horse at a walk, so as not to draw unwanted attention as she headed to town. Bypassing the busy streets that often became boisterous after sunset, Roz zigzagged through the residential districts and took the roundabout route to Delbert Brunswick's café. Dismounting, she pulled her bonnet low on her forehead and scampered down the boardwalk, sidestepping two drunken cowboys who exited one of the saloons.

Keeping to the shadows, Roz crossed the street then waited until an older couple strolled past before she ducked into the alley between the bakery and the restaurant.

The murmur of voices and sounds of dishes clattering in the café serenaded her as she waited for Delbert Brunswick to appear at the back exit. Roz nearly leaped out of her skin when an unidentified noise startled her. She grimaced distastefully when a rat scurried past her to dart behind a trash bin.

Roz heaved a gusty sigh of relief—and gasped when a masculine arm closed around her neck, making it impossible to breathe. She opened her mouth to gulp air and scream at the top of her lungs. Before she could emit a sound, the man clamped a thick cloth over her face.

The unfamiliar scent filled her nostrils and burned her throat. When her eyes began to blur, Roz tried to lurch forward, but her assailant held her fast. He ruthlessly forced her to inhale the potent scent that shut down all thought processes and deprived her of the will to resist.

Not so much as a groan escaped her as her legs buckled and she plunged into the waiting abyss of dark silence.

Eli scooped up the clothes he had asked Roz to purchase for him that morning. He dressed in the brown felt hat, dark trousers and collarless brown shirt that were standard attire for miners. Slipping silently from the house, Eli strode to the stables to fetch his horse. He hadn't seen Roz since midmorning, which was just as well. The woman preoccupied his thoughts entirely too much and the temptation of spending the previous night in her room had left him tossing and turning and cursing the hungry need that constantly tormented him.

Eli was thankful to have something to distract him this evening and relieved to be away from the house for the first time all day. He was taunted by erotic visions that refused to grant him peace. The fact that Roz had been at the newspaper office all day, and he had been left to bide his time, made him more restless and twitchy than usual.

Her constant companionship had become such an integral part of his days and nights that it felt unnatural not to have her underfoot. Eli shuddered to think what sort of withdrawal he was going to suffer when he returned to the only life he had ever known and left that green-eyed siren behind.

"Hell!" Muttering at the riptide of emotion that swamped him, Eli piled onto his horse and rode toward town in the cover of darkness.

Eli tethered his horse at the hitching post near a saloon then pulled his hat down to shadow his face. With a hunch-shouldered posture, hands crammed in his pockets, he ambled down the boardwalk.

He had intended to veer into the saloon, where the tinkling sound of piano music and rowdy laughter wafted onto the street, but a fleeting shadow caught his attention. A man, dressed in a flowing cloak that made it impossible to distinguish his size and stature darted from the alley beside Brunswick Restaurant.

Eli's first impulse was to track the phantomlike figure, but he was curious to find out what sort of disaster
had been left in the mysterious man's wake. Quick-
ening his step, Eli entered the alley beside the café.

Veering around a tumble of wooden crates and trash
bins, Eli made his way toward the rear exit of the restaurant. His blood ran cold and foul oaths burst from
his lips when he spied the crumpled form of a female
sprawled in the dirt. Eli took off at a dead run, and
then crouched down beside the all-too-familiar body—
and saw the bloody knife resting in the palm of her
hand.

Frantic, he checked her for wounds and found none,
then he gave her a jostling shake. "Roz, damn it, wake
up," Eli demanded in a quiet hiss.

Moaning groggily, Roz opened her eyes and glanced
up at him in a disoriented daze. "Eli? Wha'rya
doin'ere?" Her voice came out garbled while she
gaped witlessly at him. "Wha' hap'ed?"

"I was hoping you could tell me." He propped her
into a sitting position then grabbed her shoulder when
she toppled sideways. "I thought you were tucked
safely in your room for the night. What—?"

And then he noticed the sprawled body that was lying just beyond the steps that led to the rear entrance
of the restaurant. "Son of a bitch!" His voice dissolved
into colorful profanity as he bounded to his feet to
check on the victim's identity and condition.

It didn't take a genius to deduce that the knife in
Roz's hand had *everything* to do with Delbert Brunswick's motionless sprawl. Sure enough, Brunswick was

as dead as a man could get—and Roz was holding the murder weapon.

"Omigod!" Roz choked out as she wobbled unsteadily toward Eli.

"Dear Lord!"

When the horrified voice erupted in the darkness Eli bolted to his feet to pull Roz protectively behind him. He sighed in relief when Charles Matthews stepped from the shadows. The whites of his rounded eyes glowed in the shaft of light filtering from the back door of the café. Shock and disbelief radiated from his rigid stance as his gaze bounced back and forth between Roz and the lifeless body.

"What are *you* doing here?" Eli questioned Charles.

"Following you," he replied as he rushed forward to confirm his worst fears about Brunswick. His astounded stare zeroed in on the knife Roz had clamped in her hand. "My God, Roz, what have you done?"

Her baffled gaze swept down to the dagger clutched in her fist. Then, as if she just realized what she was holding, she dropped the weapon. It thunked in the dirt.

Horrified, she gaped at Eli. "I didn't do anything, I swear," she chirped. "I only—"

Voices drifted from the back exit of the café. Eli quickly hooked his arm around Roz's waist to jerk her out of view. Thankfully, whoever had been stirring around near Brunswick's back office retreated. Clutching Roz's clammy hand, Eli half dragged her deeper into the alley. Charles was hot on their heels.

When Roz staggered, Eli scooped her up in his arms, ignoring the jarring pain in his mending thigh. "You okay?'' he murmured as he brushed his lips over her forehead—and caught a whiff of a familiar scent.

Chloroform. Damn it to hell! Roz had been set up, just as surely as Eli had become the scapegoat for two previous murders.

"I'm feeling a little woozy, if you must know," Roz panted as she cuddled against him. "I didn't do it, Eli."

"I know, sweetheart. I believe you."

"Wish I'd been that confident of you at first," she mumbled regretfully then kissed the side of his neck. "So sorry 'bout that."

"Do you think Lieutenant Harper might be involved in this? He's certainly vindictive enough to want revenge after being jilted," Eli speculated.

Roz inhaled a breath and shook her head in an effort to clear her fogged senses. "Considering the vicious intent I saw in his eyes last night, I'm not sure I wouldn't put it past him. But I have the inescapable feeling this has something to do with Albert Thompson's demise."

Charles surged ahead of Eli's limping strides. "We'll take Roz to the newspaper office until she gets her bearings. And this is the last straw. We are calling in the detectives."

"No," Eli and Roz said in unison.

After Charles unlocked the door, Eli hurried inside to deposit Roz in a chair. He pushed the tangle of spring-loaded curls away from her face and knelt in front of her. "Now then, what were you doing at Brunswick's when you were *supposed* to be at home?"

he fumed. "Damn it, Roz, you *promised* you wouldn't venture out alone!"

Roz avoided his accusing glare and swallowed past the odd taste in her mouth. "I stopped by the café for lunch today to ask one of the waitresses if any of Delbert's employees, who matched your height and weight, had quit or simply not shown up for work the past two weeks. She informed me that a man named Hal Freedman had disappeared unexpectedly and no one knew what had become of him."

"So you presumed Freedman was the imposter the town marshal pulled from the river," Eli inserted.

Roz nodded. "I asked Delbert if I could discuss the disappearance of his employee, but he put me off by saying he was too busy with customers. I kept badgering him until he finally agreed to meet me behind the café, *after* the evening crowd had thinned out. I was waiting for him in the alley when someone grabbed me and stuffed a rag over my face." Roz shrugged helplessly. "That's the last thing I remember."

"You shouldn't have gone off alone," Charles chided her. "You could have been killed!"

"Delbert seemed extremely uneasy about talking to me in public at lunch," Roz defended. "He insisted that he wouldn't divulge any information if I didn't come alone tonight."

Eli turned his disgruntled gaze on Charles. "Why were you following me? *You* should have been keeping an eye on your daughter."

Charles flashed him a fulminating glance. "I wanted to make certain you weren't headed to one of the bordellos."

Roz's jaw dropped to her chest and she peered at Eli who was staring at Charles in total bewilderment.

"Why in the hell would you think that was my destination?" Eli demanded.

Charles averted his gaze. "Suffice it to say that I had my reasons. The question is, why did *you* end up in the same alley where Brunswick met his Maker and Roz was left holding a murder weapon?"

"I saw a cloaked figure sprint from the alley. I debated about following the suspicious-looking character, but I decided to retrace his path instead." Eli glanced at Roz. "Damn good thing I did or Roz would have found herself locked in jail and your family would have been scandalized."

"Which suggests," Roz murmured pensively, "that whoever hired your imposter, then disposed of him when he no longer served his purpose, must have seen me ride out to the bridge. The sniper tried to discredit me by framing *me* for murder, as well."

Eli nodded grimly. "That would be my guess. But if it wasn't Delbert Brunswick who hired his employee to pose as my look-alike, then who did?"

"Perhaps Ennis Paxton," Roz speculated. "My friend, Gina, told me at the party that both Delbert and Ennis had been aggressively courting her mother. Maybe Ennis decided to dispose of the competition, in hopes of acquiring control of the prosperous hotel and restaurant."

"Paxton," Eli repeated consideringly. "He's the beady-eyed braggart who owns one of the other hotels in town, isn't he?"

Charles nodded his gray-blond head. "Ennis arrived

in Denver about six years ago. He hit a vein of silver and sank his wealth into a new hotel that catered to other prospectors. *Gouged* them is more accurate,'' he added with a distasteful snort. ''Talk around town is that Ennis grubstakes miners for a fifty-percent cut of their profits. He has developed the reputation of being ruthless at getting what he wants. If Ennis cast his greedy eyes on monopolizing the hotel industry, then acquiring Thompson's elegant hotel would be the perfect place to start.''

Eli came to his feet then drew Roz up beside him. She clung to him when a feeling of light-headedness washed over her again. Blast it, this evening had not gone according to her expectations. She had hoped to come away with valuable information, after her private conference with Brunswick.

No such luck. If anyone else had recognized her when she veered into the alley behind the restaurant she could become the prime suspect for murder. Now she knew how frustrated Eli felt when he had been set up. It made her extremely determined to find out who was behind this killing spree that was undoubtedly motivated by the quest for prestige and wealth.

''I'll fetch the horses and take Roz home,'' Eli volunteered. ''Charles, you better hang around town until Brunswick's body is discovered to make sure Roz isn't implicated.''

Charles looked as if he wanted to object, but he finally nodded his consent.

When Eli strode off, Roz turned her disapproving stare on her father. ''A *brothel?*'' she questioned in disbelief. "Eli is trying to find out who framed him and you thought he was headed to a *brothel?*"

Charles had the grace to look embarrassed. He shrugged his thick shoulders and refused to meet her gaze. "I have made certain the two of you have kept a respectable distance. I was testing him. I happen to be very concerned about his intentions toward you."

Roz cast him a withering glance. "When this mystery is resolved I'm certain Eli will be in a galloping rush to shake the dust of Denver off his heels. But you are mistaken if you consider him untrustworthy and dishonorable, for he is nothing of the kind, Papa."

"I—" Charles swallowed his comment when Eli appeared in the doorway. Grabbing his jacket, Charles followed Roz outside to boost her into the saddle.

Feeling lethargic and mightily overwhelmed by the shocking events of the evening, Roz followed Eli through the back streets of town to reach home. There were dozens of unanswered questions buzzing through her mind and frustrated impatience had her squirming in the saddle. Curse it, someone had silenced Delbert before she could pry information from him. What had Delbert known that might have gotten him killed?

The instant Eli set her to her feet, his mouth seized hers in a brief but potent kiss. Her thoughts scattered in the breeze and she breathed him in, tasted him thoroughly—until he reared back and scowled at her.

"Do not scare another ten years off my life—ever again," he demanded sharply. "And if you ever go tramping off alone at night again, especially on my behalf, you can expect a tirade of temper, the likes you have never heard!"

She blinked up at him in feigned shock. "I'm not sure my delicate ears can endure another round of your obscenities."

His eyes gazed down on her like blue flames. "I'll have you know I have been holding back."

"Couldn't prove it by me. I swear profanity is your second language, not Spanish," she smarted off. "And I would appreciate it if you would stop yelling at me. I've had a bad night, you know."

He stuck his face in hers and bared his teeth. "It could have been worse. And if you don't stop infuriating me by trying to get yourself killed, you won't have to worry about someone else disposing of you— because I'm liable to strangle you myself!"

On that loud note, Eli glared ominously at her, grabbed the horses' reins and stormed off toward the stable.

"And good night to you, too," Roz snapped before she wheeled around and walked into the house.

Two hours later, Eli was thrashing in bed, tormented by the fiasco that had placed Roz in jeopardy and left him feeling wild and frantic. His vast and varied experiences had taught him to handle every situation— but that was before he dealt with the prospect of seeing Roz hurt or tossed in jail like a common criminal. He had wanted to grab hold of her and shelter her against him when he found her sprawled in the alley.

He had also wanted to kill her for scaring him half to death and leaving him so rattled that he couldn't think straight.

Restless, Eli flung aside the sheet and stepped into

his breeches. Before he realized it, his footsteps had taken him through the window to the narrow brick ledge that spanned the west side of the house. His back scraping the wall, Eli inched sideways until he reached the window to Roz's room.

He was breaking every promise he had made to himself, he knew. But after the unsettling emotions that had bombarded him this evening, Eli wanted Roz in his arms. He wanted to re-create those magical moments they had shared in the cabin and lose himself in the pleasure that surpassed everything he had ever known.

After he slipped silently into Roz's room, a feeling of contentment overcame him. Wherever she was seemed to be the place he needed to be. He could list a score of reasons why he shouldn't slide into bed beside her, but he swore that holding a gun to his head couldn't have discouraged him. Not tonight. The prospect of losing Roz had hit him right where he lived and left him reeling with aftershocks.

A faint smile quirked his lips as he eased down onto the edge of the bed to study Roz's moonlit features. Frothy golden curls cascaded across her pillow. Her arm was flung across the empty space beside her and she had kicked off the sheet. Hopelessly drawn to her, Eli bent down to skim his lips over her satiny cheek and eyelids. Then he savored the velvety texture of her lips in a gentle kiss.

He recalled how frustrated he had been the night of the party when dozens of men had claimed Roz on the dance floor and he'd had to stand aside and watch. The only time he was allowed to spend with her, to touch her as he ached to do, was when he sneaked in like a thief in the night, defying her father's demand to keep his distance.

When Roz moaned softly and her lips opened invitingly beneath his, it didn't seem to matter that the evening had bordered on disaster and that he was tired of pretending to be someone else. Right or wrong, hell to pay or not, he wanted to reclaim Roz as his own, to bury himself so deeply inside her that nothing else mattered for those wild, wondrous moments that caught and captured time.

Eli discarded his breeches and slid into bed beside her. "I'm sorry I yelled at you," he whispered apologetically.

"I'm sorry I frightened you," she murmured.

When her hand dipped beneath the sheet to enfold his erect flesh, desire burned through him and he swallowed a tormented groan. He asked himself how and when he had become so dependent and vulnerable to the touch of this one woman, but his thoughts derailed when she boldly stroked him and left him burning with tormenting need.

"This time I want to show you how much pleasure you gave me that first night," she whispered against his chest.

A wave of fire swept through his body as she worked her tender magic on him. Lips as soft as rose petals feathered over the muscled ridges of his belly. His entire body trembled like leaves beneath a raging thunderstorm as she kissed and caressed him.

Eli forgot to breathe when her questing hand drifted over his hip and swirled over his inner thigh. She cupped him gently again and the erotic pressure of her fingertips sliding over his throbbing length left shock waves of pleasure streaming through him.

Sweet mercy, he thought on a ragged breath. Her touch, the whisper of her sensuous lips on his flesh was frying him alive. When she measured him with the moist tip of her tongue, Eli practically melted into the mattress. Red-hot pleasure expanded inside him as she made an intimate study of his body—and tested him to the very limits of his self-control and sanity.

When she took him into her mouth and suckled him, flicked at him with her tongue and nipped gently with her teeth, it was all he could do not to howl in sweet torment. Need clawed at him like sharp talons, and the world around him exploded with sensation after maddeningly erotic sensation.

A silvery drop of need betrayed his attempt at control. She tasted his need for her then shifted above him to bring her mouth back to his. He shared the taste of his own need in a kiss that was so gentle yet potent that his senses reeled and his body practically melted into mush.

Eli had never allowed a woman to touch him as intimately as Roz had, never wanted a woman to have this much control over his body and his emotions. But he was ready to give Roz the moon, a sky full of stars—and anything else she wanted. He was completely at her mercy while she kissed and caressed him. She took him from one mind-boggling pinnacle of desire to the next and left him quivering in reckless abandon.

"Say you want me," she whispered as she stroked

his aching flesh. "That's all I ask of you, Eli. Just the wanting."

He replied with a scalding kiss that stole her breath away. He rolled above Roz, bracing up on powerful arms, nudging her thighs apart with his muscular legs. The scant light from the window reflected off his intense blue eyes and highlighted his handsome features that were riveted with desire—desire that *she* had summoned from him, just as surely as he had enflamed her with ardent need for him.

"I want you like hell blazing," he growled huskily. "Always have. If you don't know that by now, then you haven't been paying attention. You make me crazy, woman, and denying myself is driving me insane…and I intend to show you what that feels like."

Roz bit back a moan when his skillful hands glided over her collarbone, the taut peaks of her breasts, her belly. When he bent his dark head to take her nipple into his hot, wet mouth, pleasure coiled tightly inside her. While his hand moved over her body with tender impatience Roz writhed beneath him, willing him ever closer to that place where she wanted him most.

Her breath caught when he dipped his finger inside her, teasing, tormenting. She wanted to feel his body joined to hers—now and forever. That was the only thought to spear through the tantalizing web of pleasure he was spinning around her.

Desperate, she reached for him, aching to recapture that special closeness she had discovered once before. She *needed* to be a part of him and *wanted* him to become the living flame inside her.

"Come here," she said on a ragged breath. "I need you now...."

He didn't disappoint her. He uncoiled above her and settled his muscular body exactly over hers. The blind rush of desire swept over her as his hard satin length filled her. Each penetrating thrust drove him deeper inside her and brought her ever closer to that lofty plateau of ecstasy where time stood still and rapturous sensations blazed like the midday sun. Roz gave herself up to the urgent rhythm of passion as they moved as one, seeking wild, sweet release in each other's arms.

She held on to him in breathless desperation. She felt the corded tendons and muscles of his shoulders flex and contract as he drove into her, withdrew and then buried himself to the hilt.

The darkness exploded like molten lava erupting from a volcano. Kaleidoscopic colors flared before her eyes as scalding sensations burned through every fiber of her being. She muffled her shattering cry of release against his shoulder and dissolved into a pool of fire beneath him, around him.

When Eli hissed out his breath and his body clenched tightly inside her, she felt the uncontrollable shudders of his release pulsing through her. She clung to him as emotions so profound and intense that they defied description descended upon her, draining her strength and depriving her of all thought.

She drifted across a sea of sublime contentment, held in the arms of the man who had stolen her heart without trying. She would do *anything* in her power to see him exonerated of the charges against him, to know that he was free and happy.

Even if it meant giving him up and letting him go.

The thought prompted her to clutch Eli close to her heart, to hold on to him for just another moment before the memory of their passion carried her off into dreams. With a quiet sigh, Roz surrendered to the wondrous exhaustion that claimed her.

When Roz's arms fell away from his shoulders and Eli heard her methodic breathing, he dropped a light kiss to her lips then eased away. He wouldn't allow himself to fall asleep in her bed, for fear he wouldn't awake until dawn—and run the risk of Charles's wrath when he discovered that Eli had joined her in bed.

This was *not* the time to face Charles's fury, Eli mused as he stepped into his discarded breeches. The man who had tried to frame Roz for murder was lurking in the shadows and Eli needed no more distractions until he pinpointed who was responsible for the series of deaths in Denver.

Quietly, Eli crossed the room then eased a hip over the windowsill. He made his way back to his room via the ledge.

Tomorrow, he promised himself, he would dedicate his time and efforts to hunting down the man who had tried to drag Roz into his evil scheme and ruin her reputation.

Eli awoke the following morning, driven by a relentless sense of purpose. He was going to snoop around and keep surveillance on the remaining suspects, even if he had to prance around like a dandy and distribute his pretentious smile all over town.

Immediately after Roz and Charles left for work to

write the story about the mysterious demise of Delbert Brunswick, Eli trussed himself up in his fancy garb. He strode to the stables to ask the groom, Ramon Vasquez, to saddle his horse. Eli raced off to town, hoping like hell that he could come up with a few positive leads to solve this case—quickly.

After Roz's near brush with calamity, Eli couldn't solve this case fast enough to suit himself.

The citizens in Denver, he quickly discovered, were abuzz with the news of Brunswick's death. Eli heard all sorts of speculations about whom the responsible party might be. To his enormous relief, Roz's name hadn't been linked to the restaurateur's demise.

As Roz had speculated, Ennis Paxton's name came up regularly in the conversations Eli overheard. He was on his way to Paxton's hotel to question a few employees when Jubal Rhodes emerged from the telegraph office.

Once again, a sense of recognition bombarded him—and then flitted off before Eli could mull over how and when he might have encountered Jubal Rhodes. Maybe he had seen him in passing at one of the mining camps he owned in the mountains. Maybe Jubal had nothing whatsoever to do with the murders, but his name *was* on Charles's list—which made him subject to suspicion.

Eli intended to leave no stone unturned and ensure Roz could walk the streets without fearing that she was marked for disaster—or death.

"Ah, Señor Quintana," Jubal said as he sauntered forward. "Good to see you again. I suppose you have heard the news flying around town."

Eli nodded slightly. "Roz and Charles informed me this morning that one of the gentlemen I met at the party had been stabbed behind his café. Do you know if the marshal has come up with any suspects?"

Jubal shook his gray head. Not an ounce of emotion registered in his hazel eyes. He didn't seem particularly disturbed about Brunswick's passing. "Several of Brunswick's employees have been questioned, but there are no eyewitnesses. Marshal Stokes doesn't have much to go on at the moment." He sidestepped around Eli. "If you will excuse me, I'm expecting a shipment of supplies."

Something dark and foreboding seethed inside Eli as he watched Jubal stride down the boardwalk. He had no evidence that Jubal had any connections to the deaths. All Eli had was this instinctive feeling of recognition that had disturbed him the night of the party when he had caught sight of the man emerging from the shadows on the terrace.

Something about the way Jubal moved, or the way he held himself... Eli shook his head in frustration. The fuzzy images that assailed him were indistinctive and refused to solidify in his mind.

Impulsively, Eli followed Jubal down the street then paused when the man glanced back and sent him a smile that Eli couldn't translate. It was almost as if Jubal were silently taunting him or challenging him—Eli couldn't figure out which.

When a flash of blue and gold skirted the perimeters of Eli's vision, he glanced sideways to see Lieutenant Harper striding determinedly down the opposite side of the street. When the soldier veered into Thompson's

Hotel, Eli wondered if Harper had decided to turn his amorous attention on Roz's best friend. Eli wouldn't have been surprised. Gina Thompson had inherited money and property—both of which Harper seemed obsessed to claim as his own.

After Harper disappeared into the hotel, Eli turned back to Jubal, who was scrutinizing him thoroughly. Not to be outdone, Eli tossed Jubal the same kind of enigmatic smile he had received.

Jubal stiffened momentarily and something flickered in his eyes. Apprehension? Recognition? Maybe. Whatever it was prompted Eli to broaden his grin, just to see how Jubal reacted.

Scowling, Jubal jerked open his office door then disappeared from sight.

Damn, that was the strangest *non*conversation Eli ever remembered having. He decided to forego asking questions about Ennis Paxton's possible involvement in Brunswick's death and appease his curiosity.

Reversing direction, Eli made a beeline toward the newspaper office. He was suddenly very intrigued about Jubal Rhodes and his rise to power and fortune. Surely Charles Matthews could shed some light on the subject.

Eli paused in the doorway to see Roz, head bent in profound concentration, writing an article for the paper. A smile quirked his lips as he watched her work. Annoyed as he was with her for traipsing off to conduct her private interview last night, he had to admit that she appeared to be in her rightful place, amid the hustle and bustle of employees who were printing and stacking advertising flyers.

If Eli had ever entertained the whimsical notion that he could whisk Roz off to the mountains and she would be content leading a simpler life, that hope died while he watched her in action. No doubt about it, Rozalie Matthews had found her true calling and she approached journalism with the same passion that inspired her father.

"Señor Quintana, what are you doing here?" A blush rose to her cheeks then she busied herself with the papers on her desk.

Eli shook off the warm sensations that spilled through him and tried to concentrate on portraying his role. "I was hoping your father could provide me with some information. Is Charles here?"

Roz shook her head and sunlight glowed like a halo around her blond hair. "Papa has made it his mission to follow the story about Brunswick's murder. Perhaps I can be of help."

Eli preferred to keep Roz away from further pursuits for information that might lead her into trouble. "No, thank you, *querida*," he murmured, playing his role as a visiting aristocrat for the benefit of the men who were whizzing around the newspaper office. "I will stop by later to see Charles."

On that parting note, Eli ducked out of the office. He would have to delay speaking with Charles. In the meantime, he would find out what he could about Ennis Paxton's possible connection to this most recent murder.

Chapter Eleven

When Roz went upstairs to bathe and retire for the evening, Eli sought out Charles. He found the older man ensconced in his study, perusing his accounting ledgers. "I need some information," Eli requested.

Charles glanced up, started by Eli's silent approach, then set aside his reading glasses. "Does this have something to do with Ennis Paxton? Ask away. I devoted the afternoon to making contacts and questioning several of my acquaintances about any hard feelings that might have arisen between Paxton and Brunswick. Sure enough, the two men clashed at least twice in public yesterday because of their rival pursuit of the Widow Thompson."

"I discovered the same thing," Eli reported. "I eavesdropped on a conversation between a scruffy-looking character and Paxton while I was standing outside his office window at the hotel this afternoon. I overheard Paxton claim that without Brunswick around to fawn over the widow, he was certain he could take control of the elegant hotel, with or without a marriage."

Charles frowned pensively. "It's certainly possible that Paxton might have been the sniper," he speculated. "He's a former prospector who battled claim jumpers for several years before he struck it rich." He stared curiously at Eli. "Did you get a good look at Paxton's companion? Can you identify him?"

Eli nodded. "The man who swaggered from the back exit and skulked down the alley was a thick-set, grizzly-looking man with shaggy brown hair and beard. He was wearing buckskins and he was armed to the teeth."

"Sounds like the same man I heard described by Paxton's hotel clerk," Charles commented. "From what I gather, the ruffian is the hired muscle that collects the interest due from miners that Paxton grubstakes. Those who don't pay their debts promptly can expect to get roughed up and robbed. Paxton seems to have quite a lucrative operation going."

"So it wouldn't be surprising that Paxton's henchman was sent to dispose of Brunswick and Roz ended up at the wrong place at the wrong time," Eli surmised.

Charles winced. "That girl was damn lucky she was able to walk out of that alley alive."

Eli heartily agreed. The prospect of Roz being injured in her effort to help him solve this case unnerved him. Eli promised himself that no matter what else happened he would *not* permit Roz to be the price he paid to bring the killer to justice.

"There's one thing about that incident that doesn't quite add up," Eli said as he absently massaged his mending leg. "Why did Paxton's goon come prepared to disable Roz with chloroform? How could he have known she would be there?"

Charles shrugged uncertainly. "Maybe Paxton has a well-paid informant who saw Roz corner Brunswick inside the café earlier in the day. Or maybe the chloroform was meant for Brunswick and Roz became the scapegoat who was targeted to take the blame for the murder."

"Whatever the case, I think it's time to take the information we have acquired about Paxton and his henchman to Marshal Stokes," Eli advised. "If nothing else, Paxton's underhanded tactics of victimizing miners that are indebted to him should be exposed and stopped."

"I spoke to Stokes on my way home tonight," Charles replied as he leaned back in his chair. "Paxton is going to be answering all sorts of probing questions about his business practices. I suspect he will also be scrambling to provide an alibi to explain his whereabouts during the time Brunswick was attacked and killed."

"Good. The sooner we figure out who is responsible for these deaths the better I'll like it," Eli muttered.

Charles drummed his fingers on the desk and scrutinized Eli for a contemplative moment. "After you've been exonerated, what do you plan to do, McCain?"

Eli met Charles's curious expression and said, "I'll be leaving Denver to lead wagon trains headed west or ride shotgun for the stage. Six months ago I was approached by an acquaintance who asked me to go back to work as a railroad detective that headquarters at Colorado Springs." He shrugged nonchalantly. "There is always work for a man who knows his way through mountain passes and across the frontier."

"What about my daughter?" Charles questioned, his pale green eyes drilling into Eli.

A wry smile kicked up the corner of Eli's mouth. "She wouldn't make much of a guard or scout. I think she's better suited as a journalist, following in your footsteps." He stared deliberately at Charles. "I've read a few of her articles. She definitely has a gift."

"Yes, she does," Charles agreed. "I've given her free rein to write whatever stories interest her."

That was good to hear. Eli wanted to leave Denver, knowing Roz would be permitted to pursue her calling without her father placing frustrating restraints on her. Now that Roz had spread her wings and gained the independence she treasured so much, Eli wanted nothing to hold her back. Not professionally anyway. He just hoped like hell that she observed caution when beating the streets, chasing down a story for the newspaper.

Charles surveyed Eli's dark clothing and moccasins. "I presume you intend to go snooping about tonight, in an attempt to corner Paxton's henchman."

Eli shook his head. "Actually, I was hoping you would let me sort through old newspapers to see what I can find out about Jubal Rhodes. For some reason he seems familiar, but for the life of me I can't figure out why. This might not have anything to do with the murders, but I am compelled to satisfy my curiosity."

Charles put his ledger in the drawer of the desk then came to his feet. "I'll have my stable manager keep an eye on Roz while we're gone. After last night's fiasco, I want to make sure Roz is well guarded."

Eli couldn't agree more. Someone needed to keep

watch on Roz. She had become far too bold and daring for her own good. There was no telling what she might decide to do when Eli wasn't around to provide protection.

That was just one more reason why it would be difficult to walk away from her, Eli mused as he followed Charles outside to fetch Ramon Vasquez. As if he needed another reason. Leaving Roz behind was going to feel unnatural. He had grown accustomed to having her nearby. Accustomed to watching out for her. Accustomed to wanting her—and fighting the losing battle with his self-restraint that landed him in her bed the previous night.

Eli sighed in exasperation. He had the inescapable feeling that even when that green-eyed daredevil was out of sight she was never going to be far from mind. She wasn't the kind of woman that a man could easily forget. Eli's tormenting obsession for Roz was proof positive of that.

Dressed in her nightgown and robe, Roz padded down the hallway to let herself into Eli's bedroom. To her dismay the room was dark and Eli was nowhere to be found. Muttering irritably, Roz reversed direction. No doubt, Eli had ridden into town, hoping to gather more incriminating information to solve this case so he could shed his role as the Spanish aristocrat and head for the hills.

When Roz descended the staircase she was surprised to see Ramon Vasquez sitting in the foyer. The stout Mexican who was in charge of caring for their horses and keeping the carriages in good working order glanced up and smiled in greeting.

"I assume my father has gone out for the evening." *And left a posted bodyguard to insure I stay put,* she thought begrudgingly.

"*Sí,*" Ramon replied as he shifted in his chair. "Your father and Señor Quintana said they had business in town."

Roz stared at the groom in amazement. "They left together? Did they say where they were going?"

"No, *señorita,* but I am to remain on guard until they return. I was told to make certain you stayed home."

Well, so much for her newfound independence, Roz mused resentfully. It looked as if she would be allowed to make a few *un*important decisions without her father or Eli's intervention. Damnation, would they never understand that she longed to be considered their equal, not their responsibility?

"I think you are unhappy, *sí?*" Ramon said perceptively. "But I would be most unhappy if you did not cooperate and I lost my job." He tossed her a placating grin. "I would be very grateful if you did not disobey your father's wishes and make my duties difficult."

Roz decided Eli and her father had backed her into a corner. If she eluded Ramon to trail after the sneaky twosome, the groom would have hell to pay for losing track of her. "Curse them both," she scowled as she whirled about and marched up the steps.

Did they think she would be content to twiddle her thumbs instead of taking an active part in this investigation that affected her as much as it did Eli? He wasn't the only one with an ax to grind, after all. She could have been arrested for murder, too, if Eli hadn't shown up in the alley in the nick of time to rouse her and spirit her off in the darkness.

Feeling restrained and restless, Roz returned to her room. Despite the fact that she wasn't the least bit sleepy, she flounced on her bed and stared at the shadows on the wall.

Ten minutes later, when Roz heard footfalls in the hall, she bounded to her feet and grabbed her robe. She might not have been included in the jaunt to town, but she damn well intended to be updated on any information they had gleaned.

Roz whipped open the bedroom door, prepared to fire a round of questions at her father. She recoiled and shrieked in alarm when a darkly clad figure, his face concealed by a black hood, pounced at her. Roz kicked and clawed in an effort to escape, but the intruder snaked out a gloved hand and grabbed her by the hair. He applied enough painful pressure to force Roz to her knees, causing her hip to slam into the nightstand.

The table teetered then toppled to the floor. The lantern shattered. Glass and kerosene scattered in every direction.

"Ramon!" she screeched frantically. "Help!"

Hoping Ramon would arrive on the scene, Roz battled for all she was worth. She lashed out, thrusting her doubled fist into her assailant's crotch. He howled and cursed, but he refused to release his death grip on her. Roz struck out with her feet, pelting his shins repeatedly, then tried to heave herself upright to plow into him like a battering ram. Her captor sidestepped and

Roz grimaced when slivers of glass and kerosene sent pain shooting through her bare feet.

The unseen blow from the butt of a pistol sent her to her knees again. Stars exploded before her eyes and a new wave of pain pounded against her skull. Jaw clenched in fierce determination, she made one last-ditch effort to pry his fist from her hair, but a second blow to the back of her head rendered her senseless.

Roz collapsed onto the floor in an unconscious heap.

Charles lit two lanterns then carried them through the newspaper office to the second-story storage room that was stacked with shelves from ceiling to floor. Nineteen years of photographs and newspapers—that represented his career as a journalist in Denver—lined the walls.

Eli silently groaned as he panned the walls. He was probably searching for a needle in a haystack. It could take days to thumb through the papers. He wasn't even sure he knew what he was looking for—and wouldn't know until he found it. If ever.

"Where do you want to start?" Charles asked as he set both lanterns on the long planked table that bisected the room. "Five years ago? Ten? What is it that you're—?" His voice dried up when the click of boot heels on the staircase indicated that someone had entered the office and was rapidly approaching the upper story.

Pistol drawn, Eli darted behind the open door the moment he saw the shiny badge that reflected the light. He scowled, hoping the marshal hadn't arrived to report another murder.

Marshal Stokes drew his six-shooter. "Charles?" he called out. "Is that you in there?"

Charles emerged from the shadows. "Yes, I'm doing a bit of research this evening."

The marshal ambled forward to prop a bulky shoulder against the doorjamb then he sighed audibly. "Helluva day. I spent most of it questioning folks about Brunswick's murder. Thought I'd let you know that I came across two witnesses who claimed they saw a man in a cloak and wide-brimmed hat scurrying away from the restaurant about fifteen minutes before Brunswick was found sprawled in the alley."

Eli was relieved that he wasn't the only one who had spotted the unidentified man. He didn't want to have to be the one to report the information to the marshal. The less association he had with the law official—until this case was solved—the better.

"Well at least you have *one* possible suspect," Charles said as he strategically positioned himself beside the door to ensure Eli wasn't seen.

"Better than that actually," Stokes replied. "When I went to question Ennis Paxton about his whereabouts at the time of the murder he wasn't in his office. I took a look around and found a dark cloak and wide-brimmed hat stashed at the back of the closet." He stared grimly at Charles. "There were splatters of dried blood on the cape. Brunswick's blood, I suspect."

"Have you placed Paxton under arrest?" Charles asked.

The marshal scowled and shook his head. "I had planned to, but when I went to his house the butler said that he had gone out for the evening."

"You might try the Widow Thompson's place," Charles suggested. "I hear Ennis has been making a nuisance of himself over there, trying to get his hands on the hotel."

"That's where I was headed when I saw the light in your newspaper office. Thought I'd better check it out." Marshal Stokes pushed away from the doorjamb. "Guess I'll see if I can run Ennis to ground and place him under arrest."

When the marshal exited, Eli stepped from his hiding place. "I would like to have ten minutes with Paxton," he muttered resentfully. "If he's the man who set me up then tried to implicate Roz, I would like to know if the reason I was targeted as his scapegoat was personal or if I was simply a convenient mark."

Charles grabbed a stack of newspapers and carted them to the table. "I'm guessing it had more to do with convenience. You weren't well-known around town and your distinctive style of clothing made you easy to describe."

"You're probably right," Eli agreed as he hauled a hefty stack of newspapers to the table. "If Paxton wanted to throw suspicion on a newcomer, I fit the bill. He must have gone looking for a man who was about my size then dressed him up to do the dirty work. Even better if the imposter worked for Brunswick and he might be implicated if something went wrong."

"If Paxton disposed of Thompson then he could make a play for the elegant hotel and the grieving widow," Charles speculated sourly. "Paxton must have disposed of his rival suitor and decided to blame it on Roz since she was waiting in the alley to speak with Brunswick. Damn, I hope the judge hangs that conniving bastard high.''

"But why would Paxton dispose of Frank Mason?" Eli mused aloud. "What would Paxton have to gain from that?"

"Since Frank Mason's general store caters to outfitting miners with equipment and provisions, Paxton could buy the business. He has been gouging the fortune seekers with high-interest loans and he can also make a killing by jacking up the price of their supplies.''

Charles shook his head and sighed. "Paxton is already one of the wealthiest men in town. His obvious obsession for prominence and power might have compelled him to take control of every facet of the mining industry.''

"From digging and processing ore to selling supplies and housing miners when they venture to town," Eli murmured as he panned an old newspaper. "I was the perfect mark for a man who schemed to eliminate every obstacle in his path on the road to controlling the town.

"Why not blame a half-breed drifter who rarely stays in the same place for more than a week at a time?" Eli's gaze shifted to Charles. "That's why you object to my association with Roz, isn't it?" he asked point-blank.

Charles glanced up from the newspaper he was studying. "You mean because a man of your background and profession isn't good enough for her? No offense, McCain, but you *aren't* good enough for her.''

His faint smile eased the sting of rejection. "Of course, there isn't a man on the continent, maybe not even on the planet, who is deserving of a man's daughter. I knew Harper wasn't the best match, but I thought he'd do.'' He frowned, disgruntled. ''Turns out I was wrong about his ultimate intentions toward her.''

''And you were in a hurry to counter your wife's arranged marriage,'' Eli added.

Charles nodded his head. ''The woman still makes me crazy. Roz is right. I have been contrary and spiteful, just to annoy Sophia. Roz got caught in the middle of our ongoing feud.'' He smiled regretfully. ''But that's all changed now. Roz has a good head on her shoulders and I am trying to loosen my hold on her. As for your mixed heritage and your association with her—''

His voice evaporated as he leaned down to take a closer look at the article that had caught his attention. ''What the hell?''

Eli glanced sideways to see what had distracted Charles. '''Five years ago Lieutenant Harper was listed as missing in action,''' Eli read aloud, '''along with three men in his regiment. He disappeared after a confrontation with a gang of outlaws near Raton Pass in northern New Mexico.''' He glanced bewilderedly at Charles. ''How can that be?''

''It also says here that Harper's family offered a reward for information about him,'' Charles read on, then scowled. ''He was thirty-five years old at the time of his disappearance. The Harper *we* know doesn't look to be that old now!''

Alarmed, Charles stared at Eli. ''Do you suppose that fortune-hunting sidewinder stole Harper's identity and relocated near Denver so he wouldn't be recognized?''

"Wouldn't put it past him," Eli muttered. "I can tell you from previous experience that his battle strategies are seriously lacking. He blundered through every assignment while I worked with him. Whoever he really is, he didn't come up through the normal ranks of the military."

"Marshal Stokes and the Rocky Mountain Detective Agency are going to hear about this," Charles vowed vengefully. "I'm going to offer a reward to find out who is impersonating a military officer and make certain he's punished to the full extent of the law!"

After Charles simmered down—somewhat, at least—Eli asked, "Have you come across any articles about Jubal Rhodes yet?"

"No, are you looking for something in particular?"

Eli shrugged. "No, I'm just wondering where he came from and when he arrived in Denver."

Charles lurched toward the shelves to grab another stack of papers. "Let's start with the papers I printed when I first arrived. As I recall, Jubal had just begun his rise to fame and fortune. Maybe we can track him through the expansion of his mining business. But since Paxton looks to be the culprit responsible for these murders, I don't know how Jubal could possibly figure into this. All the motive and evidence seems to point to Brunswick and Paxton's mutual desire to expand their businesses."

"I'm not sure he does," Eli murmured. But there was still something about the man that put his senses on alert.

An hour later Eli came across a yellowed, engraved sketch and an article that hailed Jubal Rhodes as one of the first prospectors in the area to hit a bonanza. Eli held the lithograph closer to the light, then staggered on his feet when he stared at the younger version of the wealthy mining mogul. A hidden pocket of memory burst to life then flitted away before he could grasp it firmly.

"Are you okay?" Charles questioned when Eli struggled to draw breath. "Damn, you look as if you've seen a ghost. What the devil did you find?"

The newspaper in Eli's hand drifted back to the table. He braced himself against the onrush of half-forgotten memories that floated up from the dark recesses of his mind and transported him back in time. He squeezed his eyes shut, calling up the hazy image of his father, seeing him through the eyes of a confused, terrified child. The pain of losing his Spanish-Indian mother and being bundled off to roam the mountains with his white father rose from its shallow grave, bringing with it a turmoil of emotions that buffeted Eli from every direction at once.

Twenty years had come and gone and Eli thought he had banished those bittersweet memories to the furthest reaches of his mind. He had vowed to put the past behind him and had considered himself born anew after Simon rescued him from the blizzard and raised him as his own. But the haunting nightmare from so long ago boiled up like a geyser. Harsh voices and impatient shouts accompanied the terrifying visions, rolling toward him through a long, winding tunnel.

"McCain?" Charles gave him a jarring nudge.

"You better come over here and sit down before you fall down."

Eli half collapsed in the chair and drew a restorative breath. He flashed back to that fateful night a lifetime ago and remembered being jerked awake, remembered his father yanking him from the warmth of his pallet and shoving him through the rip he had cut in the back of their tent. At the time, Eli spoke Cheyenne and only a little Spanish and English. His father had growled words at him that he hadn't been able to translate.

When Eli had been forced outside, a cold blast of wind had sent shivers all the way to his soul. His father had roughly dragged him toward his pinto pony. Snow had swirled in the darkness as Eli's father stumbled against him then jerked him up to toss him on the horse.

Eli remembered the startled steed plunging off into the black abyss of night. He had hung on for dear life, shivering in the icy wind and wishing for his coat and moccasins to ward off the bitter cold.

Eli clenched his jaw when the photograph of the man's bearded face, capped with shaggy dark hair, rose up like a shadowed wraith in his mind's eye. Suddenly Eli realized why the sight of Jubal Rhodes had struck a distant chord of memory and left him with a host of uneasy sensations.

"Hand me that newspaper," Eli demanded hoarsely. "You don't happen to have the original photograph that this sketch was made from, do you?"

"It should be around here somewhere." Bemused, Charles wheeled around to fetch the paper that lay open on the table.

While Charles pawed through the box of photos, Eli surveyed the whiskered face and close-set eyes that had been captured for a moment in time by the yellowed sketch. He wanted to make absolutely certain that this was the man he recalled from childhood.

"Here," Charles said, handing him the original photograph. "Now, what the Hades is going on?"

After a moment, Eli raised his tormented gaze to Charles. "Although I only crossed paths with this man a few times over two decades ago, I think Jubal Rhodes was acquainted with my father. He might even have been my father's partner."

"Your father's partner?" Charles echoed, then quickly read the article. "You must be mistaken. It doesn't say anything about Rhodes having a partner. I vaguely remember writing this article about how Jubal hit the mother lode and the assayer's office speculated that the pure vein of ore would be worth millions. Turned out it was, too."

Eli's mind raced in circles, trying to force each fragment of memory into slow motion. His father's rough, impatient handling. The garbled command to ride away and never come back. The swaying shadows that seemed to leap out at him as his horse zigzagged through the trees. His cry of terror when he was catapulted from his horse and slammed into a boulder.

"I think we need to get you home," Charles insisted as he took the paper from Eli's hands then tucked it into his pocket. "You look as if you could use a stiff drink, and Ramon is probably wondering how long his bodyguard shift is going to last. Not to mention that Roz will inevitably pitch a fit because we are tramping on her newfound independence and didn't invite her along on this fact-finding mission.''

Numbly, Eli climbed to his feet. He shook his head, trying to clear the jumble of confusing memories. Then he recalled his encounter with Jubal Rhodes on the street earlier that afternoon. He remembered Jubal's smug smile that indicated he knew something that Eli didn't…. Until Eli turned the tables on him and returned that sly grin. Jubal had shifted uncomfortably then ducked into his office, lickety-split. Eli wondered if Jubal might have remembered him, too—and maybe he had been assailed by the same frustrating sense of recognition that he couldn't place.

Eli's befuddled thoughts scattered when Charles guided him onto the street to reach the horses. Eli snapped to attention then shrank back against the clapboard wall of the office when he saw the marshal pelting down the boardwalk, heading directly toward them.

''Is there a problem?'' Charles asked as he strode off to distract the marshal before he spotted Eli.

''Don't know for sure,'' Stokes replied. ''Just having trouble tracking down Paxton. He didn't make a visit to Widow Thompson at the hotel. He might have gotten wind of the fact that I'm looking for him and decided to lie low. But I damn well intend to locate him before someone else winds up dead around here.''

When the marshal hurried away, Eli mounted his horse and reined toward the stately mansion on the edge of town. First thing in the morning he was going to confront Jubal Rhodes. He suspected the man held the key to twenty years of unanswered questions. After all these years of searching, Eli intended to find out why his father had heartlessly abandoned him.

Once his curiosity had been appeased and Paxton was incarcerated, Eli could clear his name and reclaim his identity. Then he would have no reason to remain in Denver. He could leave town, knowing Roz would be safe—as safe as an independent female like Roz could be when she was prone to go rushing off to gather facts for a story.

But for certain, Roz would no longer need his protection, Eli reminded himself. Charles would watch over her like a hawk and would no doubt be greatly relieved to have Eli as far away from Roz as he could possibly get.

The thought of never seeing Roz again left an empty ache expanding inside him. But Eli reminded himself that he had to sever all ties with Roz. It could be no other way. He had to ride off and they both had to know—and accept the fact—that he was never coming back. *He* could never fit into her world and *she* didn't belong in his.

Groaning sluggishly, Roz battled her way from the dark pit of unconsciousness to find her hands lashed to the pommel of a saddle and her feet bound to the stirrups. The horse she was riding faltered momentarily then collided with the rider beside her. As the horses veered apart, Roz struggled to get her bearings in the darkness.

The sharp blows to her head made thinking difficult, but she was cognizant enough to realize her captor was leading her away from the distant lights of town. She glanced at her assailant, certain she knew the identity of the man whose face was hidden behind that black hood. This was same man who had grabbed her while she waited behind Brunswick's café for a private interview.

Her suspicions were confirmed when her captor leaned over to grab a handful of her unbound hair, forcing her head sideways so he could stuff a cloth over her face. The same drugging scent that had overwhelmed her that night in the alley saturated her senses and left her drifting toward helpless oblivion.

Roz tried in vain to remain conscious, but she could feel her lethargic body slumping over the horse, see the hazy fog of darkness closing in around her. Her last thought was that she wouldn't see Eli again and she never had worked up the nerve to tell him she loved him.

Now it wouldn't matter that he didn't return her deep affection. She wasn't going to live long enough to suffer through the heartache and disappointment of watching Eli walk out of her life forever.

A sense of impending doom settled over Eli when he saw Ramon Vasquez stumble dazedly from the house, rubbing the back of his head.

"Damn it, what's wrong now?" Eli scowled. If disaster had befallen Roz during his absence he would never forgive himself.

"What's happened?" Charles called to his groom. "Where is my daughter?"

"I do not know, *señor*," Ramon mumbled as he wrapped his arm around the column of the porch to hold himself upright. "Someone sneaked up behind me and clubbed me over the head. When I came to, I crawled upstairs to check on Rozalie, but she was nowhere to be found."

"How mad was she when she realized we had placed her under house arrest while we were gone?" Charles wanted to know. "Could she have knocked you senseless?"

Ramon shook his head—very carefully. "No, I don't think so. She wasn't pleased to learn that you left her behind, but I think she would have sneaked off without pounding on my skull."

Eli was off his horse in a single bound, dashing toward the front steps. Knowing that Ennis Paxton was still on the loose left him with a fierce sense of urgency in locating Roz. Eli was ready to swear that dealing with the ruthless machinations of *so-called* civilized men was worse than battling inclement weather and predators in the wilderness.

Eli faced the very real possibility that Paxton had sneaked in to drag Roz off in the darkness. Damn it, he should have left Roz at the cabin with Simon to watch over her, Eli thought in retrospect. She wouldn't have gotten caught up in the events surrounding Brunswick's death and hauled off to only God knew where! Eli predicted that Paxton had seen his chance to pounce on Roz while Eli and Charles were in town. Paxton probably intended to use Roz as a shield if a posse came looking for him. No one would dare take shots at him, for fear of hitting his hostage.

The dismal thought caused a coil of emotion to twist in Eli's gut. He would gladly exchange places with Roz if that would guarantee that she survived. He would give his life for hers without hesitation. Whatever it took to bring her back home where she belonged he would oblige.

Eli burst into Roz's room to see the nightstand upturned and lantern oil and glass littering the floor. "Damn it to hell!" he roared furiously.

Behind him, Charles clutched at his chest and wobbled on his feet as he surveyed the damage that indicated a struggle. "God! If that bastard harms one hair on her head, I'll—"

His voice evaporated when Eli snatched up the folded paper that lay in the middle of the bed. "What does he want? What does it say?" Charles demanded apprehensively.

Eli read the note that had been pasted together from the bold typeset of a newspaper. If this was some sort of cruel irony aimed to infuriate Charles it was definitely working. A stream of foul obscenities exploded from Charles's lips when he saw the familiar print.

"That son of a bitch!" Charles snarled viciously. "Paxton must have heard that I was tracking down information about his link to Brunswick's death. Damn it, he plans to take out his revenge on me by abducting Roz." He stabbed his index finger against the paper in Eli's hand. "And what's this supposed to mean? 'Wait for further instructions at High Lonesome'?"

"It's a small outpost of a mining district in the mountains," Eli explained grimly. He tossed aside the note and spun on his heel. "I'll gather my gear. You need to ride back into town and alert the marshal."

"No," Charles refused adamantly. "I'll send Ramon

to contact Stokes and report the abduction to the detective agency. I want every available lawman in the area on this case. And I am *definitely* going with you!''

Eli halted to stare into Charles's determined expression—once again reminded of the striking similarity between father and daughter. The look of apprehensive concern in Charles's wild-eyed stare left no doubt about how deeply he cared for Roz. Even his avid dedication to his career paled in comparison to his protective feelings for his daughter.

At least Charles and Eli had one thing in common, he mused as he headed for his room. They were both hopelessly devoted to seeing Roz returned unharmed.

''I'll meet you downstairs in a few minutes,'' Charles called after Eli. ''And don't you dare leave without me!''

The threat was lost on Eli. His mind was buzzing with all sorts of worst-case scenarios—none of which bode well for Roz. It was all too easy for a man to lose himself in the wild tumble of mountains—and shove an unwanted companion off a towering cliff to ensure she couldn't testify against him.

Eli didn't know how he would react if Roz got hurt—or worse. He didn't want to find out the hard way, either.

The grim thought prompted Eli to hurriedly cram his belongings into his saddle bags then strap on his holster. Paxton might have had a head start in reaching High Lonesome, but Eli knew every cross-country path through the mountains. He damn well intended to be lying in wait when Paxton arrived to leave his next note at the mining camp.

While Eli was giving Ramon instructions, Charles hurtled down the front step and raced across the lawn. "Whatever he told you to do, Ramon, do it," Charles said on a seesaw breath. "You're in charge of the place while we're gone."

"Sí, señor." The groom wobbled off to fetch his horse and deliver the message to town.

"If you lead the way into the mountains and make sure my daughter survives this ordeal, you can name your price, McCain," Charles insisted as he mounted his waiting steed.

"All I want is your promise that you won't hold Roz back again," Eli bargained. "If she—" He stopped speaking abruptly to rephrase the comment. "*When* Roz returns I want your word that you won't try to marry her off to anyone that doesn't have *her* stamp of approval, even if her mother is putting pressure on her again. Plus, I want your promise that Roz will be allowed to write whatever stories for the paper that draws her interest, woman or not."

"Done," Charles said without hesitation. "And you will be entitled to a hefty reward for rescuing her. You can count on that, too. Whatever you want, you can have."

"I don't give a damn about the money. All I care about is getting Roz back in one piece," Eli said before he dug in his heels and sent his horse thundering toward the foothills of the Rockies.

Chapter Twelve

Two hours later Eli glanced over his shoulder to see a posse, carrying torches, following behind them. The superintendent of the Rocky Mountain Detective Agency, Thomas Lake, hadn't wasted any time mounting a force, Eli mused as he urged his horse up the steep incline. Of course, considering Charles's offer to name any price, Eli wasn't surprised to see immediate results.

"How much farther?" Charles questioned as he followed the difficult path.

"A half hour's ride," Eli informed him. "I suspect we'll be walking into a trap. I think you should join the detectives and circle the area. If Paxton eludes me, the posse should be able to surround him on all sides so he can't use Roz as his shield of defense."

"You can't go charging in alone," Charles argued as he clung to his horse that was scrabbling for footing. "That's suicide!"

Eli reined his winded steed to a halt and stared somberly into Charles's shadowed face. "This is what I *do*," he said emphatically. "I'm used to working alone. I prefer it—"

His voice dried up when a lone figure emerged from a clump of pines. Eli grabbed Charles's arm when he went for his pistol. "Wait," he ordered.

Eli watched the mountain man stride toward them, leading his mule. "What are you doing here, Simon?" he asked in surprise.

"I've been hanging around all week, waiting for you to show up," Simon replied. "I wanted to make sure that things didn't go badly in town. I thought I might have to spring you from jail." He gestured to the west. "I set up camp on the west side of the ridge."

"Is this the man Roz told me about?" Charles questioned as he surveyed the bulky figure in front of him.

"You must be Charles Matthews," Simon presumed.

Charles scowled. "This daredevil son of yours thinks he should ride into High Lonesome alone to capture the bastard who abducted my daughter. Talk some sense into him."

"Can't," Simon replied. "There are times when one man is more effective than a mounted posse." He stared at the bobbing lights that were strung out on the winding path below. "Might as well send an engraved invitation that reinforcements have arrived. That only serves to make a man desperate and unpredictable."

Simon glanced up at Eli. "I'll lead the posse over the ridge and post them as lookouts around the camp." He swung onto his mule. "Charles, you should come with me."

Eli watched Simon make his way toward the approaching posse, with the disgruntled Charles following reluctantly behind him. Nudging his horse, Eli trotted along the perilous trail that most miners avoided because the slightest misstep could cause horse and rider to take the short way down the mountain.

A half hour later, Eli dismounted on the outcropping of rock that provided a bird's-eye view of the isolated community where several canvas tents and shacks had been erected around a central campfire. A muted curse tumbled from Eli's lips when he saw a riderless horse approach the edge of camp. No doubt, Paxton had left a note on his steed and was hiding in the underbrush.

Damn it, where had he stashed Roz?

A moment later, Eli caught sight of the dark figure that scurried between the boulders, heading for higher ground. Eli tethered his horse then made his way over to the edge of the cliff. Pausing momentarily he listened to the sound of pelting footsteps. He followed Paxton as he zigzagged through the trees, making his way toward what looked to be an abandoned mine shaft.

Eli had the uneasy feeling that Roz had been tucked inside the tunnel. It was going to be next to impossible to reach her without confronting Paxton first. Grabbing his rifle, Eli drew a bead on his target and fired. Paxton stumbled forward in the dirt. Eli cursed soundly when the man pushed onto his hands and knees then took off toward the mouth of the cavern.

Frantic to intercept Paxton before he reached Roz, Eli raced off at a dead run. When he heard the telltale click of a trigger he dived and rolled in the dirt.

A bullet whizzed over his head. Another shot ricocheted off the boulders beside his hip. Again, Eli reminded himself that the sniper was a crackshot. If not for the swaying shadows of the night, Eli might have become an easy target and found himself plugged by the oncoming bullet.

Eli wasn't sure how badly he had wounded Paxton—certainly not badly enough to bring him down and keep him down. The ruthless bastard refused to surrender without an all-out firefight.

Amid the rapid-fire exchange, Eli leaped from one boulder to the next, gradually making his way closer to the tunnel. He swore viciously when another shot rang out, indicating that Paxton had come armed with at least two pistols—and had dug in at the mouth of the mine to blast away when someone approached.

Grabbing more cartridges from the pouch on his belt, Eli reloaded his six-shooter. Then he scooped up a rock and heaved it to the east. Paxton fired off another round when he heard the sound that implied Eli had come within twenty feet of the entrance of the shaft.

Stalemate, Eli thought in irritation. There was nothing else to do but pitch more rocks to throw Paxton off track and make him waste most of his ammunition.

Roz was jostled awake by the report of a pistol that echoed through the stone passageway. Levering into an upright position she braced against the wall and stared up the vertical shaft where she had been stashed for safekeeping. Her hands were tied behind her back and her bare feet were coiled in rope. The rock floor was amazingly warm and steamy water trickled from the crevices in the stone.

Roz could definitely understand why miners usually

dressed in the minimal amount of clothes when they descended into the mines. The heat rising from the bowels of the earth was oppressing. It didn't help the light-headedness that caused her vision to go in and out of focus.

Shaking her head to clear her fuzzy thoughts, Roz shifted her attention to the light source that flickered eerily against the stone walls. The distant gunfire faded into silence, alerting Roz that she didn't have much time. Determined to give herself a sporting chance before her captor returned, Roz rolled across the cavern floor.

Crouching on her knees, she glanced over her shoulder and used her fingertips to jiggle the lantern globe. Although the hot glass singed her fingers she managed to remove the globe from the flame. Contorting her body, she held out her arms to burn the ropes from her wrists. She bit back a cry of pain when the flame seared her skin, but she continued to hold her hands over the base of the lantern until her wrists were free. Mission accomplished, she hurriedly untied her ankles then hobbled toward the crude rope-and-timber ladder that led up to the horizontal passage above her.

Ignoring the pain in her feet, she ascended to the horizontal tunnel—and cursed mightily when a hand snaked out to grab her hair and send her sprawling on the floor. Too late, she realized that her captor was back and his disposition had deteriorated.

"Damn you and that half-breed bastard," Paxton said in a ragged hiss. "I swear he has as many lives as a cat."

Roz didn't have time to register what Paxton said

because he rammed his knee painfully into her spine, keeping her pinned to the floor. He shoved his pistol against the back of her head, discouraging her from attempting escape.

Confound it, she had worked herself free of the ropes and crawled from the pit, only to be recaptured and used as a shield against Eli who had somehow managed to track them from town and engage Paxton in a gun battle a few minutes earlier.

Vile profanity flooded from Paxton's lips when a shadow skimmed the wall then disappeared behind one of the thick timbers that supported the ceiling of the shaft. Roz flinched when Paxton raised his pistol to fire off another shot—so close to her head that she swore her eardrums had burst.

"Come out where I can see you, bastard," Paxton snarled. "You want her alive, McCain? Throw down your rifle."

McCain? Roz suddenly remembered that Paxton had called Eli a half-breed who had as many lives as a cat. Paxton *knew* who Eli was—and had undoubtedly known all along.

Roz winced when Paxton grabbed her hair then jerked her upright. He yanked her back against him, using her as his armor of defense. His pistol stabbed into her cheek and the click of the trigger shattered the uneasy silence.

A tense moment ticked by and Roz clenched her teeth when Paxton wrapped her hair around his fist like a rope, tilting her head to yet an uncomfortable angle.

"You coming out, McCain, or shall I blow her head off, right before your eyes?" Paxton jeered viciously.

"No!" Roz shrieked, refusing to let Eli risk his life to save hers. "Go back!"

To her dismay, Eli eased away from the heavy wooden trestle and hovered thirty feet away. Close enough to get himself shot, damn him!

Then, to her startled surprise, Paxton jerked the black hood off his head. His fiendish laugh echoed through the tunnel. But it wasn't Paxton who held a gun to her head and jeered at Eli. It was Jubal Rhodes. Roz gaped at the gray-haired aristocrat in bewildered confusion.

"You should have died years ago," Jubal sneered hatefully. "I knew I had to get rid of you that day last month when I saw you walk past my office. That damn talisman you wear around your neck and the Cheyenne brand on your wrist assured me that it was you." He glowered at Eli. "But it was those blue eyes that you inherited from Marcus that confirmed the truth. I knew my secret would never be safe as long as you lived and breathed."

Eli tried to hold the tormenting memories at bay while he stared down at Jubal who was crouched behind Roz. He still didn't understand why Jubal had marked him for death and, with Roz's body shielding Jubal's torso, Eli couldn't determine how bad this murdering bastard had been hit.

The man had to be losing blood and he would undoubtedly become desperate when his strength began to fail him. If Eli could keep Jubal talking, he might be able to get the drop on him when his condition worsened.

"Marcus survived long enough to reach the tent and

send you galloping away before he collapsed,'' Jubal muttered resentfully as he clasped Roz tightly against him. ''Took more than one bullet in the back to put Marcus down for good.'' His eyes glowed with long-held hatred. ''You're as hard to bring down as he was.''

Eli finally understood what had happened that night twenty years ago. Also understood that Jubal was trying to prey on his emotions so he would react rashly. But Eli swore he wouldn't give this murdering son of a bitch the satisfaction. Instead, Jubal's words cleared up the bitter feelings Eli had held for his father all these years.

His father hadn't been ruthlessly discarding him. Marcus had been trying to *save* his young son's life before Jubal could murder Eli in his sleep. Wounded though Marcus obviously had been, he had made it to the tent to send Eli riding to safety.

Obviously Marcus had something that Jubal had wanted desperately enough to take a man's life—and his son's, if he could have gotten off a shot that cold winter night.

''You killed my father for the gold, didn't you?'' Eli accused bitterly.

Jubal bobbed his gray head and scowled. ''The greedy bastard wanted to dissolve our partnership six months earlier. I figured he'd found a vein of ore and didn't want to split it with me. After his Cheyenne squaw died and he had you to care for, I suspected he was making plans to take the gold and move into town.''

Eli was suddenly, vividly aware that the pieces of

the puzzle that was his past was the cause of his present problems. Jubal had set him up, not because he was a new face in town who wore a distinct style of clothing, but because he was the son of the man Jubal had killed to claim the gold Marcus had discovered.

"You changed the course of Eli's life forever," Roz muttered angrily. "You disposed of Marcus and everything you have amassed—and flaunted in everyone's face to make you feel important—isn't even yours! You are a murdering fraud, Jubal."

"Shut up, bitch," Jubal growled.

He yanked roughly on Roz's hair then jabbed the pistol barrel against her temple. The look he gave Roz made her a firm believer in hell—and convinced her that Jubal was the resident demon.

"It's *your* fault that McCain didn't keep running for his life when he had the chance. I made sure he would take the blame for Thompson's and Mason's murders, but then you came riding out to the bridge to see both men dressed identically."

"So you killed Hal Freedman to ensure he didn't cause you any complications," she presumed.

"I could have dragged off Freedman's body and buried him before anyone realized McCain had a look-alike, but *you* were there to spoil everything!" Jubal muttered sourly. "Then you came back to town, passing McCain off as a former acquaintance with wealthy connections and made it more difficult for me to get to him."

"So you decided to pit Brunswick and Paxton against each other to divert suspicion away from you," Eli speculated.

"I had to get rid of Brunswick, just as I have to get rid of the two of you," Jubal snarled. "Brunswick found out that Freedman was conducting business for me. He tried to blackmail me when Freedman turned up missing and Thompson and Mason ended up dead."

"So you set up Roz to take the blame for Brunswick's death. When that didn't work, you stashed your cloak in Paxton's office. What did you have against him?" Eli questioned harshly.

"Nothing personal." Jubal smirked. "Just never did have any use for two of my rivals who tried to upstage me."

"You are a real piece of work, Jubal." Ever so slowly, Eli eased his hand toward the dagger on his thigh. "I'm curious to know what it is that passes for your conscience."

"Keep your hands where I can see them," Jubal snapped. "I'm not squeamish about shooting a woman, especially one who fouled up my plans. I've spent twenty years building an empire and reputation in Denver. I refuse to see my dreams destroyed by a half-breed brat that should have died alongside his stingy father and a snoopy bitch who wouldn't leave well enough alone."

Roz could feel the warm dampness of blood saturating the back of her robe. She wasn't sure how badly Jubal had been wounded, but she was certain the injury had yet to zap his strength. He still held a fierce grip on her. She didn't how long Jubal could hold out, but his hateful tone of voice indicated that he had no intention of allowing Eli to walk out of the mine shaft alive to claim the fortune that had been stolen from him twenty years ago.

Everything Jubal had acquired was built on murder and theft. If he had been desperate enough to gun down Marcus McCain and attempt to kill his son then he would stop at nothing to hang on to his fortune and remove anyone who stood in his path.

"I don't want your blood money," Eli assured Jubal. "Let Roz walk out of this tunnel alive and I will gladly exchange places with her. This feud is between you and me—"

Eli sprang sideways to retrieve his rifle and draw Jubal's undivided attention. When the pistol swerved away from Roz's head she thrust up her hand, misdirecting the shot. It zinged off the rock wall and echoed down the passageway. Before Eli could grab his weapon Jubal fired off another shot that shattered the butt of the rifle and sent it skidding out of Eli's reach.

While Eli scrambled to his hands and knees, preparing to pounce, Roz wrestled Jubal for control of the pistol. Before Eli could dash forward, Jubal clutched the back of Roz's robe and hurled her over the ledge. She let out a shriek as she flew pell-mell into the pit. She groaned in pain when she landed on her left arm. Defiantly, she crawled toward the lantern, determined to distract Jubal before he could put a bullet in Eli.

Jubal's furious howl echoed through the cavern when the airborne lantern arced through the air and clattered beside him. Glass shattered. Kerosene splattered on his clothes—and they caught flame instantly.

As far as Eli was concerned the vicious bastard could burn alive. All Eli cared about was getting to Roz.

His heart had stopped beating and icy dread had clutched his gut when Jubal had launched her over the ledge and sent her tumbling into the pit. Eli had no idea how far she had dropped or how badly she might have been hurt. But he knew that she was conscious enough to retaliate because the lantern had soared upward to land beside Jubal.

Lurching to his knees, Jubal held his pistol in one hand and slapped at his flaming coat with the other. "If I die then we all die!" he screeched like a madman.

Eli dived for cover behind an outcropping of rock when Jubal turned his fury and his gun on Eli again. There was a sinister sneer on his lips and a mutinous gleam in his eyes as he fired off two shots that thudded in the timbers beside Eli's head.

Eli groped for the rifle that lay a few feet away. Despite the shattered butt of the weapon, Eli shoved a cartridge into the chamber.

Jubal wrested free from his flaming coat and hurled it at Eli. Lurching sideways, Eli jerked the rifle into firing position and took Jubal's measure.

The bullet plugged Jubal's chest and he staggered on his feet. He screeched in fiendish fury when he looked down at the deadly wound.

It wasn't until Jubal bowed his neck and slammed his shoulder into the timber that supported a soft pocket in the ceiling that Eli realized his intent. Eli stopped breathing when the timber creaked and groaned. The eerie sound echoed through the passageway like the toll of doom.

"No!" Eli bellowed at the top of his lungs and scrambled to his feet. Before he could reach the supporting beam, it gave way. Rock and timber crashed down and the earth trembled and shuddered. Dust rose like a black fog and rats scurried from the crevices to seek safety in the tunnel.

Eli stared in horror as the narrow shaft collapsed on Jubal, trapping Roz in the vertical shaft beyond. Choking dust rolled over Eli as he reflexively scrambled away from the tumbling stones. He shielded his face and head as debris rained down in the inky black darkness.

His soul turned wrong side out when he realized that he might never see Roz alive again. As fury and despair avalanched upon him, Eli let out a roar and cursed Jubal Rhodes straight to the hottest fires in hell.

"Roz!"

Charles's wild howl rolled toward Eli from the entrance of the shaft. Footfalls echoed along the stone floor and torches flared in the darkness. Swearing profusely, Eli dragged himself forward with his arms, trying to free his legs from the rubble.

"Oh, God!" Charles gasped as the torchlight flared against the timber-and-stone barrier that closed off the tunnel. He glanced around frantically. "Where is she?"

Eli didn't bother to reply, just floundered to his feet to hurl away the stones that stood like an insurmountable obstacle in his path. He prayed to Indian and white deities alike that the cave-in hadn't reached the vertical shaft where Jubal had hurled Roz.

There was only one other time in Eli's life that he

had been so terrified that it paralyzed his thought processes—the night his father had scooped him up and tossed him onto his horse to thunder into the darkness. But this was a hundred times worse, he realized as he tossed aside boulders in panicky desperation. He was suffering every torment of the damned, knowing that he was responsible for every disaster that had befallen Roz the past two weeks. Her association with him had been the curse of her life.

And maybe the cause of her death...

The horrifying thought plowed through him like an unseen blow to the solar plexus, robbing him of breath, taking him to his knees. Dust blurred his eyes as they welled up with unshed tears. It wasn't the fog of dust hovering around him that choked him up. It was dozens of emotions—so many converging at once that he couldn't sort them out and deal with them one at a time. They simply overwhelmed him with their intensity.

"Roz!" he roared as he blindly crawled up the pyramid of rock and debris.

He heard nothing. Nothing but the sound of his own heart thundering in his ears. Nothing but his anguished voice rebounding off the stone walls to assail him from every direction at once.

"Charles?" Eli turned his head to see that Charles had half collapsed against the wall and that Simon had rushed over to lend a supporting arm. Charles's pale green eyes were gleaming with terror and shock.

"I'm sorry," Eli murmured as he watched the expression of fatalistic defeat settle on Charles's pale features.

"Help is on the way," Simon said soothingly as he propped up Charles then veered around the handful of detectives that filled the passageway. "The miners heard the shots and the rumble of falling rocks. They're bringing their tools and carts to shore up the ceiling and clear the shaft."

Eli was too frantic to wait until the miners arrived. He didn't know how much air was left to sustain Roz, didn't know if she was dead or alive. Only one thought blazed in his mind—get to her.

Snarling a curse at Jubal, Eli clawed at the sharp-edged rocks until his hands bled, until Simon reached over to still the desperate motions of his arms.

"You can't move a mountain alone," Simon told him. "The miners will be here in another few minutes—"

Timbers creaked and groaned. The unholy sound filled the dust-clogged chamber. Every man in the shaft stopped moving, stopped breathing, when the earth shifted and settled—and threatened to bury the rescue party alive.

Eli reeled in fury and frustration as he replayed the confrontation with Jubal over in his mind. He should have known Jubal intended to bring down the mountain around them when he realized he had lost everything—his fortune, his reputation, his life. Eli should have gone for his dagger and dared Jubal to take his best shot.

Perhaps Roz might have had a fighting chance while Jubal was distracted. Or maybe Eli should have come charging into the shaft, forcing Jubal to deal with him directly, instead of sneaking toward that vicious bastard, hoping to catch him unaware. But Eli had allowed his churning emotions and his fear for Roz's safety to cloud his judgment.

God, if only he could rewind the hands of time and try a different tact. Maybe Roz wouldn't be trapped behind a wall of rock, buried under a pile of stone— like Jubal Rhodes.

Eli bit back a roar of rage. Roz had saved his life, stood beside him, stood *up* for him when no one else believed in him. She had rallied her father's support around him and put herself in jeopardy to gather information that might solve the crimes.

And Eli had repaid her unfaltering faith in him by allowing her to be kidnapped then buried alive in the bowels of the earth.

"No, damn it," Eli snarled as he shook loose from Simon's grasp.

He refused to let Roz take up permanent residence in a three-by-six-foot slice of this fallen mountain! He sprang onto the pile of boulders like a pouncing panther, spearing his hands between the rocks that sat at the top of the rubble. He was desperate to unearth a space large enough for him to crawl through.

Summoning every ounce of strength he possessed, Eli clasped both hands around an oversize boulder and heaved it aside. He barely had time to sidestep when two more jagged chunks of rock bounced toward the floor. A plume of dust rose to form another cloud at the top of the shaft.

"Give me a torch," Eli demanded hurriedly.

One of the detectives, a wiry man with bushy eyebrows and a handlebar mustache, extended the torch.

His apprehensive gaze darted to the hollowed-out arch where dust dribbled from the crevices of rock—giving fair warning that the mountain was going to topple down on them at any moment.

Eli reached out to snatch the torch from the wary detective then thrust it through the small portal he had made between the pile of stone and the unstable ceiling. Cursing mightily, he shoved away another boulder—and another—until the torch flared up, indicating that he had cleared a route to reach the air pocket beyond the barrier.

Voices rumbled through the tunnel as the miners hurried forward to begin bracing new timbers in the unstable shaft. Eli heaved himself upon the pyramid of rocks then wedged his shoulders through the narrow space he had cleared away from the ceiling. Dirt and pebbles dribbled onto his head as he slithered forward with nothing but the flickering torch to light his way through the suffocating cloud of dust that was trapped beyond the rubble of stone.

"Roz! Can you hear me?" Eli called out as he tumbled down the backside of the pile of jagged rocks.

He was met with more silence.

Another part of his soul shriveled up inside him. Afraid to look—and afraid not to—Eli scrabbled over the fallen stones to reach the vertical shaft. His heart slammed against his ribs—and stuck there—when he realized the shaft was filled with rock.

Holding the torch above his head, he panned the cubicle—and staggered to maintain his balance when he saw Roz's crumpled body in the corner, half covered with rock and timber.

"Did you find her, McCain?" Charles called from beyond the barrier. "Is she alive?"

Eli didn't reply because he didn't have the answer. Wasn't sure he wanted to climb down the ladder and touch her—for fear he would have to give up hope and face the grim reality that he had lost someone who meant more to him than life itself. Someone whose life *he* had destroyed.

He should have died beside his father twenty years ago, Eli thought as he rolled over the ledge to find footing on the frayed ladder. Then Roz would never have become embroiled in Jubal's ruthless attempt to protect his secret.

Bombarded by a riptide of emotion, serenaded by distant voices and the sound of rough timbers being pounded into place to secure the crumbling ceiling, Eli stepped off the ladder to hobble over the mound of rock. He pushed away the stones that restrained Roz's legs then sank down on his haunches beside her.

"Roz?" Eli held up the torch to see a discolored knot the size of an egg on her forehead. Her blond hair was covered with dust. So were her gown and robe.

Holding his breath, praying nonstop, Eli pressed his fingertips to her neck. He sagged in overwhelming relief when he found an erratic pulse. Everything inside him collapsed like the mine shaft when he assured himself that she was still alive.

"I found her, Charles!" Eli called out as he clutched Roz's limp body against his. "I think she'll be okay."

At least he hoped.

Shouts of relief rose up on the far side of the barrier and Eli finally managed a smile. Roz wasn't in the best of shape. Her left arm looked as if it might be broken. Scrapes and bruises marred her arms, legs and cheeks. Rope burns surrounded her wrists and ankles and cuts from glass lacerated her feet. But she would recover, Eli told himself. She was tough and resilient. Strong will alone was enough to make her fight her way back.

A quiet moan tumbled from her lips as Eli hoisted her into his arms. Eli wished Roz would open those glorious green eyes and peer up at him, for even a split second, but she simply slumped against him like a feed sack. He shifted her body and draped her over his shoulder so he could navigate the uneven pile of rocks that led to the ladder.

Eli tossed the torch over the ledge and reached out to grab the ladder. Despite the pressure on his aching leg, he ascended from the rock-strewn pit.

Two men, whom Eli presumed were detectives, reached down to lift Roz's motionless body from his shoulder. Then they clutched his arms and pulled him upward until he could gather his legs beneath him.

"Never saw a man move a mountain with his bare hands before," the detective with the handlebar mustache said. "Hope I never have to be inside one of these caverns to see it again." He thrust out his hand in greeting. "I'm Thomas Lake. Glad to meet you, McCain."

Eli shook hands, but he wasn't in the mood for chit-chat. He was anxious to get Roz outside to breathe fresh air and let Simon work his healing magic.

Retrieving Roz from the other detective's arm, Eli scrabbled upward to the narrow opening. Several men were waiting on the other side to pull Roz through. Eli scrunched through the confining space and heard Charles swearing and praying simultaneously as Roz was carried down the pile of rocks and carted through the tunnel.

Another eerie groan echoed through the passageway and dust dribbled from the ceiling again. A dozen men scrambled for their lives. Eli reached back through the opening to grab Thomas Lake's hand, giving it a hard jerk to pull him to safety.

Wild shouts resounded as the miners abandoned their tools and carts in their haste to flee. When Thomas stumbled over the uneven pile of rocks Eli jerked him upright and shoved the detective ahead of him. Dodging the discarded equipment, Eli and Thomas pelted through the tunnel, hearing the impending rumble behind them.

"You saved my life," Thomas panted as he burst outside to grab a breath of fresh air. "Thank you."

Eli mumbled a quick "you're welcome" before he shouldered his way through the congregation of miners that waited at the entrance to ensure the last two men were safe. Everyone scrambled backward when the earth shook beneath their feet and a fog of dust belched from the mine shaft.

"That's why we abandoned the site," Eli heard one of the miners say as the crowd made fast tracks toward camp. "Too damn unstable. We lost ten men in that cursed tunnel last winter."

Eli snaked his way through the crowd then sank to his knees beside Simon who was inspecting the oversize bump on Roz's head.

"Maybe a concussion. A broken arm for certain,"

Simon diagnosed. "We shouldn't move her until morning."

Eli nodded his dusty head. "Whatever she needs, she gets."

"She gets to live, thanks to your relentless persistence." Simon smiled faintly as his dark eyes swung to Eli. "If you had taken my advice and waited for the miners to shore up the tunnel she would still be in there. So would most of us. But I was concerned about your safety. I was afraid you were going to perish alongside Roz." He nodded pensively. "That is a grim reminder that when you allow emotion to override common sense you flirt with disaster."

Eli didn't need to be reminded of how close he had come to seeing Roz buried alongside Jubal Rhodes. And may that bastard roast in hell. Jubal had destroyed too many lives to protect his secret and Eli was damn happy that bastard had died as brutally as he had lived.

When Roz was placed on a stretcher and carried to camp, Eli was right beside her, clutching her hand, willing her to regain consciousness, if only for a moment—but she didn't.

Eli was there all through what was left of the night, acting as her personal guardian angel and protector. Charles was right beside him, jabbering constantly, as if Roz could hear every word he said.

Along toward dawn Charles collapsed in exhausted sleep. But Eli kept the vigil. Never in his life had he wished for the power to take someone's pain and bear it as his own. But he would do it for Roz if he could—gladly. Unfortunately, all he could do was hold a cool compress to the oversize bump on her forehead and clutch her hand, *willing* her to respond to his touch.

Eli sent a silent prayer of gratitude winging heavenward when Roz finally stirred sluggishly. Her dusty lashes fluttered up to stare right through him. Considering the blow that she had sustained to her head, he wondered if she remembered her own name, wondered if she even recalled the nightmare she had endured— *because of him.*

A faint smile curved his lips when her beguiling gaze finally focused on him, registering recognition. "Hey, Green Eyes. About time you came around," he murmured as he bent to take her mouth in a gentle kiss. "I distinctly remember telling you not to scare me half to death. Damn if you didn't go and do it again."

Her answering smile was a bit wobbly around the edges. When she tried to speak, her voice cracked and she sputtered for breath. Eli grabbed the tin cup to offer her a drink.

"Eli, I have to tell you—"

He pressed his forefinger to her lips to shush her. "Save your strength, *querida*. You can tell me later."

She shook her dusty blond head then held his hand tightly in hers. "Just in case there isn't a later—"

"There *will* be," he broke in firmly. "You're banged up, but you're going to be fine."

"I want you to know that you are the love of my heart, Eli McCain," she wheezed. "Our debt to each other has been paid in full. Now I can let you go and you are free of your obligations to me. I only want you to be happy."

"Roz, don't love me. I'm the curse of your life…"

His voice trailed off when she slumped on the cot. He didn't have the chance to tell her that he would *never* be free of her, even when he left her to the life that suited her so perfectly in Denver—a life far removed from the mountains that were so much a part of his existence.

She couldn't possibly love him, he refuted silently. He had done nothing to deserve her affection. He had dragged her across rugged terrain to endure a violent thunderstorm, forced her to hole up in a crude cabin and nurse him back to health. If anything, her conscience had hounded her until she convinced herself that she should love the man she had allowed to introduce her to the intimacy of passion. Time and distance would grant her objectivity and perspective, Eli assured himself. One day she would realize that she had mistaken lust for love.

Rising to his feet, Eli ambled outside to fetch his horse that he had tethered a short distance from the camp. Now that he was sure that Roz would recover, he needed to make a clean break—for her own good, as well as his own. He was a complication Roz didn't need in her life.

Eli swung into the saddle and heaved a weary sigh. He was going to do Roz a favor by riding out of her life because that was for the best.

Clinging to that noble thought, Eli rode west.

Chapter Thirteen

Four days after the life-threatening ordeal at High Lonesome, Roz managed to sit up in bed without nausea and light-headedness overcoming her. The blinding headaches had subsided gradually.

A week later she was walking up and down the upstairs hallway, determined to regain her strength. The cumbersome splint on her left arm was taking some getting used to, but *not* having Eli within touching distance left her feeling empty, lonely and restless.

Roz had tried to prepare herself for this inevitability. She had known Eli would leave after his name had been cleared. But accepting the fact that she would never see him again was killing her, bit by excruciating bit.

Dispirited, Roz paused in front of the bedroom where Eli had stayed. Bittersweet memories swamped and buffeted her as she stared into the vacant room. She had felt vital and alive while her life was entwined with his. Even the bad times had been filled with a sense of purpose, an innate sense of belonging to the man who had come to mean the world to her.

Now that he was gone she couldn't seem to find another sense of purpose. Even the challenge of becoming a reputable journalist didn't hold the thrill that it once had. Her father, bless him, had encouraged her to write several installments for the *Daily Chronicle,* detailing Jubal Rhodes's elaborate scheme to dispose of Eli McCain in order to protect his evil secret, his reputation and fortune. Roz had poured her heart into the story, determined that every Denver citizen knew the details of Eli's life and understood the terrible injustice that had befallen him.

Writing the story had occupied her time and her thoughts, but once she had completed her assignment she was at such loose ends that she didn't know what to do with herself.

"Señorita Rozalie? How are you feeling today?"

Roz shook herself from her depressing thoughts and pivoted to see Ramon Vasquez smiling apologetically at her—again, same as he had all week. The poor dear man had been so upset that she had been abducted and suffered injury during his watch that he visited her daily, offering her fresh-picked bouquets of wildflowers and begging for a list of duties he could perform for her to compensate. She had tried to assure Ramon that she didn't hold him responsible for her painful ordeal, but his guilty conscience continued to give him hell.

Roz nodded appreciatively when Ramon thrust another fistful of flowers at her. "Thank you, Ramon, but this really isn't necessary. I'm feeling much better." She mustered a cheery smile. "In fact, I'm feeling so much better that I would like to take a horseback ride so I can enjoy some fresh air.''

"I do not think your father will permit that," Ramon replied. "He will want the doctor's approval before you leave the house."

"My father," she said very deliberately, "is not the one who has been cooped up and going stir-crazy for a week."

Ramon bobbed his dark head. "If that is your wish then I will saddle your horse, *señorita*. I will even brave Señor Matthews's anger, if he is displeased. It is what I deserve for letting you get kidnapped while I was guarding you."

His obsidian eyes were so full of sympathy and concern that Roz smiled and patted his hand. "Please believe that I don't hold you responsible, Ramon. And I really am feeling better. Truly. I would very much like to put this incident behind us and see life return to normal around here."

"Whatever you wish, *señorita*," he murmured.

What she *wished* was that Eli McCain would come striding into the house and… And what? Roz asked herself as she walked into her room to dress for a long-awaited outdoor excursion. She vaguely remembered rousing after the mine cave-in to tell Eli how she felt about him. She had released him from all obligations. He had repaid his debt by saving her life.

They were even, she reminded herself as she shed her robe and nightgown. She had never asked more from Eli than the moment, never tried to tie him down. Holding on to him would have been as cruel and selfish as confining a wild creature to captivity. Eli McCain was a part of the frontier. If she asked more than he was capable of giving, it would only lead to resentment—and that was the last thing she wanted him to feel for her.

Roz had told herself—and her father—repeatedly that she didn't want or need a husband. She had wanted to be her own person and she had been granted her wish. Now she had her independence—and it wasn't nearly enough. She was so incredibly lonely and dissatisfied that it was spoiling her mood and her disposition.

Huffing out a breath, Roz wiggled into her riding skirt and tackled the chore of thrusting her splinted arm into her shirt. Odd, wasn't it? she mused. For years nothing had been more important than breaking free of the chains and restraints her parents placed on her. Now she had her precious independence and freedom and it didn't seem so precious anymore.

In fact, it didn't come close to satisfying her.

It was all Eli McCain's fault, she thought resentfully. Damn him, why hadn't he asked her to ride off into the sunset with him? Being anywhere with him was better than fighting this incredible sense of loss.

Much as she hated to admit it, she knew why Eli wouldn't want her underfoot. She would have been a burden in Eli's world. He liked being a nomad, roaming from one place to the next. What would she possibly do with herself if she trailed along behind him? And why would she want to when she knew that he didn't love her, didn't need her to be a part of his life?

Roz was on her way downstairs when she heard the front door swing open. Her father glanced up at her and frowned disapprovingly when he noticed her riding attire. When she tilted her chin and arched a challenging brow, daring him to forbid her from leaving the house, he relaxed his rigid stance and even managed the semblance of a smile.

"Suffering from cabin fever?" he asked.

"Of the worst sort," Roz replied as she descended into the foyer. "The walls have been shrinking in on me." She shuddered distastefully. "Sort of like having a mine shaft cave in on you. Instinct urges you to scramble toward wide-open spaces to inhale a breath of air."

Whatever objection Charles might have raised evaporated with her comment. Roz knew she had made an inarguable point.

"I brought the newspaper home with me," Charles stated. "I thought perhaps you might want to see the last installment that you wrote about your ordeal and McCain's exoneration in final print." He unrolled the paper and, smiling proudly, read aloud. "'Eli McCain, who was unjustly implicated for murder, has restored his honorable reputation and saved several lives in the process.'"

Roz smiled as her father continued to read her the article that summarized Jubal's fraudulent rise to fortune and his attempt to dispose of Roz and Eli before they exposed him for his long list of crimes.

"Everyone in town is abuzz with outrage. You have swayed public sentiment in McCain's favor," Charles reported. "The judge even came by the newspaper office after he read the last installment. You know he has a very strong sense of fair play and he began legal proceedings to have Rhodes's property and accounts transferred to their rightful owner.'' He grinned wryly. ''Whether McCain likes it or not, he is legally entitled to the fortune Rhodes has amassed the past twenty years.''

''Eli considers it blood money,'' Roz assured Charles.

Her father's shoulder lifted in a shrug. ''But it *is* his money, bought and paid for with his father's life. The judge plans to see to it that the fortune is McCain's, to do with as he pleases. I for one wouldn't want to argue with the judge when he is hell-bent on serving justice.''

Charles escorted Roz onto the porch then added, ''I've been doing extensive research to find out who Lieutenant John Harper really is. I sent telegrams to law officials in five states to puzzle out what happened to the real John Harper.''

Roz nodded pensively. ''I always thought there was something about the man that didn't fit the military persona.''

''McCain said the same thing,'' Charles replied. ''Now that things have simmered down around here, I turned the matter over to the Rocky Mountain Detective Agency.''

Roz smiled playfully. ''Never let it be said that you don't sniff out a story like a bloodhound, Papa. I'm sure that if there is something to hide in the lieutenant's past, you and the detectives will figure it out.''

''Yes, well, I *had* to turn the case over to the detectives,'' Charles informed her. ''Business has been brisk this week and I have had to double our print. You will be pleased to learn that the *Daily Chronicle* has surpassed the local competition."

"Congratulations," Roz said as she watched her father beam in delight.

"Thank you. With the rise in the number of subscribers I'm thinking of enlarging the paper. Of course, I will have to hire another reporter to track down more stories." His eyes twinkled down on her. "I was hoping I could count on you to pass along the society articles and obituaries to someone else and help me fill the news with current events and a few human-interest stories like the piece you did on McCain."

Roz gave her father an one-armed hug. "I can't think of anything I want more." Well, except to have Eli back in her life, but that was never going to happen, and she would make herself miserable wishing for the impossible. "I am anxious to report back to work fulltime."

Anything to take her mind off Eli. Thinking of him had brought her close to tears a number of times. Would it ever get easier? How long was this empty ache that consumed her heart and soul going to torment her?

As if Charles had read her thoughts, he wrapped a comforting arm around her. "I know this isn't easy, honey," he murmured. "But maybe it is better this way. Maybe McCain did you a favor by leaving."

Roz blinked back the mist that clouded her eyes. "Was it easier when Mother left? Here you are six years later and I'm not sure your feelings have changed all that much."

Charles sighed heavily. "You're right," he admitted. "But I can assure you that over time the hurting is easier to bear. Unfortunately, forgetting takes the longest time.''

He gestured to the horse that Ramon led toward the house. ''Go cure your severe case of cabin fever and I'll tell the cook to prepare a late supper. Don't be gone after dark. Please? And don't break your other arm.''

When Roz rolled her eyes at his overprotective tendencies, he smiled placatingly. ''It's going to take some time for me to loosen my hold after last week's nightmare. I thought I was going to lose you forever. But I *am* trying not to smother you.''

Roz kissed her father's cheek then strode off to mount her horse. She had the unshakable feeling that she, like her father, had difficulty letting go when it came to matters of the heart. If he couldn't get past Sophia, Roz doubted that she was going to have better luck at putting her memories of Eli behind her.

Halting beside the creek to let her horse drink its fill, Roz blew out a frustrated breath. Why did Eli McCain have to be so irresistible and unforgettable? She had been much happier back in those days when her suitors hadn't spiked her interest or touched her emotions. Unrequited love, she decided, had the power to make you absolutely miserable.

''Wherever you are, Eli McCain, I hope you're happy,'' she murmured to the darkly handsome image that floated across her mind. ''Letting you go is the hardest thing I have ever had to do…. And I'm not doing it well a-tall.''

Eli dismounted then slung his saddle bags over his shoulder. He stared up at the log cabin where a thin curl of smoke rose from the chimney and drifted in the wind. After two weeks of guiding would-be miners and businessmen through mountain passes to reach the latest mining camp that had sprung up at Bonanza Ridge, Eli was thankful to be home for a few days.

He had encountered extremely rugged terrain and several difficulties when the inexperienced wagoners attempted to ford fast-moving streams. A half-dozen greenhorns had taken a dousing in the chilly water before Eli had been able to pull them to safety.

Oh, yes, there had been plenty of difficulties to occupy his time and his thoughts, he mused as he hiked toward the cabin. But each evening, when he sprawled on his bedroll, an incurable case of loneliness had descended on him. The image of bright green eyes sparkling in an angelic face had tormented him. It seemed that his quality of life had dropped off considerably since he had walked away from Roz.

"How much longer?" Eli asked himself as he stalked up the front steps. "When will these memories fade?"

He would like to ask Simon that question. Simon was wise and experienced and he usually had all the answers. Eli would be eternally grateful if Simon could fix this one tormenting problem as easily as he patched up wounds. Unfortunately, Eli wasn't sure that wounds of the heart were Simon's specialty. After all, Simon had taken to the hills for some mysterious reason and Eli was pretty sure that it had something to do with a woman.

So where did that leave him? Wallowing in loneliness and misery, that's where. Doing the right thing for Roz was having one hell of an impact on his life—and not in a good way.

Eli pushed open the door—and stopped dead in his tracks. His jaw dropped to his chest as he glanced around the sparsely filled cabin. He gaped at Simon who had shaved off his beard and mustache and trimmed his long hair.

"What the devil is going on?" Eli asked as he panned the cabin again.

Simon removed the last of his leather-bound books from the shelf and stuffed them into a pouch. "*I'm* what's going on, son," he said enigmatically.

Eli let his saddle bags drop to the floor with a thud. He turned his bewildered attention to the cot that Simon had stripped of its bedding. The older man's personal belongings were crammed in two knapsacks that were propped against the wall.

"You're leaving?" Eli asked stupidly.

Simon nodded his gray head. "It's time. I was waiting for you to show up so I could say goodbye."

Eli's mind reeled. He had already walked away from the woman whose memory was driving him just short of crazy. Now Simon was leaving? After all these years?

"*Why?*" Eli choked out.

Simon smiled ruefully as he gestured for Eli to take a seat at the sawbuck table. "I need to tell you a story, Eli."

Eli parked himself in a chair. He had the feeling that, after all these years, Simon was going to confide his reasons for seclusion.

Simon strode over to pour two cups of coffee then plunked down across from Eli. "Twenty-four years ago, I left San Antonio, Texas, and just kept riding until I reached these mountains," he said, then sipped his coffee. "My family owned a ranch near there."

Eli stared at Simon, trying to picture him as a cowboy.

"The neighboring ranchero was owned by a Spanish don who had a daughter, his only child." A faint smile curved his lips and a faraway look encompassed his weathered face. "As children we were inseparable. Since she was younger I always looked out for her."

Simon grinned wryly. "You would have liked her. She was spirited and lovely beyond description. Strong-willed, too. Much like Rozalie."

Eli nodded. He could easily imagine a Spanish beauty who shared Roz's unforgettable traits. No doubt, the woman had stolen Simon's heart and her memory continued to haunt him.

The smile on Simon's face vanished, taking the sparkle from his dark eyes. "When she came of age, I asked the don for her hand in marriage. But Elena—" His voiced broke and he cleared his throat. "I haven't allowed myself to speak her name in twenty-four years." He hauled in a deep breath and continued. "Elena's father refused my request because I was Anglo and he had arranged a marriage between Elena and another Spaniard to keep their bloodline pure."

Eli sipped his coffee and tried not to notice the look of angry torment in Simon's eyes.

"Elena refused the match, defied her father's wishes and fled to our ranch. She insisted that we leave together, before her father sent her away. But her father knew exactly where to find her and he went straight to my father. They both believed in following the traditions of our separate cultures. Our two families made acceptable neighbors, but that was as far as it went. It didn't matter that Elena and I loved each other,'' Simon murmured.

Eli watched a turmoil of emotion provoke Simon to clench his fists. It was a long moment before his friend could continue.

''I was furious that my own father had no concern for my feelings. He decreed that I would take a wife of his choosing to carry on our family tradition. That night I packed my saddle bags and headed for the Drago ranchero to whisk Elena away—and the devil take our fathers and their unfair decrees.''

Eli waited for Simon to proceed, but there was such a long pause that he glanced up to see unshed tears shining in the older man's eyes.

''I arrived to discover that Elena had defied her father, as I had defied mine. She had also gathered her belongings, determined to return to me. But the don caught up with her and bound her up like a captured fugitive. He took an entourage of caballeros with him to transport Elena across the border to Mexico. The marriage took place immediately.''

Eli wondered how he would deal with the prospect of Roz marrying another man. For sure and certain, he wouldn't want to be within two thousand miles after he had lost her forever. He understood why Simon had searched for a place that was vastly different from his ranch. A place that wouldn't remind him of home or the woman he had been forced to leave behind—in body but never in spirit.

"And so I kept on riding," Simon said eventually. "I turned my back on my family's wealth and prestige, because a father that refuses to support his own son can't possibly possess true affection for him. I turned my back on my father, just as he turned his back on me when he refused to help me fight for the only thing I wanted more than life."

"Is your father still alive?" Eli questioned.

Simon shook his head. "He has been gone for ten years. My younger sister and her family manage the ranch," Simon informed him. "For the past few years, since the telegraph has reached Denver, I have contacted my sister."

Eli almost hated to ask. "And Elena?"

"Her husband passed on two years ago. Last year she returned to the ranchero with her daughter's family," Simon replied. He stared straight at Eli. "I've tried to convince myself that I have another life and that too much time has passed to take up where Elena and I left off, but I want to see her. I need to know if I still matter to her. She was the love of my youth, and if there is a chance that we can grow old together then I want to be with her."

"I don't blame you," Eli murmured. "But that doesn't mean that I'm not going to miss you."

Simon smiled ruefully. "As I will miss you, son. More than you can imagine. But watching you fight to pull Roz from the jaws of hell in that collapsed mine shaft drove home the point that we should never give up our hopes and dreams. If Elena and I have only five years, ten years—whatever fate grants us—then the torment I've lived with will be worth every lonely day. My feelings for her compel me to make a new start, if she will have me.''

He reached out to lay his hand on Eli's shoulder. ''You made all these years bearable and gave them purpose. I had no child of my own, but I *chose* you. Yet, in the end, Eli, a man is never truly at peace unless he follows the path that leads him back to his own heart. *Elena* is my heart.''

Eli understood completely because, lately, he had been on the most intimate terms with nearly unbearable loneliness.

''I hope you don't keep running from where you left *your* heart,'' Simon said, emotion crackling in his voice. ''I don't wish my life on any man, certainly not a man who is my son in every way that counts.''

Eli watched Simon push himself upright then amble over to his unmade cot. His jaw dropped open when Simon pried up two floor planks then reached down to retrieve four pouches.

''What the hell is that?'' Eli asked, bewildered.

''A hobby,'' Simon replied with a lackadaisical shrug. ''I've collected placer gold from the sandy deltas of mountain streams during my travels.'' He grinned at Eli's astounded expression. ''This is part of your inheritance.''

He carried the heavy pouches of gold dust to the table and thunked them down at Eli's fingertips. ''You happen to be a very wealthy man, son. You will one day inherit half of my cattle ranch in Texas. And if you don't accept the fortune that Jubal Rhodes stole from your father, then you are a fool.''

Eli shook his head adamantly. ''Blood money,'' he maintained. ''My natural father's life was sacrificed to build Jubal's empire. I want nothing to do with that bastard's fortune. He can take it to hell with him for all I care!''

Simon chuckled at Eli's ferocious scowl. ''And miss the chance to show benevolence to disheartened prospectors who need a generous grubstake so they can chase their rainbows to find a pot of gold? You told me that this Paxton character had been cheating prospectors with high-interest grubstakes. Justice will prevail if you offer grubstakes with minimum interest. You might drive Paxton right out of business.'' He grinned wickedly. ''Now wouldn't that be a shame?''

Bad as he hated to admit it, the prospect of cutting into Paxton's profits held tremendous appeal.

''Selfish greed was Jubal's curse and it turned out to be the death of him,'' Simon went on. ''Your father intended to provide a better life for you and he would have wanted you to accept what he died trying to protect.'' His onyx eyes bore down on Eli. ''If you had a child of your own, would *you* deny him what you worked so hard to provide?''

The image of a dark-haired boy with luminous green eyes and unrestrained spirit leaped to mind. Eli tried to shove aside the vision, but it refused to be vanquished.

''No,'' he said quietly. ''I would want my child to have every benefit that I could provide. I would want him to grow up in a home where he knew he was wanted and loved, not uprooted and bundled off to one place then the next like extra baggage.''

"Like you were," Simon said perceptively. "You were afraid to cling tightly to those you held dear because cruel twists of fate kept snatching them away from you. First your mother, then your father. And you kept an emotional distance from me in those first years that we were together.''

Simon always seemed to know what was in Eli's heart, though Eli had never confided that he was leery of lasting attachments—just in case they were taken away as they had been in the past.

And sure enough, Eli mused. Now this old man was going to abandon him.

Eli shook himself from his tormented thoughts when Simon picked up his gear and carried it to the porch. "That's it? You're leaving now?" he asked, frustrated.

Simon chuckled at Eli's disgruntled tone. "You have a choice, son. You can ride to San Antonio with me or you can roam these mountains for years on end. Or better yet, you can follow your heart.''

"I'm not sure I have one left, if I ever had one at all," Eli grumbled.

"You have one all right. You've just lost it. Same as I did. But fortunately, you know exactly where you left yours." He grinned as he carried an armload of his belongings toward the mule. "I just hope you don't wait twenty-four years to recover it.''

Accepting the inevitable, Eli scooped up the rest of the knapsacks and strode toward the mule.

"When you see that feisty lass again—and if you have any sense whatsoever—you will tell her that I stopped running from my past and I went to claim my future.''

''Simon?''

Emptiness that seemed to carry the same weight as a boulder settled in Eli's belly. He dropped the satchels and headed straight for Simon, clasping him a hug that testified to the long-standing respect and affection he felt for the man who had saved his life and raised him as his own. They clung to each other for a long moment before Eli made the symbolic gesture of stepping away and letting go.

''I'll be expecting to see you in the near future,'' Simon murmured. ''If you decide to head south, ask directions to Foster Ranch. It won't be hard to find.''

Eli studied Simon for a moment, still trying to visualize this rugged mountain man in spurs, chaps and wide-brimmed hat.

Simon chuckled at Eli's speculative expression. ''Believe it or not, I grew up roping, riding and herding cattle. But I left that life behind and ran from the painful memories. I've discovered that you can't run from who you are inside, Eli. Take my word for it. Go back where you belong.''

Eli glanced toward the rustic cabin that had been home for twenty years.

''You're looking in the wrong direction and we both know it,'' Simon said sagely.

''And *do* what?'' Eli asked, staring helplessly at Simon. ''*Be* what?''

Simon strapped his belongings on the mule. ''You're adaptable, son. You've always excelled at sensible solutions. I'm sure you will figure something out.''

Eli stood there, watching Simon lead the heavily laden mule down the mountain. His world shifted around him, leaving him feeling more alone than ever before. Now Simon was abandoning him in hopes of reclaiming the woman who had been stolen from him so many years ago. Eli was left with a small fortune in gold, the promise of a deed to part of a Texas ranch and the rightful ownership to mines and several businesses in Denver.

Suddenly Eli had more wealth at his disposal that he knew what to do with. He also had his own life savings that he had never had the time or the inclination to spend while he drifted from one locale to the next, searching for links to his uncertain past.

He had everything that fortune seekers ever dreamed of.

Yet, he had nothing but a severe case of loneliness to keep him company. He was right back where he had started twenty years ago.

The frustrating thought had him swearing profusely as he stalked back to the cabin to pour himself a drink—or four.

Chapter Fourteen

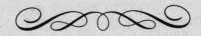

Roz left work early at the newspaper office so she could assist Gina Thompson with the decorative changes at the hotel restaurant. The grand reopening was scheduled for this evening. Roz was thrilled beyond words that Gina and her mother had decided to take on the challenge of managing Denver's finest accommodations and café.

Stepping back, Roz surveyed the new artwork of rugged mountain landscapes that Mrs. Thompson had purchased from a local artist. "Perfect," Roz exclaimed as memories of her travels with Eli leaped to mind. She could come in here and stare at the paintings, imagining that Eli was out there somewhere.

Gina came to stand beside her, smiling proudly at the changes they had made in the restaurant. "I'm so glad you encouraged me to try my hand at running Papa's business," she murmured. "I feel as if I have a purpose for the first time in my life."

Roz used to know what that felt like. The past few weeks, however, had been an emotional struggle. Dealing with the inconvenient splint on her arm was nothing compared to the unbearable loneliness that followed like her own shadow.

"Come quick! You're missing all the excitement," the young hotel clerk called out as he poked his head into the recently remodeled café. "I just heard that one of the detectives at the agency placed Lieutenant Harper under arrest. He was brought in from the garrison."

"Serves him right," Gina grumbled as she pulled a face. "The man has been making me crazy. He's been showing up three times a week, regular as clockwork, and dogging my footsteps. He claims that he's suddenly developed an infatuation for me." She smirked skeptically. "I find that rather hard to believe since he followed you like a pup until you showed him the door. There is a word for men like that."

"Yes, fortune hunter of the worst sort," Roz declared.

"I wonder why the lieutenant has been arrested?" Gina mused aloud.

Roz wasn't sure, but she had no doubt that her father had something to do with it. Charles had made it his mission to gather background information on John Harper—or whoever he really was. Apparently the detectives had finally gathered enough evidence to warrant an arrest.

Curious, she ambled into the hotel foyer. Gina was a step behind her. Roz stared in amazement at the crowd of bystanders who had gathered around the office that housed the Rocky Mountain Detective Agency. As expected, Charles Matthews was pelting down the boardwalk to witness John Harper's incarceration.

Roz grabbed a notepad from her reticule and started off down the street. This was one story she was anxious to write. She'd had her fill of the lieutenant trying to use Gina and her to make the social connections that he constantly obsessed over.

Her heart stalled in her chest and she stumbled to a halt when her gaze landed on the rider who dismounted to pull Harper from his horse. Roz couldn't breathe, couldn't even remember why she needed to. Her gaze was glued to the tall, muscular detective who half turned and stared over the crowd. When his gaze locked with hers, Roz felt as if she had taken an unseen blow in the midsection.

Eli McCain was back in town? He was working for the detective agency? When had this happened? She was supposed to be a journalist who kept up with the goings-on in Denver. How could she not have known?

Her accusing gaze swung to her father who glanced in her direction then quickly looked away. Charles had known, she realized. But he hadn't bothered to tell her. Why not? Because he preferred there was no further association between her and Eli? Probably. He had tried to keep them apart while Eli was staying at their home and obviously nothing had changed.

And what of Eli? she thought as hurt, rejection and disappointment welled up inside her. Obviously, he had gotten over her quickly enough. After a month of separation he showed up in town—and hadn't bothered to contact her.

Well, that said a mouthful, didn't it? *She* wanted to

be the place he came first when he returned to Denver. *She* had been pining away for him and *he* had gotten on with his life and taken a job with the agency. Temporarily, no doubt. You couldn't keep the man in the same place unless you nailed his moccasins to the floor. He had been born wild and free and he intended to stay that way.

"Where are you going?" Gina asked as Roz whirled around and started off in the direction she had come. "Isn't that Eli McCain?"

Roz was finished listening to whatever Gina had asked. She strode off to fetch her horse and make a beeline toward home. This was not how she had imagined her first encounter with Eli—if it ever came. Her secret fantasy centered on Eli striding into her home and promising to love her forever and ever. She hadn't quite figured out how they would share their future together. But none of her dreams entailed Eli showing up in town and maybe—or maybe not—dropping by to say hello when he got around to it.

She wished she hadn't seen him at all, she mused as she piled onto her horse—and cursed the cumbersome sling and splint. Her whimsical fantasy had been so much better than the demoralizing realization that she had never been more than a chapter in Eli McCain's eventful life. She hadn't been the first place he'd come because she wasn't his first priority.

Tears rolled down Roz's cheeks and her heart caved in on itself. Her emotions boiled like a cauldron as she thundered toward home. She had half a mind to board a train and head east to marry that highfalutin lawyer her mother had earmarked for her. Then she wouldn't have to wonder if she and Eli could have found common ground.

The spiteful thought vanished as quickly as it came to mind. No, Roz reminded herself as she blotted her tears on the sleeve of her gown. Denver was where she wanted to be and Denver was where she would stay.

She wasn't going to marry anyone—ever. Not for love or convenience and certainly not for spite. She was her own woman now. She didn't need a man—Eli McCain to be specific—tormenting her thoughts and her emotions. She wasn't his number one priority and he would no longer be hers, she vowed resolutely.

Roz was still trying to get her rioting emotions under control an hour later when her father returned home. She greeted him with a mutinous glare and did her best to ignore him, but Charles strode up to her in the parlor and forced her to deal with him.

"Aren't you going to ask what charges have been brought against the so-called lieutenant?" Charles asked before Roz sidestepped around him to pace back and forth across the carpet.

The urge to stamp off half-mad was tempting. But the last time she had done that she had ended up witnessing a murder and had been carted off by Eli—and fell helplessly in love with him. She had nearly sacrificed her own life to find the culprit who had framed him and this is the thanks she got—a broken heart.

"I don't particularly care what Harper is charged with," she said as she glanced at her father who had propped himself against the doorjamb to watch her wear ruts in his rug. "Just so he is charged with something and is forced to leave Gina and me alone."

"The man impersonated a military officer and stole his identity," Charles said, as if he hadn't heard her. "His real name is Robert Shields. He is wanted in New Mexico for mail fraud and horse theft. The scam of advertising the sale of a miracle remedy for gout caught up with him in Santa Fe five years ago. The U.S. Marshal Service came looking to arrest Shields and he lit out on the first horse within reach. While he was hiding out in the mountains he came across a doomed army patrol that had been ambushed by a band of outlaws."

Roz halted. Aggravated though she was, curiosity got the best of her. "So he stole the lieutenant's credentials and the uniform and passed himself off as an officer?" she presumed.

Charles nodded his gray-blond head. "According to the commander at the fort near Denver, Harper reported for duty, carrying what turned out to be forged orders. Since the post was short on much-needed officers, the commander didn't ask too many questions. But the army is taking serious offense to Shields's charade. The man deprived Harper's family of information and the fallen soldier of a proper military burial."

"Sort of like never knowing if your father abandoned you because he considered you a burden and inconvenience or if he had perished trying to save your life from a greedy murderer," Roz murmured, thinking of Eli's long quest for information about his father.

"I expect so," Charles replied. "Considering the evidence collected against Shields, Judge Milner will make sure that swindler spends a dozen years in the penitentiary."

"Good place for him," Roz agreed when she finally

cooled down enough to stop pacing. "At least the man won't be pestering Gina and swearing undying love for her, when all he wanted was to get his hands on her inheritance and launch himself into high society."

Her gaze zeroed in on Charles. He winced because he knew exactly what was coming, she predicted.

"Why didn't you tell me that Eli was in town? You had to have known. You have been in constant contact with the agency and you put up a reward for information on Harper."

Charles shifted uncomfortably beneath her penetrating stare. As well he should have, Roz thought sourly.

"I was told not to say anything," he mumbled.

That really hurt! Roz wheeled away before she burst into tears again. Apparently Eli had intended to go about his temporary job and avoid her. Did he think that would make it easier on her now that he knew how she felt about him?

Roz suddenly remembered that Simon had warned her that Eli might use her own anger against her to break all ties between them. Well…it had worked. She was spitting mad. And Hurt. And indignant. And that was only the condensed list of the turbulent emotions that were boiling inside her.

"If it helps—"

Roz rounded on her father. "Nothing helps!" she railed, unable to ground her flying emotions. "I thought I was making headway, thought I was getting past my feelings for him, slowly but surely. I could have been better prepared if I had known that he had returned to town."

Charles shifted awkwardly from one foot to the

other. "I don't think McCain was counting on drawing such a crowd when he arrived in town, after he chased down Shields who tried to make a run for it. McCain wasn't particularly pleased to discover that he had become a local hero and that everyone in Denver knows his life story."

"If he's half as aggravated as I am then I'd say we're even," Roz said dourly. "I—"

Her voice fizzled out when the front door swung open and the source of her frustration invited himself inside. Roz stared at Eli's neatly clipped raven hair, clean-shaven face, the familiar attire that set him apart from a crowd and she felt her heart clang against her ribs like a Chinese gong.

Just the sight of Eli McCain held the power to turn her wrong side out and expose every emotion. She wanted to wallop him upside the head with her splinted arm. She wanted to fly into his arms and hold on to him until he made her let him go.

The two diametrical thoughts kept her rooted to the spot. She simply stared at him and wished she had never laid eyes on him because he had hurt her—all the way to the depths of her soul. How could she love him so much and still want to strangle him? she asked herself in exasperation.

Eli stared into those livid green eyes and knew Roz was silently wishing him to perdition. He hadn't planned for Roz to learn that he was back in town by seeing him riding down main street with his fugitive in tow. Of course, he hadn't known that he had become a household name who would be instantly recognized, either.

"I distinctly remember telling you that I didn't want my name and my story splashed across the front page of the newspaper," Eli said as he met her hostile glare. "Thomas Lake, the superintendent of the agency, just showed me the installments that you wrote. And thank you *so* much," he added caustically.

"And thank *you* so very much for not doing me the courtesy of notifying me that you were back in town," she snapped back at him. "You left High Lonesome while I was unconscious and didn't bother to say goodbye."

"Maybe I should leave the two of you to—" Charles inserted, only to be cut off by the slashing gesture of Roz's splinted arm.

"No, you stay here to make sure I don't kill him," Roz muttered. Her gaze dropped to the package in Eli's hand. "What is that? Some sort of peace-treaty gift that you hastily picked up on your way over here? If it is, I don't want it."

Eli tossed the package on the sofa. "I told you that I intended to replace the gown you were wearing when I whisked you away from the sniper."

Well, so much for gratitude, he thought as he watched Roz stare at the package as if he had offered her a poisonous snake.

"I would have preferred that you mail it to me," she said sourly. "But now that you have delivered it in person, you can leave. For good."

Damn it, this wasn't how Eli had envisioned his return to Denver—his first encounter with Roz, specifically. It was fairly obvious that the affection she claimed she felt for him—after she survived that nightmarish ordeal in the collapsed mine shaft—had been twisted emotion speaking.

Eli had wrestled with the dilemma of Roz Matthews for a month—and nearly drank himself blind. Eli had finally reached a decision and he had come looking for work that might keep him in the area indefinitely.

Not that *Roz* cared that he had compromised and was trying to make a place for himself in *her* world.

Simon had said to follow his heart. Bad advice, Eli thought angrily. Roz looked as if she wanted his heart fried in lard and his body chopped up in bite-size pieces to feed to the buzzards.

"Perhaps I should fetch us a cool drink," Charles suggested as his wary gaze bounced back and forth between Eli and Roz. "I think some of us need to cool down."

"I am as cool as I intend to get...until our unwanted guest makes himself scarce," Roz said sharply.

"We definitely need drinks." Charles shot off like a cannonball, leaving Roz and Eli involved in a visual duel at twenty paces.

"I mean so little to you that you couldn't bother to tell me you were in town?" she asked bitterly. "Or were you afraid that I would make a fool of myself over you and you didn't want to deal with that?"

"I had business to attend, arrangements to make," Eli explained stiffly.

"All of it far more pressing than seeing me," she burst out, then whirled around to present her back to him.

The comment gave Eli hope that she *did* have feelings for him, that it had been more than the rush of adrenaline and the intense, life-threatening situation at High Lonesome that had prompted her to whisper that she loved him.

Feeling himself on more solid footing, Eli ambled over to unwrap the package and display the expensive green satin gown he had selected at the boutique.

"Do you like it?" he asked as he held up the garment for her inspection.

Roz sniffled then glanced over her shoulder. "Yes, you will look splendid in it," she smarted off. "However, I would suggest slippers rather than moccasins to complete the ensemble."

Eli bit back a grin. Roz was in usual form. Quick wit and sassy mouth.

"I was hoping *you* might wear it this evening. Charles told me that Gina's grand reopening at the restaurant is tonight."

She turned to face him. Her delicate chin shot up. "I'm not the least bit hungry."

"Of course not. What was I thinking?" He grinned at her. "You are too busy chewing on me to have much appetite left."

"Very amusing, McCain," she said, then glared at him.

His attempt to tease her into good humor wasn't working. He tried a different approach. "Simon said to tell you goodbye. He decided to stop running from his past and go back to Texas."

He had her now. He could see lively curiosity overshadowing her anger with him.

"Texas?" she repeated interestedly.

Eli nodded. "Back to Elena Drago, to be specific. I received a telegram from him when I rode into town."

Her eyes sparkled with curiosity and Eli gestured toward the new gown. "If you agree to join me for supper I will be happy to provide all the details."

She recoiled again. Damn it, he'd come so close. Eli drew himself up and inhaled a deep breath. This was not how he had pictured this encounter, but if he didn't go for broke right now, they might be engaged in a stalemate that lasted all night.

"Just answer one question," he requested.

"No," she replied.

He cocked a dark brow. "*No,* you won't answer or *no* is the answer to every question I ask?"

"Papa!" Roz called out. "Where is that cold drink you promised? I want to throw it on McCain so he'll take the hint and leave!"

Charles did not miraculously appear. Smart man. No need to get caught in the cross fire.

"I want to know if you meant what you said that night at High Lonesome," Eli blurted out.

"About setting you free from your debt? Absolutely," she replied shortly.

"No, the other part."

"McCain, you are sorely testing my temper," she scowled. "What is it that you want from me, precisely?"

Eli swallowed hard and laid his heart—and his future—on the line. He hauled in a bracing breath and spoke the words he hadn't voiced since he couldn't remember when. "I want to know if you really do love me because I sure as hell love you. I came back to see if I could fit into your world. Partially at least. The assignments I take with the detective agency will occasionally require overnight forays in the wilderness. I don't expect you to give up your passion for journalism, but we could—''

His breath came out in a whoosh when she flew across the room and leaped into his arms. The wooden splint clanked against his skull when she tried to wrap her arms around his neck. The pain, however, didn't override the pleasure of having Roz meshed familiarly against him for the first time in weeks.

"You love me?" Tears streamed down her cheeks and put a crackle in her voice. "You really mean it? Truly?"

The apprehension that had been hounding him dissolved in two seconds flat. Eli clutched Roz possessively to him, savoring the long-awaited feel of her lush body pressing ever closer to his. God! He felt as if he had been holding his breath for a month. Suddenly he could breathe again and he was no longer going through the meaningless paces of existence.

He nuzzled against her neck, absorbing the sweet, enticing scent that belonged uniquely to Roz. He felt his heart begin to beat—after hanging in his chest like a shriveled peach for weeks on end. Suddenly the world was a far better place than it had been.

"My life has been an endless string of disappointments, hardships and challenges," Eli murmured. "Simon taught me to deal with it, to get from one day to the next. But then I met you and I want more, need more."

"Oh, Eli—"

He interrupted her, determined to make her understand that he desperately needed her to be a part of his life. "I know how independent you've become and that you have your heart set on being a spinster, but I was wondering if you could compromise. You really need to marry me because I don't want to live without you."

When she simply stared at him, her jaw gaping, Eli felt the need to fill the awkward silence. "It seems I have inherited a palatial mansion and I have all sorts of records to keep since I'm grubstaking prospectors with no-interest loans. I can't keep up with all the bookwork and charity donations while I'm on assignment with the agency. I was hoping you could help me out...as my wife—"

Eli was glad that she silenced him with an enthusiastic kiss because he knew he was jabbering nonstop. When Roz leaned back in his arms and smiled radiantly he was pretty sure that her answer was going to be yes.

"Oh, Eli, I'm so pleased that you are going to use your rightful inheritance to help those who need a sporting chance. However," she said, her green eyes twinkling with mischief, "it is going to cost you to get me to agree to this compromise of marriage."

"Whatever it takes," he said without hesitation.

Her expression became serious and she said, "You have to promise to love me for the rest of my life."

He shook his head. "No, I'm going to love you for the rest of *mine*. Whether I deserve you or not, I tried living without you for four endless weeks. It was pure hell. You are my heart and, as Simon says, a man has to follow his heart or he has no life at all."

Then she kissed him for all she was worth and his hands glided down her curvaceous body, memorizing her by touch, by heart and soul.

"Ahem…"

Eli lifted his head to see Charles holding two glasses of lemonade. There was no censure in his eyes, Eli noticed. But he wasn't sure how Charles would react when he learned that Eli had every intention of marrying Roz—with or without his permission.

To Eli's amusement, Roz eased from his embrace and stood squarely in front of him, as if protecting him from her father. "Papa, Eli has asked me to marry him and I have agreed."

Eli waited with bated breath and felt Roz leaning rigidly against him. Charles studied them for a long silent moment, saying absolutely nothing. The suspense was killing Eli and he decided to play his trump card before Charles objected to the marriage.

"Charles, you told me the night Roz was kidnapped that I could name my price if I brought her back alive," Eli reminded him. "Your daughter is the price I demand."

Another long moment ticked by. Finally Charles broke into a grin. "Well, I suppose a deal is a deal. And at least Roz didn't pick a shyster guilty of mail fraud, theft and impersonating an army officer." He raised one of the glasses in toast. "You have my blessing. I wish you better luck in love than I had."

"Thank you," Eli murmured.

"Just one more thing." Charles's expression sobered. "Do you love her, McCain?"

"I'm absolutely crazy about her," Eli admitted as

he looped his arms possessively around her waist. "There is something I have been wanting to ask you though. Why did you think I was headed to the brothel the night I found Roz in the alley, waiting to become a murder suspect?"

Charles grinned sheepishly. "I was testing you. I spent the week making certain the two of you weren't alone together. I had to know if you were the kind of man who looked elsewhere when he was denied."

A disapproving frown puckered Charles's brow as he continued. "And if you hadn't saved Roz from the murder accusation and moved a mountain to rescue her from the jaws of death, I would have you whipped. I am not so naive that I don't realize what has been going on between you two. And just so you know, I don't care if you're half white and half—" he waved his arms in expansive gestures, slopping lemonade on the floor "—and half mountain goat! I'm going to fetch the judge immediately and we are going to see this matter settled."

Roz grinned at her father. "Excellent idea. Why don't you nab Judge Milner on his way out of the courthouse and meet us at the restaurant's grand re-opening?"

"And leave you two alone? I think not," Charles said, and smirked.

Roz scooped up the gown Eli had purchased for her, then grabbed his hand. "I'm going upstairs to dress. With this cumbersome splint I will need Eli's help."

When Charles opened his mouth to object, Roz flung up her splinted arm to forestall him. He stared speculatively at the splint that could easily become a weapon. Setting aside the glasses of lemonade, Charles heaved a gusty sigh.

"McCain. I give her to you for safekeeping. Now *you* can deal with her defiant streak." He smiled wryly as he spun toward the door. "I think I might be getting the better end of this bargain."

"I think you are, too," Eli said, chuckling.

The conversation with Charles flew right out of Eli's head when Roz flashed him an inviting smile that stripped the breath from his lungs and left him hard and aching in the time it took to blink. He followed Roz upstairs, peeling off articles of clothing as he went.

And when they were naked in each other's arms, Eli forgot to tell Roz that Simon and his new wife, Elena, were in Colorado Springs and would arrive on the evening train. He forgot everything except the burning need that this spirited beauty constantly aroused in him. Her loving touch gave him life, filled his heart and soul with immeasurable joy and pleasure.

"I love you," he whispered as he stretched out on the bed beside her.

Roz cupped his face in her hands and stared into those mesmerizing, sky-blue eyes that shimmered with affection and unmistakable desire. She had gone from the very pit of dejection to the towering peaks of sheer delight in the course of two hours. She knew beyond all doubt that she had discovered the greatest power a woman could attain. She had love. This unique and special man was all she needed to make her life rewarding and complete.

"I love you, too, Eli," she whispered back to him.

"And I'm going to show you just how much, starting now and lasting until long past forever."

Roz's worshipful kisses and caresses sent Eli higher than any mountain precipice he had ever scaled. And he returned each loving touch, giving all that he was to the woman who held his heart. He thought fleetingly that whatever he had been—up to this point in his life—did not begin to compare to the man he had become now that he had Roz's promise of love until the end of time.

Eli swore there and then that no matter what difficulties they encountered in their future, nothing would keep him away from this green-eyed, blond-haired siren. Different lifestyles be damned. He would truss himself up like a dandified aristocrat to attend parties with Roz—as long as they came home together to make wild sweet love.

Since Eli hadn't allowed a barrier of fallen rock to stand between them, he knew that nothing would ever come between them again.

"Mmm," Roz murmured in the aftermath of breathless passion. "I do believe that you meant what you said."

Eli dropped a kiss to her smiling lips. "I meant every word. You are my heart," he assured her huskily.

Roz glanced toward the window, watching the last rays of sunset filter through the drapes. "We should get dressed for supper and our wedding."

"In a minute," he said as he moved suggestively above her. "I've decided we should be fashionably late. Any complaints?"

"None whatsoever," she murmured as she melted eagerly against him.

They were late for supper, but they were definitely on time for the impromptu wedding ceremony that Charles had arranged in the hotel lobby. Simon Foster and his lovely wife were also there to witness the event.

Thanks to Charles the ceremony made front-page headlines the following day. But Eli didn't object because he had been on his way to the secluded mountain cabin where he and Roz had first begun the journey into their future. They stood on the outcropping of rock at Angel's Peak, admiring the spectacular view of immense blue sky and rugged mountains. Eli felt at peace with the world because he had everything that was important.

His world was the woman he held possessively in the circle of his arms. And there she would stay—until the end of eternity.

He leaned down to kiss Roz, sealing his devotion for his new wife. "I will love you. Always," Eli whispered in promise.

"I will love you. Forever," Roz whispered back.

And they did....

*   *   *   *   *

If you enjoyed what you just read,
then we've got an offer you can't resist!

Take 2 bestselling love stories FREE!
Plus get a FREE surprise gift!